The Buffalo's Burden

A Tara Road Mansions Mystery

Monica Ronghe

Clever Fox®
PUBLISHING
Chennai • Bangalore

CLEVER FOX PUBLISHING
Chennai, India

Published by CLEVER FOX PUBLISHING 2025

ISBN: 978-93-6707-247-9

PROLOGUE

Bombay-Poona Road, India (1987)

Tyres screeched, and the fully laden truck swung wildly as it made a sudden turn off the highway onto a muddy, rutted track. The driver glanced in his rear-view mirror, there it was again! The dilapidated white Tempo van that had been behind his truck, since he left the Bombay warehouse a few hours ago, had turned in too. "If I were paranoid, I'd think I'm being followed!" He shrugged off the thought.

He had turned off the highway for a popular truck stop outside the city, located just before a major octroi checkpoint. As his truck bounced forward along the unsurfaced road, the tired truck driver saw a familiar and comforting vista ahead – puffs of grey smoke rose from a tin shack surrounded by several haphazardly parked trucks. His shoulders sagged with relief at the thought of strong, sweet tea, hot food, and stretching his cramped body on a charpoy bed. He was taking the last truckload for delivery before he went to his village to visit his family. The supervisor had given him several months' salary as a reward for working without a holiday for three years, and permission to stay in the village for a few months.

It was almost harvest season in the village, and his family would appreciate having him home; the extra pair of hands and extra money were always welcome. He was looking forward to seeing his young children, wife, and elderly parents. For three years, he had lived in the city, shared a small room with three other truck drivers, cooked and cleaned for himself. It had been hard but wages in the city were good.

He stopped his truck on the outskirts of the motley collection of trucks and cut the ignition. He could see some familiar faces amongst the truck drivers on the charpoys, napping, eating, chatting, and playing cards. Smoky fumes from the shack wafted through the window and greeted his nostrils. Smells of wood, kerosene, and coal mingled with aromas of fresh rotis and spicy lentils tinged with diesel fumes belched by a truck in the far corner. Two elderly truck drivers and an unkempt youth were desperately trying to coax life into its engine. Some drivers were redistributing goods and packages between their trucks before getting to the octroi checkpoint to save on taxes. They worked quickly, with minimal conversation, and the drivers mostly nodded or pointed at the packages. They soon returned to their charpoys for a final snooze or a bidi before leaving the truck stop. These proceedings were occasionally punctuated by a loud guffaw from the card game, an occasional shout for more tea from the shack, and a noisy phlegm-clearing cough from the bushes at the far edges of the truck stop that served as an open-air bathroom.

The newly arrived truck driver jumped down from his truck. Nonchalantly, he raised a hand in greeting at the noisy group of card players as he strode past them and stretched out on an unoccupied charpoy, lazily lighting a bidi. He had hardly taken a drag, when he heard footsteps next to his charpoy. Without looking, he automatically held out his hand, expecting a grimy glass of piping hot tea from the young boy wielding an enormous galvanised kettle.

So, he was surprised to hear a rough male voice say, "*Arrey! Arrey!* Don't sleep, *dada!*"

Not recognising the voice, the truck driver opened his eyes and glared, "Why not?" He sullenly took in the unfamiliar figure before him. The tall, young man was dressed much like all the other drivers at the truck stop.

The young man was taken aback by the truck driver's rudeness but answered earnestly. "*Dada*, I've been following you since you left the warehouse this morning. They loaded one of my packages on your truck. I only drive a small Tempo and deliver things in the city all day. Today, I have spent much of my time and petrol just following your truck on the highway. I had hoped you would stop sooner. If I don't do ten deliveries a day, my family goes hungry, *dada*."

The truck driver frowned. Now he would have to waste time driving back to the warehouse to get his own correct package instead of enjoying his break at this truck stop. As if reading his mind, the Tempo driver suddenly remembered something and triumphantly said, "I've got your correct package in my Tempo. You won't need to go back for it. Take that, give me mine and then you can sleep, *dada*."

The truck driver looked at the young Tempo driver with tired eyes. All he wanted to do was get some sleep. Reluctantly, he pushed himself off the charpoy and stood up. The Tempo driver was already leading the way. Together they hefted a package off the Tempo and hoisted it into the truck. Then they carried the misplaced parcel from the truck to the Tempo. Keen not to waste any more of his time, the Tempo driver promptly climbed into his seat and waved as he drove away. The truck driver returned to his charpoy and lit a new bidi, gestured to the tea boy to pour him a glass and hoped no one was going to disturb him again.

✦ ✦ ✦

CHAPTER 1

Tara Road Mansions, Bund Garden Road, Poona (1987)

A large white Ambassador slowly wound its way through the Bombay-Poona Road traffic as it headed into Poona city. It was a private taxi because it had a red 'T' painted in curlicue brackets. The driver wore a white uniform and a peaked cap; his passenger was a smartly dressed young girl in her mid-twenties, who was intently studying a blue file. The driver beeped loudly at a meandering cyclist, startling both, his passenger and the cyclist. The girl in the taxi closed the file with a start and glanced at her watch. It had been almost five hours since they had left Bombay. Her mind vividly retraced the last 24 hours.

Yesterday at 11 am, she had received a terse and urgent telephone summon from her boss. At the gate, they had said, "Go straight to the main office, you're expected." Everyone seemed curiously alert and tense. Events from the last few days had been unsettling. Disturbing. A consignment worth two million dollars had gone missing on their watch. A day later, their main suspect was found dead in his car; his body riddled with bullets.

"Why on earth have I been summoned?" She wondered for the hundredth time as she took the steps, two at a time. She had never worked with the consignments team; her expertise had always been investigating people. The only reason she knew about this missing consignment was its staggering value. As she had knocked on the open door, she had felt the tension in the dimly lit, silent room. She had pulled herself up and stiffened; her spine tingled as she walked in and greeted her boss. He was alone, looking out of the window. His bulky figure was a dark silhouette blocking the bright daylight outside, making the room seem smaller and darker. As her eyes adjusted to the light, she saw his taut shoulders and muscled hands clasped tightly behind his back.

"You wanted to see me, sir?" She asked with a smile in her voice.

She was shocked when he spun around with an angry shout, "Yes! Two days now and that bloody consignment is still missing! Stolen right under our noses! It started off exactly as planned from here at the Bombay warehouse. It was headed for Poona under our protection and surveillance– the customs officer, the delivery truck, the truck driver, the delivery address in Poona – everything and everyone was known. Yet, such a large consignment has simply disappeared on my watch!"

He sneered, "Don't worry, I had assured them. I will see it safely to its destination. I have overseen several such operations in the past. I staked my reputation on it. And just like that, it's gone. Disappeared. Just like that!" He snapped his fleshy fingers and swore again, this time more crudely. "Find it! Just find the damned thing!" She flinched as he banged his muscular fist on the large wooden table between them.

"Why me? I don't know anything about consignments," she thought but did not dare voice her sentiments as she met his furious gaze, taking in his weary expression and angry, bloodshot eyes. In the ten years that she had worked with him, she had never seen him like this. His voice was always low, polite, quiet, in control; his movements were usually measured, deliberate and slow. She stood still and quiet, instinctively knowing there was more to come.

His loud, angry voice continued, "To top it all, the timing of this stolen consignment is shit! Total shit! The one time we lose a consignment in years, we have a new police commissioner breathing down our necks. He's hell bent on a clean-up of all the departments. He sacked the old Assistant Commissioner within hours of taking charge. Now the new Assistant Commissioner is tasked with looking into every active unresolved case. The size of this consignment and its eye-watering value is going to catch his eye very quickly and it's so recent, it'll be right on top of the pile of our failures. We need to keep a low profile and find that consignment quickly and quietly without attracting their attention. We must tread very softly but resolve this missing consignment issue as soon as possible. So, by the time he gets to us, everything is shipshape or close to it."

"We?" She enquired softly.

He ignored her question and simply thrust a blue file at her, "Paperwork! Consignment details, docks clearance, transport company used, petrol stations, even routine truck stops. We had thought of everything to ensure a smooth operation, and yet it's been stolen," he spat out each word in disgust. The fury in his voice was unmistakable. She tried to muster the correct response to this outburst as she tried to piece all the information together, while he rambled on. "My best men are chasing all these details very quietly in Bombay and Poona, trying to figure out where our plan was breached and the whereabouts of the consignment. I need you to approach it from a different angle, undercover but in plain sight. You're one of my best people. No one, dealing with consignments, has ever seen or heard of you. Get to Poona. You are going undercover; your name is going to be Preeti Rao, an educated young girl who works at the famous Halo Advertising Agency. The agency has been informed about your cover and your need to keep erratic work hours. Preeti Rao will live alone in her brother's house at the brand-new Tara Road Mansions. I called in several favours and managed to get you in there. Remember, no late nights, no boyfriends, not even noisy get-togethers with girlfriends. The fewer people connected with you while you're there, the better. It will mean you can get closer to the residents of Tara Road Mansions, that is important. Everyone should think highly of you, trust you, confide in you, and never suspect a thing."

Not daring to interrupt, Preeti stared as she thought, "What was the connection between the consignment and Tara Road Mansions?"

He continued, "All the residents of the new houses at Tara Road Mansions are suspects. At the moment, they don't seem to know each other, but they could be pretending and actually be well-known to each other. Why else would this housing project by a brand-new developer be snapped up so quickly within hours of going on the market, especially at those astronomical prices? The developer Tarun Tejani is new to the real estate market but owns Tejani Transport, a well-respected, well-established national transport company. Most of the residents moved into the houses within days of each other, around the time that the consignment disappeared. We have just found out that all the residents were offered free truck services by Tejani Transport with two dedicated trucks. Most of the residents took up this offer to move their furniture and other household things. These two dedicated trucks are the very same two trucks that were used to transport the consignment until it disappeared. All this cannot be a mere coincidence. Somehow, I think this is all connected, and we are missing that link. Find me that link or the consignment! Was the consignment taken to one of the residents' former houses, or offloaded at one of the Tara Road Mansions houses?" he shrugged.

"You must watch, observe, and befriend all these neighbours. Get inside their houses, look in the places they show you and snoop in places they don't. They have all moved there recently, so their houses and their routines will still not be quite set. I am hoping you can find a chink in their cover-up, something that we can widen and investigate. Everyone at Tara Road Mansions is a possible person of interest. Just now, we have no idea of the whereabouts of the consignment. But such a big consignment will definitely move, although they may cool it a bit first.

Two million dollars is a lot of money. Successes will be counted and inefficiency scrutinised. Heads will roll over this. Make sure it's not mine," he said sharply, "Or yours!" He added suddenly in a much lower, sinister voice. She waited, expecting more instructions. But unexpectedly, he sat down heavily in his chair, suddenly exhausted with tension and rage. Unsure of what to say, she had nodded and taken the proffered file. She had spent the rest of the day preparing to go to Tara Road Mansions as Preeti Rao.

By the time she sat in the taxi bound for Poona the next morning, she had read the file several times and knew all the information about the consignment, the driver, the contacts at the docks and customs etc. She had also seen photos and newspaper cuttings showing that in the early 1900s, Tara Road Mansion had been an oversized three-storey building with beautifully manicured gardens, outhouses, and pavilions overlooking a bend in the river and a large stream. It had been leased to Poona's prestigious Boat Club as an exclusive vantage point for their members to watch the river regattas in luxury. The gardens had leisurely paths to the stream and then to huge colonnaded pavilions on the riverbank. She had seen paintings and photographs of the pavilions displayed prominently at the century-old Boat Club on the city's outskirts. The pictures flaunted governors, film stars, and scions of industry relaxing in huge velvet armchairs, watching the regatta on the river. The ladies dressed in floor-length dresses and high hairstyles. Their slender fair arms holding ornate binoculars with golden rims. These tableaux of full-dress uniforms and elegant, glamorous clothing were completed by turbaned, stiff-backed waiters bearing silver platters of food and drink.

Over the years, the bend in the river had run low; now all that remained was a large, deep stream. The still-famous and highbrow Boat Club regatta committee had moved the race route to a different stretch of the river. As Tara Road Mansion was no longer useful, the Boat Club had withdrawn its patronage and the property had fallen into disrepair for decades until recently, when it was demolished and developed into a cluster of swanky homes by Tarun Tejani, who named the development Tara Road Mansions.

The file also contained a double-page newspaper cutting from *Poona Business News*, which said "Tara Road Mansions: Five unique double-storey houses with large customised, landscaped, established front and back gardens at an iconic site overlooking a large stream. Calm and quiet in the heart of the city." The architect's rendition of the new development was beautiful. It showed an old tree-lined lane leading to the original distinctive black and gold wrought iron gates. A large driveway wound around a tiny landscaped roundabout and branched out to the five driveways of the double-storey houses with the promised front and back gardens and a huge green bank behind the houses that was cordoned by a large stream as advertised.

A sketch of the ruined pavilions between the stream and the dry riverbank only added to the luxurious feeling of space and old-world charm. The open space, deep stream, large brand-new individual houses, and wide tree-lined lane, with its proximity to the bustling main street, were rare and expensive luxuries in a city residence. The end of the newspaper article said Tara Road Mansions had found buyers within an hour of being available, setting a real estate record for its price and selling time." Preeti had pondered this information carefully, trying to work out how it could all link with the missing consignment, the trucks used for moving, the large stream, the high real-estate prices, and the rich residents.

"Madam. Madam? This is Bund Garden Road. We will be at Tara Road Mansions in a few minutes, madam," the driver's rushed sentence burst into her thoughts. She jerked her head up at the driver's voice and nodded, and rolled down the window a little. Still holding the file, she began to observe her surroundings with renewed interest.

Bund Garden Road in Poona was a bustling street packed with the cacophony of traffic, shops, and people. Handcarts laden with fruit and vegetables did brisk business all day long by the roadside as women haggled and shopped in quick, seamless transactions. The road was crammed with revving cars, fume-belching buses, and pedestrians obstructed by rickshaw drivers arguing in the middle of the road. Flower sellers seated cross-legged at the edge of the pavement could barely keep pace with their fast-selling jasmine and marigold garlands. Between the garland sellers and rickshaw rank sat a dusty red post box cemented to the ground. Its round black top and angled posting slot gave it the appearance of a squat red sentinel in a black peaked cap.

Beyond the pavement, the shops were almost comical in their proximity and diversity, as if a child had arranged them thoughtlessly. Mawani Sweets exhaled aromas of traditional sweets and savoury fried snacks next to the smart Cantonment Civilian Commerce Office with glass doors and glossy granite steps, which in turn flanked Gleam Men's Haircutting Saloon, with its low roof and peeling lurid green paint; it shared a wall with Hanuman Stores. This ubiquitous grocery burgeoned with dusty glass cabinets, noisy freezers, and food products that encroached the pavement with bunches and bundles of wares right up to the traffic. The shopfront was festooned with strings holding dozens of shiny foil packs of potato chips, colourful shampoo sachets, condom packets, dusty multi-coloured beach balls, and plastic bats, promising all kinds of glorious fun for all ages. These stringed wares hung low and loose; they danced in the breeze, swaying wildly every time a hurrying customer bumped into them. At the street intersection, cheek by jowl were a second-hand bookshop, a small, untidy-looking laundry, and the ancient and dusty Poona Gift Emporium entrenched between a sari shop and a car mechanic's shop.

Preeti rolled down the window further. Instantly, the street was a sensory cocktail garnished with constantly honking traffic, vendors shouting prices, and easily excitable pedestrians. A wailing baby, a yelping dog, and the hydraulic hiss from an ageing bus followed a crescendo of screeching brakes, occasionally punctuating the constant hum of traffic. Mawani's fresh samosas' aromas tickled her nostrils before mingling with the smell of acrid exhaust fumes and grease from the car service centre, top notes from the flower sellers' jasmine, and a fresh whiff of clean clothing sizzling under the laundry's large hot iron.

Almost suddenly, the Ambassador turned from this busy and noisy main road into a broad, deep lane with a large green sign with big white letters, 'Tara Road (Private Keep Out).' This quiet, shaded lane seemed cooler, longer, and deeper after the cacophony of the bustling street. There were hardly any people here. Broad ancient trees formed an arching guard of honour all the way to majestic black and gold gates with 'Tara Road Mansions' freshly painted on the wrought iron curlicues. The car drove through the enormous gates and glided to a halt outside house no. 2; Preeti Rao had arrived home.

✦✦✦

CHAPTER 2

Seven well-dressed people sat awkwardly, exchanging polite smiles in the well-furnished, old-fashioned living room. Some squirmed in their seats and made movements to stand up or speak but reluctance won each case.

Finally, a rotund older woman heaved herself up, momentarily stretching the paisley print of her stiff, starched cotton saree. "Hello everyone! Welcome to our first meeting at Tara Road Mansions. Let us introduce ourselves. I am Mrs Barvay." She sounded confident and well educated, speaking convent-taught English with an Indian accent, rolling the 'r' in the middle of words and softening the 'r' at the end. Her tone had a comforting, melodious lilt, reminiscent of long-gone Anglo-Indian school teachers. "I am speaking in English because I saw everyone's last names and realised that Hindi and Marathi, not all people here can understand, so English it is." As she gestured with her arms to the room at large, several chunky gold bangles clinked on her chubby wrists; her words gently rose and ebbed the tide of her ample chest, bobbing the *mangalsutra* around her neck like a ship on a gentle sea.

"I have moved temporarily to Tara Road Mansions. Much more manageable than our family home, Barvay Mansion. Painting and renovation work is going on there at the moment," she paused for effect before continuing, "Usually my son Avi, … Avinash looks after all that. But he is away just now…" her words tumbled out hurriedly, as if she was keen to finish her sentence. She looked around the room expectantly, hoping this was enough of an introduction for herself and that someone else would volunteer to go next.

Her fair face was like a soft, smiling cushion of talcum powder, punctuated by sharp hazel eyes, coral-coloured lipstick, and a large circle of red *kumkum* on her forehead. Her jewellery and perfume, like her living room furniture, were heavy, expensive, formal, and old-fashioned. She looked around the room kindly but her astute hazel gaze assessed every person in the room.

Jumping the queue of hesitance, a young woman stood up. Her delicate silver bracelet jingled on her wrist and an elegant silver watch on the other arm glinted as she smoothed down her dress and began, "My name is Preeti Rao. I am from Calcutta; my parents still live there. I work at Halo Advertising here and live alone too, in my brother's house. He is Rohit Rao, house no. 2. He's taken his family away to the US on a three-year work contract. It's very nice to meet all of you." Preeti Rao's quiet, confident voice, her slim, petite figure in the low-heeled sandals, a pale blue calf-length dress with its demure neckline and cap sleeves, impressed everyone.

An expensively dressed, elegant couple looked at each other at the mention of Halo Advertising. The wife was rather flamboyant in a bold-patterned salwar kameez, stilettos, and chunky diamond jewellery that wobbled and winked with the slightest movement. She began nudging her husband and making upward eye rolls at him, goading him to go next. Her heavy makeup accentuated her not-so-subtle gestures. Her stiff hairspray did not allow her hair to move even a millimetre when she nodded vigorously at her husband.

He pushed away her elbow rather unkindly but stood up as Preeti Rao finished her introduction. He was tall, athletic, and dressed elegantly. Monogrammed cufflinks glinted at his wrist, drawing attention to his expensive watch when he gestured as he talked. "I am Shivram Karamlegavraokar and this is my wife Dr Rajni Karamlegavraokar." He paused to draw effect from their long, impressive surname that included two landed titles and the fact that his wife's name had the prefix of doctor. "I am the director of my own finance company and Rajni is an orthodontist. We moved to Tara Road Mansions because our children's school is a closer commute from here." He named a very posh private school and his wife looked around expectantly, but no one commented or looked awed.

She looked disappointed as she stood up to speak, "Actually, I trained in the US. Their programmes were very expensive but far superior," she simpered in a strange accent, peeved that the mention of their children's posh school had not brought forth any reaction. They had both looked around, hoping to have impressed everyone with their important-sounding name, professional success, and their children's posh school.

Mrs Barvay quietly repeated their surname in her head, trying to work out Mrs Karamlegavraokar's strange accent and had a sudden smile. She prided herself on her knowledge of surnames, castes, classes, religions, and regions of India, and their associated accents too. That almost double-barrelled surname was surely made up by combining their individual unimpressive names.

They were both from the lowest underprivileged castes and the fake American accent was just so put on, it had made Mrs Barvay laugh. "New money always shows" she thought disdainfully as Mrs Karamlegavraokar's ostentatious diamonds glinted and gleamed brazenly even as she leaned back in her chair. Mrs Barvay had many jewels, including diamonds of much better quality and superior design but she would never wear such large pieces of jewellery for a neighbours' meeting. She mentally tut-tutted the inappropriateness of it.

Next, a short bald man with aquiline features stood up and smiled. "Namaste, namaste. We are Mr and Mrs Tulpule," he said in a booming voice as he beamed around the room, indicating the lady who sat next to him on the couch. Then he continued, "We are very happy to meet all of you fellow Indians here today. India is a great country and we want our future generations to learn our rich history, culture, traditions, science discoveries, and business practices."

Mrs Tulpule sat up straighter and looking around the room, smiled at the others. "Namaste. We are being in the last house with the paddock," she said in a soft, sweet voice. The couple's simple clothes were made of cotton and khadi, and their fingers were cluttered with numerous chunky finger rings studded with unmistakably very good quality precious stones set in gold.

Mrs Barvay stared in horror at the pair, "The khadi, the rings, and all this talk about India.... Was this a politician for a neighbour? Maybe two? How crass!" Politicians meant press reporters, entourages, and bystanders. She had moved here thinking it would draw less attention to herself. "Noses like bloodhounds, those reporters." She shuddered at the very thought.

The Karamlegavraokar couple, however, looked at each other and quivered in delight. "Politicians! That would be really good for dinner parties," Mrs Karamlegavraokar gleefully whispered to her husband.

"... our two children go to a formal, local language school only for two days in the week. We only speak English when we have to; otherwise, we speak only our native Marathi. We teach our children Sanskrit and other subjects at home by ourselves only. We firmly believe in our cultural heritage and going back to basics, learning from nature, hence the paddock and our beloved Sundari. You must have seen her already, no? Oh, and my wife and I, we have a business consultancy company also. That is how we can afford to run our household," he smiled almost coyly.

Mr Tulpule's Indian English was mostly correct but had a heavy Marathi accent with excessive use of 'only' in his sentences. It lacked the polish of the other residents' English, as if he translated each sentence into English in his head before he spoke.

"Phew!" thought Preeti Rao. "Not politicians then." Politicians came with all kinds of unwanted attention along with security details, armed escorts, visitors, protestors, and the press. All these extra people would have made her task very difficult indeed.

A tight-lipped smile had passed around the room at the mention of Sundari. The word 'Sundari' meant beauty and in the past week, everyone had seen the huge black buffalo with long, curled horns, ambling nonchalantly as her owners called to her at the end of the day. She ignored their calls with an insolent toss of her large head and unceremoniously tried to lean over everyone's backyard fences to chomp indiscreetly from all the neighbours' new manicured gardens. She was dark as the night, but her nostrils and lips were deep grey, leathery and rough. The skin on her lips and nostrils had natural embossed patterns. She had a large, rough, drooling pink tongue and a huge set of beautiful white teeth set close to her lips. Every now and then, Sundari stretched her leathery, embossed lips over her top teeth in a sneer that was menacing and idiotic at the same time. Mr Tulpule, oblivious to the vibe in the room about his beloved buffalo, droned on and on about pesticides and additives unsuitable for Sundari and good quality feed and milk yields.

The elegant Mr Karamlegavraokar gave his garish wife a stricken look. "Just one more neighbour left for introductions. So far, none of them have seemed impressive or noteworthy despite them buying some of the most expensive real estate in Poona. Have we made an error in moving here?" he wondered.

Sensing no end to the boring monologue about the virtues of buffaloes and home schooling, Mrs Barvay, who had been nodding politely at Mr Tulpule, decided to interrupt inquiringly with a clichéd, "And last but not least, our final neighbour?"

The good-looking, well-dressed lady in the hijab sat up in her armchair. She was uneasy. This was a new circle of strangers. The others in the room, despite their overt differences, had plenty in common with each other. She was very conscious of being the only Muslim in the room. She stilled her trembling hands by smoothing the ends of her long headscarf resting in her lap. "Where was Ayaz when she most needed him by her side? He had talked her into moving here from his ancestral home and then he had promptly scuppered abroad!" she thought crossly.

She began nervously in a soft, well-cultured tone. "I am Hamida Ayaz Sheikh. My husband Ayaz is mostly abroad, away for work for several months at a time. So, it is just me and my children that you will see and hear. I have a small dressmaking business called *The Begum Boutique,* which I run from home. I use the ground floor as the shop and we live upstairs."

There was a soft gasp and some eyes opened wide at this revelation. *The Begum Boutique* was one of the most popular and expensive bridal boutiques in the city. No one had associated this quiet lady in the conventional Muslim attire with the owner of such a glamorous boutique. But Hamida mistook the soft intake of breath as an expression of collective shock at having a Muslim family amidst them. Without meaning to, they stared in fascinated awe, making Hamida even more uncomfortable.

Sensing Hamida's awkwardness, Mrs Barvay diverted her guests' attention, "Come, come! This way.... Let's all have some tea and snacks as we chat. Please help yourselves." She led them to a huge dining table behind an intricately carved wooden Kashmiri screen. The table was laden with food.

A large chocolate cake jostled for space next to fresh samosas, dainty sandwiches, coconut burfee, pistachio rolls, cool dahi wadas, spicy paneer tikkas, spongy dhoklas garnished with coriander, biscuits bursting with nuts and raisins sat amidst an assortment of sweet and spicy chutneys in small bowls. On the burnished sideboard was a heavy and ornate silver tea service. Ready to serve the hot drinks stood a demure maid in a cheap, nondescript salwar kameez, with neatly braided hair, tiny silver earrings, and mismatched plain glass bangles.

This was Meena, who had started work at Mrs Barvay's when the wealthy lady had moved to the newly built Tara Road Mansions. Meena's interview had been conducted in Mrs Barvay's former residence, as Meena had furtively appraised the contents of the spacious living room in Mrs Barvay's sprawling old mansion. She had almost gaped at the high quality of the items and immediately decided to take the job. Meena always stole small, expensive items from her rich employers. Only one from a pair of earrings, a bottle from a set of imported perfumes, a spoon from a tea set, a gold bracelet from a careless teenager's room etc., so it took a while for the thefts to be discovered. The pawnshop near the railway station paid good money for these items.

Meena had a good eye and a deft hand for these petty thefts. She had scrutinised the six guests as she stood behind the screen, quietly listening to the introductions with great interest. The cotton-clad couple with the buffalo held the least interest for her. The lady with the chunky diamonds was definitely worth following and that young girl in the blue dress too. "These educated, young career girls were careless and had lots of expensive things. And that lady with the bridal boutique was such a good find!" Meena had thought greedily. She had heard that the expensive bridal clothes worn by rich people had low-quality diamonds and precious stones sewn on with pure gold thread for embroidery and expensive Swar-something crystals. "So easy to steal! People with children always needed extra help, so plenty of opportunities, especially since the husband was away," she thought happily. She set herself to work, being attentive and helpful to all these guests, thinking, "If I show them today that I am very good at my job, then these people will not hesitate to offer me some part-time work."

With the practised ease of a good hostess, Mrs Barvay hospitably shepherded her guests from the lavish living room towards the sumptuous dining room. Soon it was alive with the tinkling of silver on china, muted laughter, and pleasant chitchat. Everyone settled into comfortable conversations as they sized up one another. Mrs Karamlegavraokar the gaudy orthodontist was desperately trying to befriend Mrs Barvay because she had concluded that the lavish lifestyle seen in this house could only be possible with very old money and that was definitely friendship worthy. Mrs Karamlegavraokar gushed compliments about the food, furnishings, and the house. She tried to steer the conversation to old family jewellers and lifetime golf club memberships. Mrs Barvay was amused at these ill-concealed attempts at familiarity because she did not care much for nouveau riche people. "Too showy and unrefined," she thought unkindly. She had rather liked quiet, refined Hamida of *The Begum Boutique* fame, who was standing by herself, and veered towards her.

Most residents of Tara Road Mansions quickly figured out that it was best to avoid Mr and Mrs Tulpule with their strange ideas, lifestyle, and omnivorous buffalo. However, the Tulpules were a maelstrom in themselves and Mr Tulpule managed to corner every resident and chat with them about Sundari. Mrs Tulpule rattled on about homeschooling, medicinal herbs and traditional Indian herbal remedies, without giving anyone else a chance to speak.

Sensing an opportunity, Preeti Rao discreetly asked Meena for the bathroom. Meena directed her to the downstairs powder room tucked between the living room and dining room. Preeti waited till Meena had turned away to serve some tea, then she deliberately misunderstood the instructions and went upstairs pretending to look for the bathroom. She used the time wisely and went through Mrs Barvay's bedroom and its contents very carefully. The other rooms upstairs were almost bare. They contained basic bedroom furniture and some opened boxes of bed linen. To Preeti's well-trained eye, a few minutes in each room were more than sufficient to look through their contents. In fact, fitting with Mrs Barvay's story, there seemed to be just enough furniture for a comfortable temporary stay. Preeti trod the floor tiles purposefully and tapped the walls, listening for altered or hollow spaces. But she found nothing remotely interesting upstairs and discreetly made her way downstairs to join her neighbours.

Downstairs, the new neighbours chatted about all the clichéd topics. "Where did you live before this?" "What part of India are you originally from?" "Have you set all the rooms yet?" "Did the maid from your old place agree to come here?" "Did you use the Tejani Transport trucks?" "How many trips did the trucks make to move all your things?" "Do you know any good drycleaners near here?" "Guess what we couldn't find on our first morning in our new house? ...."

Recognising this as the correct moment to keep her promise to her maid, Mrs Barvay clapped her hands for attention. The room quieted, and she pointed, "This is Meena, my maid. Although Meena lives with me, I don't need her all day. If any of you would like her to do part-time work for you, please let her know." A general murmur of approval ran through the room. A maid who was vouched for was precious indeed.

Now, Mr Karamlegavraokar stylishly clinked a teaspoon on the fine china of his teacup, "One more announcement," he beamed at them. "We are having a small housewarming party tomorrow evening at 7 o'clock. All of you are invited to our house with your families, it's Number 4," he said rather pompously.

Unable to contain herself, Mrs Karamlegavraokar squeezed in on the action, "We only had a very small religious ceremony last week before the delivery of our new furniture and fridges and all that. Now our beautiful new home is set up and we have settled in just as we had envisaged. Tomorrow morning is the formal *vaastu shaanti puja* at an auspicious ceremony with four high priests. We have invited all our relatives in the morning and all our friends in the evening. You know, that way we can look after all our guests really well."

Mrs Barvay smiled to herself and thought, "What Mrs Karamlegavraokar meant was that their relatives and friends were from very different stratas of society and they did not want to invite them all to the same gathering and feel ashamed of their family, who would definitely cramp their style."

Mr Tulpule generously gushed forth to offer fresh homemade ghee from Sundari's rich, creamy milk for the religious rituals. He was disappointed when his offer was refused politely by the Karamlegavraokars. They had already made arrangements with an expensive supplier for the large amount of ghee demanded by the high priests for the religious ritual offerings. Suddenly, everyone was exchanging notes about their own *vaastu shaanti pujas* before they moved in. Mrs Tulpule proudly told anyone willing to listen that her husband had conducted the religious rituals himself, since he knew all the Sanskrit prayers and verses, and rituals and ceremonies.

No one asked Hamida whether she had any rituals or ceremonies before moving in. No one knew whether Islam had these rituals and did not want to ask the wrong thing, so they simply evaded the issue. They certainly did not know any Muslims or their traditions. Hamida listened to the exchanges around her and longed to tell everyone that her father-in-law had organised for children from the madrassa to read verses from the Quran at the mosque. They had prayed for prosperity and peace in their new home. Her family had distributed lunch and traditional sweets in the local orphanage and her children, parents, and in-laws had eaten a delicious hearty lunch cooked by Hamida and her sister-in-law. However, it all remained unasked and thus, unsaid.

Mr Karamlegavraokar kept scanning the room for Preeti Rao but the attractive young girl was nowhere to be seen. Instead,

Mr Tulpule kept making a beeline for him and there was no escape. He listened politely and nodded patiently at the virtues of homemade cream, yogurt, and ghee while his eyes hopefully scanned the room for either his wife or Preeti Rao so he could excuse himself and escape from the buffalo conversation. But he was unsuccessful in this endeavour and soon subjected to more and more details of Sundari's feed and seasonal changes in milk production. "No easy task, I'm sure" said Mr Karamlegavraokar for the nth time, desperate to flee the clutches of his new buffalo-mad neighbour. Then he had an idea. Suddenly and smoothly, he nodded to an imaginary person across the room, made an 'excuse me' kind of gesture and left Mr Tulpule mid-sentence, still dispensing information about buffaloes.

Meanwhile, Mrs Tulpule had commandeered a corner of the dining table and was poking every plate and bowl to inspect its contents before serving herself generous portions. She was thorough in her task and tasted every item on the table, some of them twice, before she declared, "I really don't eat anything between meals."

Hamida of *The Begum Boutique* fame was now chatting easily to Mrs Karamlegavraokar, as they had discovered their children went to the same posh private school. Mrs Karamlegavraokar mentally plotted to parade Hamida and Mrs Barvay to her friends at their housewarming party the next day. Preeti Rao eventually came down the stairs, hoping to join the ladies but was whisked aside by Mr Karamlegavraokar who wanted to talk to her about Halo Advertising's rates; he had decided he was very keen for them to advertise his business and she promised to get him some information from the office. Mr Tulpule muscled in on every conversation in the room, hoping to complete the oration of Sundari's seasonal feeding schedule but could not finish his monologue delivery to anyone, it was just too long and boring.

Mrs Barvay was satisfied as she looked around the room and thought "The first gathering of Tara Road Mansions went well. This is the new beginning I really need."

✦✦✦

CHAPTER 3

While the adults were at the meeting, Hamida's children Ashu and Munni, played cricket on the grassy patch between the houses and the stream. The deep stream was a few metres wide and formed a natural boundary. Their mother had warned them not to play too close to it or try to cross it.

Soon, a tall, pale boy walked up to them from a neighbouring house. He was sucking a lollipop. "Hi" he said, offering lollipops to the cricketers. The siblings promptly stopped playing and accepted the sweet offering as the boy introduced himself as Kartik Karamlegavraokar from No. 4. The three children were about to resume their game when a girl wearing a pretty dress skipped along, carrying a headset and a Walkman. She stopped and asked for a lollipop. Kartik introduced her as his younger sister Kaveri.

"I want to bat!" she said in a petulant voice as soon as introductions were done.

Ashu and Munni looked on in complete disbelief as Kartik meekly handed over the bat and took up a fielding position. The smug girl batted a few balls then demanded more lollipops from Kartik before sauntering off. A middle-aged woman followed her. She was dressed in a plain, pale blue saree and had a water bottle slung over each shoulder. "That's our maid, Maya Bai; she looks after Kaveri and me" Kartik said flippantly as an explanation.

Maya Bai tried to catch Kartik's eye to draw him away from the new children but he purposefully ignored her. She knew her employer Mrs Karamlegavraokar did not let her children play with any new children unless they had been vetted. Maya Bai fidgeted for a few minutes then gave up on Kartik and decided to focus on Kaveri and keep her away from the new children. Maya Bai said, "Kaveri Baby, don't go far. Your mother has said not to go to the stream. Play here, only with your brother. Give me Wok Maan, it might break," she held out a hand to take the Walkman. Heedlessly, Kaveri continued walking closer along the stream, hands firmly on the Walkman in case it was wrested away from her. She stopped now and then to check that the lady in the blue saree was dutifully following her.

As the evening deepened, the children reined in their game and were about to pull out the stumps when they were surprised to see Kaveri wander back with two more children in tow. "See what I found?" she said, pointing dramatically at the two boys in her wake. "They were playing by themselves outside the last house near the stream. Look, they're boy twins! And they have a pet buffalo called Sundari," she said, dragging forth two boys who looked about eight years old.

Everyone stared at the identical twins for a few seconds in amazement before breaking into big smiles. The boys introduced themselves as Sushrut and Suhrud Tulpule and quickly joined the game of cricket. Maya Bai shuffled uneasily, mumbling, "More new children. Hope Madam never finds out about them." Eventually, she gathered her charges rather forcefully, told them it was time to say goodbye and marched Kartik and Kaveri home.

The twins stayed on to play a while longer and even pointed out the North Star and a couple of constellations to Ashu and Munni before their mothers called them home.

✦ ✦ ✦

A huge wedge of chocolate cake sat on the dining table when Ashu and Munni returned home that evening, bursting to tell their mother of their newfound friends. Their mother Hamida explained that Mrs Barvay their new neighbour had sent the cake because she lived by herself and had diabetes, which meant she could not eat anything sweet. Ashu was excited about the new friends they had made but the chocolate cake distracted him completely. He loved all sweet things! Even plain sugar. He had once eaten a kilo of sugar while no one was looking! Nowadays, his mother locked up the sugar and all sweet things. He was impressed with the huge wedge of chocolate cake. "Just imagine Munni, such a lovely chocolate cake, and she had to give it away. I feel sorry for that Mrs Barvay but very happy for us!" he added cheekily.

Then Ashu excitedly told his mother about Kartik and the twins, with Munni chiming in about Kaveri's dress and Walkman. Hamida Sheikh smiled to herself as she heard her children's excited chatter all through dinner and afterwards as they ate slices from the large wedge of chocolate cake. "Maybe moving here was going to be alright after all," she thought.

Ashu and Munni went to bed very happy and content. "Friends, chocolate cake, and lots of space to play cricket in this new place.

I'm glad we moved to Tara Road Mansions, Ammi" Ashu had said when his mother kissed him goodnight. Listening to her happy children relaxed Hamida's tense shoulders. She had been very reluctant to move out of their old Muslim neighbourhood where her husband's family had lived for seventy years. Those streets had people from their community and their religion; they knew Ayaz's family for generations, they knew her and her children. She was comfortable there, but the old Sheikh villa although quite large, was crumbling. Many parts of it were unusable. It had very large halls, few rooms, and just one indoor bathroom. It was just not practical or spacious for all of them anymore, as Ayaz, Hamida, their children, Ayaz's parents, Ayaz's brother and his wife all lived in the one, sprawling, large old-fashioned house. Ayaz was rarely home; the success of *The Begum Boutique* had meant longer and longer hours for Hamida in the boutique and the commute to the boutique from the ancestral home had become tedious. Now that Ayaz's brother's wife was pregnant with twins, they would need extra space and appreciate help from the in-laws to look after the little ones. So, Ayaz had suggested that his family move out of the ancestral home. Ayaz and his father had bought the house in Tara Road Mansions and converted the ground floor into Hamida's boutique. Hamida had strongly advocated against buying the house at Tara Road Mansions when she realised they would be the only Muslim family here. Yet here she was, with Ayaz thousands of miles away and a solemn promise from her in-laws that she could always move back to the Sheikh villa any time if she did not like Tara Road Mansions. They had promised to visit regularly and frequently, but she still felt lonely after years of the hustle and bustle of a large family residence.

Kartik and Kaveri Karamlegavraokar did not go to bed happy, although their dining table had also boasted a huge wedge of chocolate cake and they had been excited to see it too. But their mother had said, "Don't even think about touching it tonight. Too sugary and rich for this time of the day, Maya Bai will give you some of that cake after school tomorrow. Make sure you brush your teeth afterwards." The cake was put away in the fridge. Their excitement deflated as they were given their usual Friday night dinner of fish stew and chapattis, and fruit to finish the meal. Kartik furiously kicked Kaveri under the table as she almost told their mother about their new friends. He knew if their mother disapproved of any of these new friends, then they would never be allowed to play with them again. This had happened a lot in their previous neighbourhood, and he was not keen to repeat it. "If she doesn't know about these new friends, she cannot tell us to stop playing with them" he explained to Kaveri as they brushed their teeth before bedtime. They would also have to make Maya Bai promise not to tell their mother about these new friends.

The twins Sushrut and Suhrud were, of course, the home-schooled Tulpule children, who had pointed out constellations to their new friends. Their names were traditional and meaningful, but they were also hard to pronounce and ended up being shortened to ridiculous nicknames by their friends. Children in their old neighbourhood used to call them Soup and Shredder. The twins were glad no one had tried to say their names this evening, for that is how the laughing and teasing usually began. They had eaten the chocolate cake after dinner, then practised their Sanskrit verbs and verses before getting ready for bed.

Suhrud consulted his brother that night, "Should we just make up new names and tell them they are our nicknames? Something normal like other children have?"

"What if they hear our parents calling us?"

"We'll just pretend that those are our formal names used just for school and sometimes by our parents."

Sushrut nodded his head, "Yes, that would work."

"Okay, what should we call ourselves?"

"Sameer and Sunil"

"Yes! But what if the other children call us our new names in front of our parents?"

"We will just say the other children cannot say our names, just like last time."

His brother nodded in approval.

✦✦✦

As all the children from Tara Road Mansions were getting into bed, Meena finished washing the large pile of plates, cutlery, and serving dishes used that evening. When the last guests had left, Meena had cajoled Mrs Barvay into an armchair in front of the TV. She had asked for instructions to put away leftovers, then made up a tray with a cup of tea and some of the leftovers and left it within Mrs Barvay's reach. "Call out, if you need anything else. I will go and tidy up and wash everything. I don't remember which cabinets we took things from this afternoon. Maybe you can tell me later on? Everything is new to me, here."

Mrs Barvay leaned back in her chair and put her tired feet on an old leather ottoman. As she sipped her tea and watched TV, she felt quite content. It had all worked out. This new house, the new maid etc. All her old friends and acquaintances, and relatives had been quite shocked and unsupportive of her sudden move to a new, much smaller house, and letting go of her maid Lakshmi who had been with her for several decades. Mrs Barvay could not tell anyone that the old house was too big, too full of memories and constant reminders of her son Avi, and the dreams and hopes of generations of Barvays. It had once bustled with family members and house staff. Nowadays, the joint family system had been disbanded and large families were no longer the norm.

She and her husband had hoped for a large family too, but had managed to have one son and four miscarriages; every miscarriage had been a girl. She and her husband had desperately prayed every time that each baby girl survived, but it was not to be. That was years ago. She shook herself out of her reverie. This house, although tiny compared to Barvay Mansion, was huge for her alone, with several rooms she would never need or use. Here, she had the master bedroom and a large sitting room upstairs for herself, plus some empty bedrooms upstairs too. She had relegated the downstairs study as a storeroom, filling it with boxes, trunks, and sacks full of things from Barvay Mansion that she would probably not need until Avi returned. "When would Avi be back? Would Avi be back? Look forward to the future.

New beginnings!" she fiercely reprimanded her thoughts to stop herself spiralling into gloom.

In the dining room, Meena dealt quickly with the food and the washing up. She would have loved some chocolate cake, but Mrs Barvay had given it all away. There were other sweet leftovers; she could always have those. "Best ask first, brand-new job" she thought; it would definitely make a good impression. Soon she had all the pretty bone china plates and silver cutlery drying on old tea towels on the kitchen counters. She made a great show of laying all the silver spoons on a soft muslin cloth. Employers always checked these first; they were the easiest to steal. She fingered the heavy, carved, silver tea service lovingly. "These were the things that would be worth stealing, but not just now. Early days…" she thought, content with the promise of things to come.

✦✦✦

At that very moment, a rather discontent discussion was going on in the Karamlegavraokar bedroom. "Shivram, I thought we could get richer and more well-known neighbours here at Tara Road Mansions because of the prices, but other than that *Begum Boutique* lady, no one worth mentioning! I was so hopeful of that khadi-clad couple. At least some lower-level political affiliation, some celebrity press…. but nothing! Just glorified hippies, bohemians. Wonder how they can afford a house here? Or maybe they won the lottery or something? Or could there be some illegal dealings? They did say they have a business consultancy, but that means nothing really. Maybe they are consultants for buying buffaloes," she smirked. "Wagging fingers at TV programmes and good private schools, hmmph!" Mrs Karamlegavraokar removed her heavy makeup rather forcefully, directing her frustration on the cotton balls that were cleaning her face of the gunk.

"Yes, I'm disappointed too. We had purposely planned tomorrow's party after this evening's meeting so we could invite all our rich new neighbours and show them off to our friends. Not much to show off now. That girl who works at *Halo* was impressive, though. Knows her stuff. I had a bit of a chat with her, and very good-looking too. We must try and make friends with her, maybe she knows some influential people through her advertising contacts?" Mr Karamlegavraokar was more restful than his wife about their lacklustre neighbours as he calmly padded about the room, switching off unwanted lights and adjusting the air-conditioning. He believed that the situation could still somehow be salvaged.

Mrs Karamlegavraokar's hands had stilled their energetic face cleansing when her husband mentioned the *Halo Advertising* girl. She bristled at the very thought that her handsome Shivram should find that young advertising girl attractive, when she herself was so much more intelligent and attractive too. All that girl was wearing was a cheap blue dress, some jangly silver bracelet and cheap pearl earrings. Probably costume jewellery bought in some wayside shop. Real class meant wearing diamonds like her own, and gold jewellery. And expensive imported clothes and perfumes. That train of thought led her to Mrs Barvay.

"That Mrs Barvay was very boring but oooold money, Shivram. I could recognise… almost smell it. Did you see that silver tea service! And the paintings on her walls are all originals. Ravi Varma, Amrita Sher-Gil, MF Hussain even! Did you see the carpets she had? All hand-knotted kilims – silk and intricate patterns. Wonder what business her husband had... Would have been a very long time ago, though. Must ask her next time."

The make-up was finally off, and now Rajni Karamlegavraokar struggled to open an expensive new tube of hand cream and kick off her fluffy imported slippers at the same time as she sat on their huge, carved, wooden four-poster bed. "Pity her son and his family are not here. They would have been the perfect friends for our children. Still, early days...." She trailed off her sentence and sighed dreamily as her husband gently caressed her breast through her expensive French nightie. She moaned and snuggled closer, breathing in his familiar imported cologne, glad to take his mind off that Halo Advertising girl.

✦ ✦ ✦

CHAPTER 4

The day of the Karmalegavraokar *vaastu shaanti puja* and housewarming party dawned with a bright orange sky that was already quite warm. The household at No. 4 Tara Road Mansions was a hive of activity. Early morning had brought home four Hindu priests in the Karamlegavraokars' long, grey Mercedes. They looked fierce with smooth shaven heads, foreheads streaked with sandalwood lines, and grim, unsmiling faces. They wore white dhotis and cotton shoulder shawls, their sacred diagonal *jaanva* threads stretched and bounced over their bare torsos and potbellies as they hurried into the house. By mid-morning, No. 4 was resonating with priestly chanting, and the downstairs windows billowed thick, pale grey smoke of sandalwood and ghee from the sacred fire rituals. Coughing and rubbing their eyes, Kartik and Kaveri stumbled out with Maya Bai and went to play by the stream.

All morning, an endless tide of Karamlegavraokar relatives swept in. Waves of pedestrians, motorcycles, rickshaws, and an assortment of shiny new and battered old cars made relentless, dutiful appearances at No. 4. Each vehicle disgorged unimagined numbers of people from within. Most guests were traditional and conservative in dress and attitudes. Stiff-backed men always walked ahead, followed by the women a few steps behind, clad in bright sarees with long and heavy brocaded *pallus* drawn over their lowered heads. As they arrived, they all stopped to look up in awe at the Karamlegavraokar house before they hurried to the front door to add to the heap of footwear and then disappeared into the large new house. Old, frayed, dusty leather chappals obscenely elbowed dainty, elegant sandals under the weight of unevenly worn leather boots and once-smart leather slip-ons, while branded sports shoes flirted shamelessly with cheap, gaudy plastic slippers.

Ashu and Munni enviously watched these proceedings from their bedroom windows as they pretended to study. Final exams were close. Their mother had gone downstairs to *The Begum Boutique* after breakfast, leaving them uncensored, free to stop revision and stare all day at the proceedings next door. They had abandoned their books and focused on the happenings in the house next door. The siblings were fascinated by the bare-torsoed Hindu priests and the billowing smoke that made their eyes water. Then they caught a glimpse of the Karamlegavraokar couple decked in traditional garb and indiscreet amounts of gold, when they momentarily appeared in their garden to pray to the sun god, with the priests giving curt instructions. Ashu and Munni had never witnessed anything like it in their old neighbourhood. They thought it was marvellous that their friends had gone out to play by the stream with Maya Bai. They, themselves, would have never been allowed to leave the house to play outside if they had so many guests at home.

Later that morning, smoke-belching rickshaws delivered some more people in traditional clothes and huge pots of cooked food. By late afternoon, the grey Mercedes took away the pot-bellied priests. The guests left in dribs and drabs soon after they had eaten lunch, dwindling the motley collection of footwear and vehicles from No. 4. The three Karamlegavraokar cars swiftly ferried away the many remaining guests who had arrived by rickshaw and on foot.

Very late in the afternoon, Meena hurried to No. 4. Mrs Karamlegavraokar had asked her to help look after the evening guests' children. Meena had been delighted at the chance of earning extra money and unfettered access to the Karamlegavraokars' house, and guests' belongings. There would be handbags to rifle through and children's amulets and trinkets to magic away.

Early evening brought a small truck to No. 4. It was new and purred gently as it dispensed smart waiters in black trousers, crisp white shirts, dark waistcoats, and red velvet bow ties. The waiters unloaded silver salvers, long tables, stacks of starched linen, upholstered chairs, and covered trays of food. Soon, the Karamlegavraokars' backyard was transformed into a stylish cocktail party. Fairy lights twinkled in the garden, a bar was set up in one corner, food was laid out on trestle tables with pristine white tablecloths, and chauffing dishes gently warmed delicious smelling food. Jazz music and old Bollywood tunes curled out of large speakers and softly joined the evening breeze as the smartly attired waiters floated around offering silver salvers of canapes and cocktails to the first evening guests.

At the front door, Mr and Mrs Karamlegavraokar proudly welcomed their guests. He was elegant in a dark suit, and a tie from his UK alma mater. Her clothes and jewellery were expensive and loud. Jangly-belled bracelets announced her presence every time she waved her arms, and she constantly nodded to show off her large, long diamond-drop earrings.

The evening guests were rich, stylish, and modern; unlike the morning guests, these couples walked alongside and close to each other. No pedestrians, dusty rickshaws or motorcycles pulled up in the driveway now. Uniformed chauffeurs of expensive cars helped their well-dressed employers step out of the cars and carried gifts to the front door before driving away. Large professional-looking bouquets and ostentatiously wrapped presents graciously exchanged hands after much air kissing and shaking of hands. The presents were handed to Maya Bai, who put the packaged presents on display on a large table in the foyer.

Mrs Barvay watched the endless stream of cars from her living room windows. It took her back to her old residence Barvay Mansion and the many happy and sad gatherings she had organised there over the years. "Would they ever happen again now?" Her heart ached as she thought of Avi. Then with a sigh, she came back to the present. She needed to get dressed and join the Karamlegavraokars' party. Meena had laid out Mrs Barvay's clothes before leaving for No. 4. Half an hour later, Mrs Barvay emerged from her front door, wearing a beautiful green saree and emerald jewellery, and ambled across the front lawns of the neighbouring houses to get to the party. Her chubby fingers clutched a pale green sparkly purse in one hand and an ornate traditional envelope with gift money in the other. She was welcomed effusively by the hosts.

When the Karamlegavraokars welcomed their guests at the front door, they encouraged them to have a walk through their new home before joining the party in the garden. They had spent lavishly on their new home and wanted everyone to admire it. They were confident that even the most jaded people would find something to gush over. The huge kitchen with its glass cabinets showed off the latest kitchen appliances, imported china and cutlery. There were wing-tipped, button-back leather armchairs in the book-lined study, large American-style couches, hand-embroidered curtains, antique tapestries, brand-new Persian carpets, European porcelain, and twinkling glass chandeliers. The latest TV, video player, music systems, and cassette players were set up for the guests to fawn over. The Italian marble dining table, Chinese mother-of-pearl inlaid rosewood coffee tables, and polished rocking chairs on the back porch with designer quilted cushions were on display too. The children's rooms had pale matching bed linen, crisp new storybooks and ornaments on the shelves, mirrored wardrobes, and favourite storybook characters stencilled on the walls. To top it all, every room, except the kitchen, had an air conditioner.

Ashu and Munni had watched impatiently from the window since early morning, and it felt like they had waited a lifetime to go to the Karamlegavraokar party while their mother finished boutique work. As all their things had not been unpacked as yet, Munni had rummaged through her new wardrobe and some boxes to unearth her new party frock and shiny sandals immediately after lunch. If this had been their old neighbourhood, they could have simply gone next door by themselves, and their mother could have come later. But here, they knew none of the adults and had met their new friends only once. They had to wait.

Hamida had mistaken the other residents' sharp breath of awe at the mention of *The Begum Boutique*. She had thought it was because she was Muslim and therefore, had been unsure whether she and her children would be welcome at the Karamlegavraokars' party. She had wondered whether their invitation had been just a formality and that she and her children were not expected to go. She was quite sure there would be no other Muslim people at the party. She knew that in this part of Poona, it was okay to love Muslim film stars, have Muslim classmates, Muslim colleagues, and even buying clothes from *The Begum Boutique* was fine. But friendships between Hindus and Muslims were rare, and inviting Muslims to a Hindu home was socially awkward for everyone. She had heard from relatives that it was different in other parts of India, where Muslims and Hindus mingled freely, but she had no experience of that. She had discussed the housewarming party invitation in great detail with her mother and her mother-in-law that morning. They had both advised that it would look incredibly churlish if she did not go. "At least give the new neighbours a chance. After all, they have invited you. And you can always go, wish them happiness in their new home, give them a gift, make up some excuse and return home if you feel you are not welcome," she had been reminded repeatedly. Finally, she had decided to go late in the evening for a very short time. But her children had nagged all day, and now she and her children had arrived at No. 4 much earlier than planned.

However, the Karamlegavraokars were so welcoming and gracious as soon as they saw Hamida and her children that she felt guilty for her earlier misgivings. Mrs Barvay had already commandeered a table and she waved excitedly when she saw Hamida. The children ran off as they spotted their new friends. Hamida sat down with her new neighbour, glad of her companionship in the midst of this party of strangers.

Preeti had arrived carrying a huge bouquet, almost immediately after Hamida. Preeti looked lovely in a silvery-grey salwar kameez and tall heels. She had wanted to arrive once there were a few guests and stay at the party as long as she could without being conspicuous. Like Hamida's children, Preeti too had discreetly watched the proceedings all day, looking for any familiar faces among the many and varied guests. So far, she had neither recognised nor seen anyone acting suspiciously. She had been excited about this party all day because it was an excellent opportunity to walk through the whole house, linger wherever she wanted, and no one would notice her. A perfect chance to have unfettered access and cast her practised eye over each of the rooms to search for clues. She was hoping not to bump into any of her new neighbours until she had a chance to look through the whole house.

As Preeti had entered the Karamlegavraokar house, her trained eye had caught sight of a middle-aged man and woman standing in a shadowy corner where the living room doors opened onto the veranda and backyard garden. They looked vaguely familiar, but she could not recognise them, and that bothered her. The couple's sharp eyes seemed to be taking in everything and everyone from their vantage point. They had looked at her too, momentarily. The minute she caught their eye, they looked away. This happened several times in a couple of minutes. Instantly, she was alert. They just kept looking at everyone, yet made no move to approach anyone, and no one came to talk to them.

Preeti saw Hamida and Mrs Barvay settled at a table outside and decided to avoid them. She sat on a couch in the living room and smiled at some other guests, hoping to make small talk, while waiting to have a good snoop upstairs, because after this party, getting access to the upstairs rooms would be difficult. Again, she saw the nondescript couple looking at her. She remained seated for a few minutes, when the couple looked in a different direction; she stood up and walked around the living room, pretending to be interested in the expensive knick-knacks near the bottom of the stairs. Slowly, she edged towards the staircase to go upstairs, and instantly sensed the woman's eyes on her. The man began stepping forward in her direction, stepping back as Preeti lingered by the stairs and started walking around the living room once more. She wandered aimlessly in the living room again, giving the other guests a few polite smiles. Several times, she got as far as the staircase, and once, she even went up a few stairs before the woman from the couple began to walk towards her. Preeti knew this was no coincidence. "Who were they? Friends or foes? Competitors?"

The presence of the couple was very unsettling; they just stood together in a corner all evening, and did not talk to anyone except one other man. They were of average height, well-dressed, and did not look out of place in this crowd, but they were so nondescript that it made her uneasy. She observed them carefully; she needed to describe them to her boss to find out their identity. She could not move around without worrying about the couple following her, and she could not take that chance, in case she saw or found something important.

Eventually, Preeti gave up trying to go upstairs. She would have to find another opportunity to have a good look at the upstairs rooms of the Karamlegavraokar house. She headed to the garden. As she walked past the couple, boldly she smiled at them, using the opportunity to stare at them for a few moments. They smiled back amiably and then said to her, "Are you Shree and Vasu's daughter? You look so much like your parents." She was taken aback at this confidence; she simply smiled and assured them those were not her parents' names but did not tell them her own name. They apologised, further puzzling Preeti, "Were they genuine guests?"

In the garden, several people were speaking animatedly around Mrs Barvay's table. Hamida waved for Preeti to join them. Preeti nodded and began walking towards them; it seemed like a good place to park herself for the time being, ward off the strange couple, and watch everyone at the party.

Mrs Barvay's sharp eyes had noticed Preeti avoiding the couple, then talking to them and scowling as she walked away, so she asked Preeti about them. "Oh, just family friends, they're trying to matchmake. I am not at all interested in marriage for a few years," Preeti said, ever professional at keeping her cover. Mrs Barvay and Hamida were amused at the attempted matchmaking and smiled. It was a timeless and familiar story at all social functions, regardless of class, caste or religion.

Now resigned to not wandering around the house, Preeti decided to use this cosy interlude to get better acquainted with Hamida, since Mrs Barvay was constantly inundated with visitors to their table. Hamida cheerfully answered many questions about Ayaz, the children, and other members of her family. She was looking much more relaxed than she had at the residents' meeting. Hamida told Preeti about her family's textile factories and her in-laws' successful diamond business in the Netherlands and South Africa. She mentioned the inadequacies of the old Sheikh villa and the need to move to Tara Road Mansions. She said her husband Ayaz worked in a mercantile shipping company. Preeti's mind carefully stacked and filed away this information to fact check in a quieter time. Skilfully, she had got a lot of information out of Hamida but only volunteered that her own parents were currently visiting her brother and his family in America and her brother was a computer engineer.

All the men at this housewarming party were dressed in suits, and the women wore elegant sarees and expensive jewellery. The only man at the Karmalegavraokar party who wore neither a jacket nor a tie was the photographer whose camera seemed to be larger and heavier than his small, thin frame. He wandered quite freely in the throng with the video camera perched awkwardly on one shoulder and another camera slung around his neck as he wrestled with the wires and frequently set up a tripod amidst the throng. He took photos and videos of groups and individuals, including some overenthusiastic people who posed self-consciously. Preeti Rao made a mental note to ask the Karamlegavraokars to see photos and videos after the event, knowing it would pump their egos and allow her to see all the people at the party once again and perhaps a chance to have a good look around the Karamlegavraokar house too. She could also ask them about the strange couple.

In a corner of the garden, a small counter boasted food and desserts just for children. Jelly cups and ice creams hid in the little white mini freezer, while piping hot chips, vadas, vegetarian burgers, and chicken lollipops proudly sat in chauffing dishes separated by cards that read “Vegetarian” and “Non-vegetarian.” Groups of girls in smart party frocks and boys in blue jeans and Star Wars t-shirts constantly gathered around to be served, taking complete advantage of the fact that their parents were too busy socialising and would not notice how many helpings they had.

When the Tulpules arrived, the twins ran in from the door, calling out to their new friends. The twins wore mismatched, patterned cotton shirts and dungarees. “Either they had been allowed to choose their own clothes or they still haven’t unpacked everything,” Hamida thought and smiled. Their parents were in pastel-coloured starched cotton clothes, clearly setting them apart from the silks, chiffons, suits, denim jeans, and other expensive materials on display that evening. Preeti Rao and Hamida had waved at the Tulpule couple, assuming that, like them, the Tulpules would not know anyone else. They were very surprised when the Tulpules ignored them and went straight into the crowd of Karamlegavraokar guests and were instantly surrounded by the other guests, who began animated conversations with them. Preeti puzzled over this, instinctively watching who they spoke to. Hamida thought it was a bit strange too, but did not comment on it; and Mrs. Barvay frowned at being ignored by the Tulpules and continued chatting about her club, recipes, families, and everything in between.

As the evening wore on, the table commandeered by the three Tara Road residents was frequently approached by guests who knew Mrs. Barvay and some of them tried to touch her feet as a mark of respect. The air was punctuated by Mrs Barvay's loud and delighted Marathi exclamations of "*Aggobai! Tu ithe kuthe?*" followed by long conversations about Mrs Barvay's health, Avi in America, extended family, and of course, the families of the guests who had come to say hello to her.

Hamida was whisked away several times by Mrs Karamlegavraokar and proudly introduced to her friends, who promptly wanted a business card. Hamida, who had wondered whether to come to this party at all, was pleasantly surprised and did not have any cards to hand out; she had to go home to get some. She began to feel quite comfortable, welcomed, and accepted in this cluster of new people.

Preeti observed all these interactions intently, scanning for familiar faces, names, places, and other clues. The Karamlegavraokars seemed to have almost a hundred guests at their home that evening. Preeti deciphered that some of the people who talked to Mrs Barvay were relatives; others were family friends, and her son's friends from school and university. The Tulpule couple seemed to know many of the Karamlegavraokar guests too. There were a lot of hellos and namastes being exchanged with the Tulpules although no one tried to touch their feet.

Preeti made a final attempt that evening to sneak upstairs and managed to get past the watchful, weird couple. She was ecstatic when she reached the landing of the first floor, until she realised another man had followed her from the veranda and was waiting alongside her as she bided her time to make a thorough recce of the master bedroom. As she waited for the current group of people to wander out from one room and go into the next one, the man smiled and waited beside her. He was tall, with a beard and huge yellow-tinted glasses. "Who was this?" she wondered. As she stepped through the open door, about to make her foray into the now-empty bedroom, he closed the distance between them, blocking anyone else from entering the room with them. Then she stiffened in shock as both his hands quickly grabbed and groped her in the recessed doorway. Years of training and reflexes spun through her. She dug her nails into the large hand on her breasts and wriggled free, stamping her heel into his shoe as she fought to free his other hand from her buttocks. As her heel stabs caught him off guard, she heaved him aside and ran down the stairs; unfortunately, this movement caught the eye of the strange couple. She dismissed her suspicions about the bearded man with yellow-tinted glasses; he was simply lecherous. Silently, she cursed him. Getting to the first floor again, past the staring couple yet another time this evening would be impossible.

The Karamlegavraokars proudly watched the interactions between Mrs Barvay and their other guests. Judging by the number of people who went up to see her, she seemed well-respected in the old-money set. The Karamlegavraokars had also noticed the popularity of the Tulpules. Mr Karamlegavraokar, unable to contain his curiosity about the Tulpules any longer, took aside a much older financier friend Mr Dev and asked him about the Tulpules.

Mr Dev said, "*Arrey baba*, don't you know? Mr and Mrs Tulpule collectively own about 20% of our state's most expensive and expansive real estate. This includes agricultural land, plantations, forested land, and some of the city's commercial districts where they lease buildings to shops, restaurants, and banks. The very land, where these Tara Road Mansions are built and the surrounding land, including the stream, right up to the river, belongs to Mr Tulpule." Mr Dev continued, "It's lucky the river belongs to the government; otherwise, Mr Tulpule and his ancestors may have leased that to the government too, with a renewable lease." Mr Dev chortled. "Fantastic sense of business in that family, I tell you Shivram, just fantastic! Mr Tulpule's foresight and business acumen in negotiating any deal makes us all look like school children. Years ago, my uncle worked as an accountant for one of the Tulpule companies. The stories he told of their wealth were fascinating to me as a child. But I am only appreciating their true value now, after I became a financial consultant. Her family is also very rich. You know the CKK group? That's them. They are landowners with a major civil construction business here and the family also have diamond mines in Africa. Again, impeccable business acumen, and she has inherited it. Remember the government's Keshav Dam project that was stuck, mired in controversy and bureaucracy? She negotiated that deal, and her brother's company built it. I was a consultant on that project. Formidable woman! Her business brain is like lightning."

Finally, the penny dropped. Of course, Mr Karamlegavraokar knew of the very, very rich Tulpule family and the prestigious CKK group. He had never even thought of associating that information with his buffalo-crazy, khadi and cotton-clad, technophobe neighbours; their surname was ordinary enough. So Mr Dev's answer had astounded Mr Karamlegavraokar, and he struggled to maintain his poker face. He could not wait to tell his wife! Just imagine! He knew the Tara Road Mansions land had been owned by THE Tulpules. He had thought the mad eccentric Tulpule couple who were his neighbours could at best possibly be far-flung relatives of THE Tulpules. He had never considered even for a moment that they were actually THE Tulpules! The move to Tara Road Mansions had been even better than they could have ever hoped for— next door neighbours with THE Tulpules!

✦✦✦

CHAPTER 5

Eventually, when Mrs Barvay wanted to leave the Karamlegavraokar party, Preeti Rao offered to walk her home. Mrs Barvay was overwhelmed by such kindness, and Preeti Rao beamed at her own success in befriending the older lady. Preeti had completely given up on the Karamlegavraokar house for the evening and decided to try to have another look through Mrs Barvay's house. Mrs Barvay was tired, and as Preeti walked the old lady home with great care, she smiled at her own cunning plan.

Preeti asked, "Mrs Barvay, please could I use your phone to make a couple of local calls? Just to my aunt and uncle? My phone connection is not set up yet, and my mother worries if I have not been in touch daily with my aunt."

"Of course! Of course!" said kind Mrs Barvay instantly as she thought of her Avi in the same situation. Mrs Barvay mentioned going upstairs to change into more comfortable clothes, then returning downstairs to keep Preeti company. She took her time and thought this would give Preeti some privacy to make her calls. While Mrs Barvay climbed slowly to the top of the stairs, Preeti sat in the chair closest to the phone and flicked through her tiny diary, pretending to find the necessary telephone number. The telephone receiver rested cosily between her shoulder and her ear. But her ears listened to the party music still in full swing at

No. 4 and concluded that Meena would definitely be busy at the housewarming party, looking after the guests' children.

Preeti pretended to dial a call from the telephone on an old-fashioned corner table and waited until she saw Mrs Barvay disappear upstairs, heard the beep of an air conditioner switched on, and a door quietly click shut, promptly muting the whirr of the air conditioner. She leapt from her chair and briskly began inspecting the rooms downstairs.

She combed diligently through the kitchen. She tapped and scraped expertly at a couple of places that could have held false drawers or a sliding panel between the shelves. Tirelessly and systematically, she continued searching through canisters and storage jars in the kitchen, but she found nothing noteworthy. In the dining room, she looked behind the ornate paintings and inside the deep sideboard and decorative panels. She pressed, poked, and prodded everything, looking for hidden catches, concealed compartments, and secret shelves but the shelves and boxes and compartments she found were too small or empty. She left the living room for last; she would always have access to that. She scanned the darkened doorways and slipped into a room. It seemed to be Meena's room, judging by the shabby, thinning bedclothes and old bedframe. The room was tidy but the furniture was frugal and its furnishings were very plain, threadbare, and mismatched compared to the rest of the house. The few clothes in the cupboard were obviously hand-me-downs and other belongings so meagre that Preeti felt sad as she remembered her own humble beginnings. There was nowhere to hide anything here.

Across the corridor, she squinted in the dark and saw the study. Currently, it seemed to be used as a storeroom. It looked promising; full of boxes and bags and other shapes. Preeti longed to look through their contents. But not tonight. Mrs Barvay would be back any time, and she could not chance it just now, she thought. She hurried back to the telephone and sat in the chair once more because she had just heard an upstairs door click and Mrs Barvay's heavy tread on the staircase. Preeti was saying a warm goodnight to the dial tone by the time the older woman entered the living room, and Preeti hung up the phone, smiling beatifically at Mrs Barvay. "Thank you so much for letting me use your phone. I'll head home now."

✦ ✦ ✦

It was late into the night, the guests had left and Mr and Mrs Karamlegavraokar were discussing the entire day's proceedings over a nightcap. Mrs Karamlegavraokar had complained to her husband that one of his aunts had pointedly told her that their house did not face the right direction, so they were both going to die young. "Really, Shivram! The gall of the woman! She has never liked me or my children. She was very keen for you to marry her neighbour's daughter. And now she prophesies our death! She only tolerates me because you are her favourite and richest nephew." Mrs Karamlegavraokar bristled with indignation, but she had discarded her long earrings, so the effect was less dramatic than it could have been all evening.

"And did you see how many people went up to say hello to Mrs Barvay? I was right. She is o-o-o-old money. We must become her close friends." At the mention of old money, Mrs Karamlegavraokar's voice had dropped to a revered whisper.

"Rajni, my darling, speaking of old money, you know our buffalo-mad Tulpules, well, Mr Dev, you know from my old office, he said they are actually THE TULPULES…." At last, Mr Karamlegavraokar had the chance to unburden the big secret he had hugged to himself most of the evening.

"Oh Shivram, this is too good to be true. What a feather in our cap! We are neighbours with THE Tulpules!" Mrs Karamlegavraokar had cooed with joy after listening to the whole story. The social standing of their new neighbours had added veneer to the Karamlegavraokars' views about the strange habits of the Tulpules, and suddenly all their idiosyncrasies seemed acceptable, even eclectic.

"And darling, did you see the Patils' strange friends? Ajay rang me yesterday to ask if they could bring a couple of friends. Of course, I said yes. Who can refuse the Patils anything? Ajay is the share market king. But if you ask me, the friends were an odd couple. In fact, I don't even know if they were a couple or siblings or just friends. They just seemed strange."

"Strange? What do you mean, Shivram?"

"Oh, they were polite and gracious enough and were dressed really well, but just seemed to stand in a corner and watch everyone. They made no attempt to meet people or mingle or anything like that. Ajay introduced them to me, and they said hello but after that, they just stood in the far corner between the living room and the garden, silently eating, drinking, and watching. Didn't seem right."

"Shivram, you are always so suspicious. Maybe they are just introverts or felt a bit awkward because they didn't know anyone and were kind of add-ons. We didn't mind, of course, but maybe they felt as if they were added on as a formality." The conversation moved on; one by one, the Karamlegavraokars discussed all their guests until it was almost dawn.

✦✦✦

Exactly as Mr and Mrs Karamlegavraokar had hoped, everyone was impressed and talked about the Karamlegavraokar house and their housewarming party for days. The next morning, memories of the Karamlegavraokar party lingered for Ashu as he remembered sampling every flavour of ice cream and every colour of jelly, trying each of the other desserts at least twice. For once, his mother had been busy and not paid him too much attention. His sweet tooth was insatiable, and he could not have asked for a better evening. Ashu and Munni could not believe that such a grand party was just for housewarming. It had seemed more like a small wedding. With a special corner just for children's food! Their eyes still lit up, just thinking about it.

"Ammi, why didn't we have a big party like Kartik and Kaveri when we moved to this house?" Ashu had questioned his mother. "All we had were the children from the *madrassa* reading from the Quran, and Nana, Nani, Dada, Dadi, and some relatives came for lunch. And to eat? Just kebabs and biriyani- nice food but only three sweets."

Hamida smiled. Her reluctance to move here had overshadowed even the meagre housewarming that Ashu had just described. "We can think about a bigger party, once your father is back" she said, knowing that Ashu would forget everything about food and sweets and parties once his much-beloved father was home.

"Hmmm okay, but when IS Abbu coming back? He had said this time he was going away for six months but it has been longer than that now. I've told him to get me a blue remote-control car this time," said Ashu, already distracted by the sugar puffs his mother was rolling out, as he and his sister ate breakfast.

The Tulpule children, accustomed to their own rather frugal lifestyle, had been impressed by the sheer number of things that the Karamlegavraokars had managed to collect and display in their house. The Tulpule twins had been puzzled by the huge speakers of the music system and the video player. They had never encountered these things before and could not fully appreciate the intricacies of cable TV and the audio and video cassette collections that had so impressed Hamida's children. Mrs Tulpule had sampled all the food, including that in the children's corner, before declaring, "I just don't eat between meals. It's not a good habit."

Mrs Barvay rang her sister the next morning for a leisurely chat about the Karamlegavraokars' party, and to tell her of the scandalous amounts of money that must have gone into furnishing the house and hosting two housewarming dos in one day. "You know, it was rather naughty of them to have invited all the conservative, poorer relatives in the morning and their posh friends in the evening. Just as well, I suppose. Neither group would have been comfortable with the other. I watched the morning crowd from my window. *Aggobai!* So many of them, all arriving crammed in cars, rickshaws, and motorcycles, packed like sardines, they were, I tell you. They must have never seen a house like No. 4 in their whole lives! They stared at it in awe from the moment they arrived at the driveway. The Karamlegavraokars even have American modern art on the walls! Of course, I don't care for these things, and I don't understand why interlocking triangles and splashes of paint like a chicken walking on the canvas after strutting through a plate of paint should be called art or cost ungodly amounts of money. But there you go! These nouveau riche people will buy anything as long as it is expensive, huh! And *aggobai*! Almost forgot to tell you who I met – Madhav's oldest son. Apparently, he runs his father's multi-specialty hospital now. That boy could not even pass his matric exam without his father's bribes. How on earth did he become a doctor? Wouldn't want to consult him if he was the last doctor left on earth, I tell you! Money can buy all kinds of things, I guess… And that Arundhati's granddaughter, pregnant again! Yes, the third one in almost four years…*Aggobai*! If the educated people act like this, then what can we expect from the poor illiterate masses, *ho na*?"

✦✦✦

CHAPTER 6

The residents of Tara Road Mansions soon settled into their new homes and routines. Preeti Rao's keen eyes made detailed observations and meticulous notes on everyone's movements, including Sundari, the buffalo. Preeti watched keenly for clues every morning as she walked and jogged along the periphery of Tara Road Mansions. From her window, she also noted the residents' movements and visitors on different days and at different times of the day.

Summer had arrived, bringing long, hot days. Sundari loved to roam, enjoying her freedom and the juicy green shoots from the adjoining manicured gardens. As soon as her early morning milking and feeding was done, she ambled over to the neighbouring Karamlegavraokar backyard. It had a high fence with a modern design that left plenty of gaps for her buffalo-sized head, which she pushed in to reach the expensive and tender landscaped plants. Kartik and Kaveri often sat on their sunny veranda for the 'sunshine vitamin' at breakfast, and if no one was watching, they ran out and hurriedly fed Sundari their own much-detested, expensive and tasteless bran-rich healthy breakfast.

Sundari always neatly avoided Hamida's garden, which had neither a fence nor a shrub border. Ashu and Munni had begged a huge garden bed for themselves, allegedly to plant vegetables and flowers. But in reality, it was a very large, uneven, mud patch by the wall, often littered with drying mud pies, foot-high mountains and fist-deep tunnels, muddy water in plastic teacups, toy trucks, tin boats, and tiny plastic animals. The rest of the garden had roses, crotons, and other colourful leafy bushes that required little maintenance. Nothing that appealed to Sundari.

Preeti Rao's garden on the other hand, had no flowers, just a very low, leafy green border and a large patch of soft lawn; Sundari spent most of her mornings revelling on the soft lawn. It was peaceful and deserted in the morning because Preeti left for a long jog around Tara Road Mansions and the stream. When she returned home, she soon left for work.

Mrs Barvay's backyard had no fence; it was paved to form a traditional courtyard with a low herbaceous border. Several pots of flowering shrubs sat in neat clusters in the corners. The focal point of the courtyard was a large, traditional, four-sided concrete *tulsi vrindavan* altar she had brought from her former home. It had a potted tulsi plant on top, and the structure had an alcove on each side, which housed a different Hindu god. Mrs Barvay said her prayers every morning as she orbited the *tulsi vrindavan*. She was a keen gardener and tended her potted plants and borders in the paved courtyard every morning.

Sundari avoided the Barvay backyard at all costs in the morning. She had been shouted at, hosed with water, and even threatened with a stick by Mrs Barvay! Sundari would never know that Mrs Barvay was too kind to ever hit her.

However, from early afternoon, while the sun still beat down mercilessly, its direction cast large cool shadows of Mrs Barvay's house over the paved courtyard. This cool shade became Sundari's sanctuary until dusk because it was devoid of noisy children and bustling adults. The shaded, deserted, quiet courtyard had cool, clean paving, and the washing at the end of the backyard flapped at regular intervals, creating a fragrant breeze of detergent and peace.

Every afternoon at exactly half past two, Mrs Barvay left for the club in her white Mercedes. The attentive chauffeur, in his smart white uniform and peaked cap, held the door open for her; he returned her in the same style at 8 pm; and until then, Mrs Barvay's cool, shaded courtyard by the storeroom window belonged to Sundari, and Sundari alone. Only when the day cooled sufficiently into a peach-coloured twilight did Sundari rise to her feet and amble back to her shelter, where Mr Tulpule waited patiently with her evening feed.

✦ ✦ ✦

Meena had settled in well with Mrs Barvay, who affectionately called her "Ey Meenay!" and she liked that. Only her mother had ever called her 'Meenay', so it brought back many happy memories. Meena's room had been marked 'Maid's Room' in the architect's plan. It was a tiny room next to the kitchen, tucked away in a nook with a built-in cupboard and its very own, tiny bathroom. The room was just long enough for a small bed and boasted a small window. Mrs Barvay had put in an old bed and a battered mattress, thinning sheets, flattened lumpy pillows, and a faded, flowery curtain. But Meena had felt like a princess as she unpacked her small, broken suitcase of belongings and modest bedroll. She had always shared a room, first with her mother and then with other maids.

Meena had learnt over the years that the minute employers suspected theft, the first rooms searched for missing items belonged to the domestic help. This would be obvious at Mrs Barvay's, where she was the only live-in employee. So, this time, she had taken special precautions. She had started stashing her loot in the storeroom, which according to the architect's original plan was a small study on the ground floor with a window that overlooked the courtyard. The unused room was full of boxes of books and files, old suitcases, some old furniture, and several small sacks of lentils, beans, rice, sugar, and unopened beer bottles.

Mrs Barvay was severely diabetic, and "Surely old women did not drink beer! It must be for visitors," Meena thought, "so the sugar from the sack would never be needed nor anything from the box of beer. Perfect! I can safely hide my stolen things here."

In the kitchen, for Meena, visitors, and houseguests, there was always sugar from the large packet that arrived with the weekly groceries, and there were beer bottles in the fridge that were never opened. As a final safeguard, she half undid the bolt that fastened the window. The loosely secured window could now be blamed if ever she was suspected of theft. She planned to say, "That bolt was always loose. Anyone could have broken into the storeroom. Why suspect me?"

Meena had easily found part-time work at Tara Road Mansions after Mrs Barvay introduced her at the residents' meeting. Four afternoons a week, after Mrs Barvay left for the club, Meena looked after Hamida's children when they returned from school. She made sure they changed out of their school uniforms and washed their hands before they sat down to eat their afternoon snack. Then she waited with them until five o'clock, when they were allowed to put on their shoes and go off to play with the other children near the stream. She did the same things for the Karamlegavraokar children once a week when their Maya Bai had her weekly day off. Once the children went out to play, Meena swept and mopped Preeti Rao's house every day before returning to Mrs Barvay's house by dusk to start cooking an evening meal for the older lady. As Meena walked between the houses for her part-time jobs, she often saw Sundari ambling to and from her shelter, nonchalantly leaving a trail of dung pats behind her.

Meena was happy at Tara Road Mansions; life was good here. Her day was full, the money was good, and the little items she 'picked up' were a bonus. She had made a start on her secret earnings at these Mansions from the Karamlegavraokars' housewarming party. She had immediately deposited her first illicit gains in the storeroom. Her loot included one each from a pair of a baby's gold anklets and a toddler's gold bangles, expensive-looking sunglasses, and some cash from handbags left unattended.

Meena had started work as a maid and regularly stolen from her employers since she was orphaned at the age of nine. She had started with dusting and folding clothes and worked her way up to all household work and simple cooking. She always worked for large joint families for very short periods of time or while their regular maids were away. These large homes and households were always hectic and chaotic; this bought her time before people realised their things were missing. It was easy to name-drop some rich people's names she had heard at earlier jobs and say she had briefly worked for them. No one ever remembered the names or faces of the substitute maids, so there was no chance of references or confirmatory calls. Her story when she left each employer was either that she was getting married and her husband did not want her to work after the wedding or that the aunt she stayed with was moving to a different city. These were plausible excuses, and kinder employers often gave her presents of clothes, money, and jewellery for her wedding dowry.

Although Meena was pretty, she was careful never to draw attention to herself in any way. Even after discovering the theft, it took people a while to accept that the naïve-looking, simple girl had stolen so much from them. The employers often assumed they had misplaced or dropped the stolen items. By the time they talked to other family members, and the tally of lost items grew, and they considered theft a possibility, she was long gone to another part of town, and 'working' another unsuspecting household. The employers rarely made police complaints, as that meant admitting to their own carelessness and inviting the social stigma of police visits to their homes. In turn, the police were not too keen to follow up on these petty crimes as the stolen items were never recovered, even if the thieves were eventually caught.

Meena never knew her father, and when her dear mother had died unexpectedly in their small, shabby rented room, Meena was nine years old and suddenly understood the power of money. Or rather, she experienced the consequences of having no money.

Within hours of her mother's death, the landlord had thrown her out on the street. Her relatives had refused to take her in because girls meant wedding expenses and dowries, and she was penniless. Some neighbours had put her clothes and some food in a large cloth bag, insisting it was for the journey. "To where?" she had asked over and over through her tears. She remembered crying as she walked away aimlessly from the rented room and the street full of people. She could still feel the chill of that winter night when she had huddled under a vegetable cart for warmth. The fusty smell of the stale vegetables still tingled her nostrils when she remembered that night, and the intense hunger pangs as she watched people eating and drinking around a tea stall. She had vowed then never to be without money ever again. She was happy to work for some money and ready to steal some too. Over the years, she had paid small, irregular sums of money to a landlord in her old neighbourhood so she could buy a room for herself. "No one was ever going to set her on the street again and pack her some food for a journey to nowhere" she had promised herself.

✦ ✦ ✦

Every morning at eight o'clock, Hamida walked her children to the main road for their school bus. Afterwards, Hamida frequently walked to the dull red post box across the road to post a rectangular blue aerogramme to her husband. "The house is lovely and the neighbours have been so welcoming. The children have made new friends and love it here. All my fears about moving here were based on nothing; you were right, *jaan*. I should not colour everyone in the harsh brush strokes of some people. Now

I'm glad we moved to Tara Road Mansions," Hamida had written in the aerogramme after the Karamlegavraokars' housewarming party.

On some mornings, Hamida saw Mrs Barvay walk to the post box too, when she posted the pale blue square of an inland letter. Hamida and Mrs Barvay walked back together to Tara Road Mansions; they were beginning to be good friends. Hamida wondered who Mrs Barvay wrote to every week but it seemed rude to ask. The square inland letter meant it was going somewhere in India. "If Mrs Barvay wrote to her son in America, shouldn't it have been a rectangular aerogramme just like the one she sent Ayaz every week?" Hamida had pondered this until she remembered that her own mother still wrote weekly letters to an assortment of relatives and family friends in India. "Besides, the Barvays were so rich that Mrs Barvay probably spoke to her son frequently on the telephone rather than writing him a letter," she thought as she remembered that Ayaz did call when their ship was at a port but even the briefest calls were very expensive.

Fifteen minutes after Hamida and the children left for the bus stop, the Karamlegavraokar offspring set off for school in a large, silver-coloured car driven by a uniformed chauffeur. The older Karamlegavraokars set off in separate cars half an hour later. Every morning, minutes after her employers left for work, Maya Bai, always dressed in a plain blue saree, enjoyed a forbidden treat. She drank a sneaky cup of tea in an imported, fine bone china cup as she sat in a designer rocking chair on the back porch. For the rest of the day, she was relegated to standing while she worked or sitting on the floor, and her employers insisted she use a chipped, cheap mug for tea and an old steel plate for food.

The Karamlegavraokars' groceries and food arrived from the most expensive shops and suppliers in the city. Their groceries were delivered once a week in a little Tempo delivery van from the posh part of town. Preeti had chatted with Maya Bai and knew that along with the usual Indian staples, numerous expensive local and imported foodstuffs were delivered to the Karamlegavraokar household. Individually wrapped slices of Kraft cheese, Chinese egg noodles, jars of Tang, slabs of Gold Seal margarine and Amul butter, custard and jelly packets, tins of baked beans, cans of fruit cocktail, and jars of glistening strawberry jam were always on the list. Top-quality imported coffee for the Italian coffee percolator and tea leaves from China and Sri Lanka were also mentioned in their conversations. As soon as Mrs Karamlegavraokar could afford imported teas, she had snootily relegated Indian tea for their domestic staff and the children's tuition teachers.

Maya Bai had told Preeti that on occasion, Mr Karamlegavraokar secretly enjoyed a cup of strong Indian tea brewed with plenty of milk and sugar, exactly as Maya Bai made it although he now drank it in a bone china cup, of course. He had told Maya Bai it was pure nostalgia for him. The strong, sweet milky tea reminded him of childhood monsoons; the long, tiring walk from school with his siblings to their ramshackle hut, rain-soaked, splashing in puddles, muddy, tired and hungry, and then drinking the hot, strong, sweet milky tea his mother made to fill their famished bellies with warmth until their meagre evening meal. It reminded him how far education had brought him and his wife from their dusty village, poor households, and illiterate parents.

Just before eleven o'clock every morning, Meena strode out to Mrs Barvay's paved courtyard with a bucket of wet washing. She hung it in a discreet sunny corner. Invariably, she took this opportunity to peer at the other backyards, assessing their clotheslines. Silk sarees and imported clothes fetched good money, so did fancy salwar kameez suits. "Of course, I can't steal clothes from a washing line! But it's always good to know what to steal when I work part-time in those houses," she told herself.

Preeti had noted that every day as Meena hung out the washing, a neat elderly man in a traditional churidar kurta and crochet skull cap, pedalled his bicycle with great effort up to the Sheikh household. A small tiffin carrier swung lazily on the handlebars. He was Darzi Master, tailor for *The Begum Boutique.* His wizened face, long white beard, and gentle smile belied the effort it must take him to cycle. Every afternoon, he sat in the shade of Hamida's porch to eat lunch from the small, round steel compartments of his tiffin carrier. He worked in the boutique all day until it was dark. Preeti Rao and Meena's sharp eyes had noticed that every evening, Darzi Master took home small, flat, brown paper parcels gripped in the bicycle carrier.

Every evening, while Mrs Barvay was at the club and Sundari commandeered the shaded paved courtyard, the children played cricket on the long strip of land between the backyards and the stream. The cricket pitch was silent only on Wednesdays when the Karamlegavraokar children went to a music lesson and the Sheikh children's Quran teacher came to their house. The children had marked their cricket pitch by scoring lines with a stone through the mud and sparse grass. The boys had made neat holes for the stumps and the girls insisted on plugging them with bunches of twigs, leaves or flowers when the stumps were pulled out at the end of the cricket session every evening. Sundari often nibbled away at these bits of greenery in the stump holes when she ambled back and forth from her shelter.

Sometimes the children abandoned cricket for badminton with a skipping rope on the ground as an imaginary net or noisy games like *chor police,* complete with verbal sound effects for the imaginary police guns and enactments of the fugitives dying slow, dramatic deaths. They also played traditional games like *dabba ais pais* and *lagori,* but the Karamlegavraokar children were not allowed to play those. "Mummy said those games are for poor children who don't have cricket bats or other toys. Not for people like us," Kartik had explained one day. Then, in a whisper, he had added, "Let's play those when Maya Bai has her day off, so she can't tell Mummy." The other children had stared at him in complete disbelief.

Preeti could see that the Tulpules had twice as much land as the other residents of Tara Road Mansions. The Tulpule garden flourished with Mrs Tulpule's relentless efforts and Sundari's rich manure. Their front garden was full of flowers and decorative bushes. Their backyard was a huge, high-fenced, vegetable garden with a large, corrugated iron shed in one corner. To add to the intrigue, the shed was always locked with the key always around Mrs Tulpule's neck. The Tulpules constantly offered milk, milk products, and fresh herbs to all their neighbours.

Once a week, an old, battered car drove up to the Tulpule house. Mrs Tulpule, in her usual, faded, hand-spun kaftan, bustled from the shed to the car, carrying two or three shoeboxes. She carefully handed them to the driver and promptly walked back to the house. There was no conversation with this driver, no exchange of pleasantries, not even a smile or a wave. Preeti had been fascinated.

Preeti noted the Tulpules were very kind to everyone. Even beloved Sundari's large, airy shelter was always clean and dry. She was well-fed and watered, and freed of restraining ropes at her first low call. Mr Tulpule had helped Preeti carry a large bag of groceries from the tree-lined avenue to her house, Mr and Mrs Tulpule had watered Mrs Barvay's courtyard plants when she and Meena were away overnight at a wedding, they helped Hamida with a flat tyre on her car, and frequently invited Preeti to dinner, which she always accepted as a chance to access their house.

But the Tulpule family seemed to be on their own erratic timetable, except for Sundari's feeding and milking times, and the Tulpule children's game of cricket every evening. The rest of their days seemed to be oblivious to any routine or rhythm. No one ever knew when the Tulpule children could have a sudden astrology lesson in the dark with two huge telescopes set up in their paddock and their parents flipped the pages of a huge book about the solar system or an equally unexpected biology lesson at any time of the day with Mr Tulpule pointing at Sundari's body parts with a long wooden stick or looking at seeds and blades of grass through a microscope set up in a marquee on one of the ruined pavilions. The other children told Preeti they thought this was much more exciting than school uniforms and packing school bags.

The Tulpules did not own a car. The family used bicycles for errands to the main road shops. A beautiful old Morris Minor and various new, large, gleaming chauffeured cars made erratic and frequent appearances to whisk away the adult Tulpules, either solo or tandem. An old lady usually arrived in a rickshaw before they left and stayed with the children until the parents returned. Mrs Tulpule kept to herself. She just smiled and waved from the car if she saw any neighbours when she returned in the car. She did not stop to join them for a chat, even when she came out of the shed or was working in her vegetable garden.

Hamida's elderly parents visited at midday every Thursday and always stayed for dinner. Hamida's father cut an elegant figure in a small pointed fur cap and a dark, collared *achkan* tunic over a radiant white churidar. His large strides in soft leather *mojris* were always followed by the dainty, quick steps of his tiny, graceful wife. She always dressed in pastel-coloured traditional clothes, head and face covered in a matching dupatta edged in white lace, and occasionally, when the wind whipped the dupatta off her face, it exposed her fair face and neck and made her exquisite diamond jewellery wink in the sun as she raised her dainty ring-decked hands to adjust the dupatta once more. They arrived in a gleaming black Mercedes with a silver figure of Mercedes mounted on the bonnet. Their chauffeur was a scar-faced man in black livery and a silver-braided peak cap. He carried huge platters of food and baskets of sweets and fruits to Hamida's house, then returned to the car and waited patiently.

He was called to the door and given a plate of food for lunch, which he ate in the shade of the huge tree by the wrought iron gates of Tara Road Mansions. He often wandered off to smoke a cigarette by the stream but always returned shortly and resumed his post in the car, watchful and alert.

Most Saturday mornings, Hamida's in-laws and their family visited. Their car was grander than her parents' car, and they too stayed till late evening. They usually brought large bags of vegetables, fruits, and boxes of sweets. Ashu and Munni played with their cousins until their uncle and grandfather arrived in time for lunch. Delicious smells always wafted from Hamida's house all day. On Sundays, Hamida often drove the children out for the day in her car, returning in the evening, laden with shopping bags or empty picnic baskets and happy faces.

But on most Friday nights, a sleek red Impala pulled up close to the door of Hamida's house. A tall man in jeans and a t-shirt confidently loped from the long car to the front door. The outdoor lights caught the gleam of his gold wristwatch and the thick gold chain at his neck. The children always opened the door for him with squeals of delight and he fondly ruffled their hair as the door was promptly shut behind him.

✦✦✦

CHAPTER 7

Preeti Rao and Meena had noted the frequent nocturnal visitor and his reception at Hamida's house. The man often took Hamida and the children out in his car at night. Mrs Barvay loved gossip, so as an effort to make herself more likeable, Meena told her about the black Mercedes and the scar-faced man, and the younger night visitor in the red Impala. Meena thought she had seen the man in the Impala somewhere before she came to Tara Road Mansions but could not place him.

Preeti Rao, on the other hand, was worried. She, too, was quite sure she had seen the driver of the red Impala somewhere before this, but just could not remember where, and this troubled her greatly. In her line of work, people frequently changed appearances and familiar faces could be friends or foes and therefore, needed close scrutiny. Meena, Mrs Barvay, and Preeti separately pondered the identity of this man and his relation to Hamida. Preeti Rao kept trying to think where she had seen or met him.

Mrs Barvay tried to weed out possibilities as she talked to her sister, "He can't be a tuition teacher because they can't afford luxurious cars. He can't be a supplier or a boutique customer because he never has any packages and never visits during business hours, and he is always hurried upstairs to the home, not to the downstairs rooms of *The Begum Boutique*. The downstairs lights aren't even switched on for the entire length of his visit, so he has nothing to do with the boutique. He always visits alone. Don't you think, even for a family friend, a visit every week is just too much, especially when Hamida's husband is away?"

Gradually, separately, and surely, Mrs Barvay, Meena, and Preeti Rao decided that the man in the red Impala had to be either the husband who was allegedly away or a boyfriend. Then Mrs Barvay and Preeti thought of another possibility; Islam permitted a man to have more than one wife. "Was Hamida a second wife?"

Mrs Barvay gently put forth this suggestion to Mrs Karamlegavraokar, who agreed immediately. Mrs Karamlegavraokar did not particularly care whether Hamida of *The Begum Boutique* fame was a second wife or a first wife with a boyfriend, but instantly decided that if this was the quickest way to be close friends with the old lady with the even older money, then so be it. Since the Karamlegavraokars had realised that the Tulpules were THE Tulpules, knowing Hamida of *The Begum Boutique* had quite lost its lustre.

"Besides, where is this absent husband of Hamida's anyway? No one has seen him. All Hamida has told us is his name and that he is constantly away working for an international shipping company. Hamida has said nothing else. It could mean anything. That he was involved in some dodgy business, maybe he was a smuggler, maybe Hamida was his second wife, maybe they aren't even married! You never knew how people organised their lives..." said Mrs Karamlegavraokar to Mrs Barvay conspiratorially, always quick to pass judgement.

Preeti Rao left for work and returned at different times every morning and evening, always ensuring she was home by dusk. This ploy helped in keeping her 'good girl' image and let her observe her neighbours at different times on different days. The advertising world was considered glamorous and erratic. No one at Tara Road Mansions expected Preeti to keep regular office hours. Each morning after her jog, Preeti got ready and briskly walked along the tree-lined avenue to the noisy main road to look for a rickshaw to take her to work. Sometimes she walked around the Mansions talking to her neighbours, hoping to know them better. She chatted with the children playing by the stream. She often gave them chocolates or lollipops, so they welcomed her like an old friend. She was also popular with the children because she never asked to bat or bowl and always wanted to do some fielding at their cricket game. This gave her a chance to watch the houses at leisure from various angles and listen to the inane chatter of children. She always hoped they would say something that could give her a clue to the missing consignment. Every day, she walked or jogged, observing the minutiae of the inhabitants of Tara Road Mansions, hoping for a breakthrough. But she got nothing, just the summer heat that was beginning to make her evening walks uncomfortable; yet she persisted.

Preeti tried to arrange and rearrange her observations in many different ways, trying desperately to see a hidden clue, some pattern or a scheme, but the final picture still did not make sense. Nothing seemed to fit any recognisable plan or pattern. Secretly, she had been very pleased to be chosen for this difficult and urgent task. Now she wondered if the job was impossible, then told herself, "I will be successful and prove myself. Then they will have to promote me! In my usual way, I will cover every base, go a step further than the allocated task, and take possession of the valuable consignment. I have never failed at any job before this. I do love the thrill of it all. Yet, the bosses keep promoting the junior men. If I make it on this difficult task, surely, they can't ignore me?"

But much to Preeti's disappointment, so far, she had only amassed more questions than answers. "Was the missing consignment at Tara Road? Or had it already changed hands? Had they modified its form? Did it still look like the description she had been given? Were all these people interconnected?" She had made some enquiries with her boss and had other enquiries on her own. It seemed as if the consignment and everyone connected with it had simply disappeared into thin air.

The disorderly lifestyle of the Tulpules intrigued and confused Preeti's well-ordered thinking and well-trained mind. The whole family frustrated her. She was suspicious of the Tulpules because of their kindness and helpfulness. She knew they were incredibly rich and had a clear idea of their assets, which meant they could easily provide the money needed to buy the missing consignment themselves or maybe even commission its theft. They had too many irregular goings-on and some very regular activities; looking after Sundari, the constantly locked shed, the strange car that took away shoe boxes from Mrs Tulpule every week, and the gleaming cars that arrived randomly to collect and drop off the adult Tulpules. "What was in the shed that was sent out in shoeboxes? Where did they go? Who was the man who collected them? Why were the Tulpule twins home-schooled?" More questions piled onto Preeti's heap of unanswered questions.

Another puzzle for Preeti was the weekly Impala visitor to Hamida's house. And even more infuriating was the fact that she was sure she had seen him somewhere before this, but just could not pin down a context. "Who was this man? Why did he visit so frequently? Should I know him? And more worryingly, would he recognise me? If he did, would my cover remain intact or get compromised?" Preeti pondered.

She was concerned, the number of familiar faces she could not place and the questions were piling up with no answers. But the one question that actually kept her awake several nights was, "Are all these people at Tara Road Mansions in cahoots with each other and simply pretending to be strangers? Is that the reason I cannot get a breakthrough? What am I missing in my observations?"

She had heard that sometimes when an item of immense value was at stake, a group of individuals or families protected the valuables by forming an informal symbiotic community compound. If that were the case here, she would be the one who got cornered. She was dealing with dangerous people; they had already killed a man; she made a mental note to always keep her pistol cleaned and handy. She would need to plan her moves very carefully.

One night, a police siren wailed as it sped down the tree-lined avenue and turned into the Tara Road Mansions' gates. Curiosity and alarm drew several residents to their windows in time to see the direction and destination of the noisy police car with its flashing lights. They watched the car slow down to go around the tiny roundabout, switch off the flashing lights and siren and speed back down the lane.

"Disturbing the peace!" said Mr Tulpule derisively, as he strode off to check on Sundari, in case she was startled by the siren. "She gets alarmed by sudden loud noises and her milk production is affected if she gets spooked," he muttered.

"Must be for that missing husband of Hamida's or her posh-car boyfriend," said Mrs Karamlegavraokar ungraciously. Since she had now made friends with old-money Mrs Barvay and of course, now she knew the Tulpules were super rich, it left only Hamida as the culprit because unfortunately, so far, she had not found anything suspicious about that Halo Advertising girl.

"Now, now!" soothed Mr Karamlegavraokar, which further irritated Mrs Karamlegavraokar, who had not quite forgiven her husband for calling Preeti Rao pretty and intelligent.

Mrs Barvay, half-asleep as she watched TV, was initially unsure whether the police car was wailing in her American TV programme or in her real world. Meena had jumped up in panic and rushed to the window, terrified her thefts had been discovered. She thought the police were coming for her! As the car sped past their house, she composed herself before returning to the TV programme she did not understand, yet watched with Mrs Barvay.

Preeti Rao, who was listening to music and reading a magazine, had almost reached for the phone to ring her boss in alarm, as she watched the flashing police car from an upstairs window. She was worried her cover would get blown. But her panic faded as the cars slowed down in the unlit driveway, switched off the sirens and lights, turned around and drove out through the gates. She thought she heard a very soft slam of a car door, but was unsure. Then when she neither saw nor heard anything else, she decided the police may have simply come up the wrong lane, so she went back to her magazine and music.

Hamida watched from the upstairs window with her children, a bit confused at first, then absolutely annoyed. The sirens and the car had slowed down by her driveway as it circled the tiny roundabout, then switched off the sirens and gone down the road quietly as if the car had turned into Tara Road Mansions in error. She knew what that meant.

No one had noticed the door open quickly and a man jump out of the wailing police car as it slowed down to turn by the roundabout, switched off its siren and drove off. Purposefully, the man had walked up the path to Hamida Sheikh's front door and rang the bell. Hamida leapt to her feet as the children raced down the stairs to open the door. An irritated Hamida stood on the stairs as the children excitedly let the man in.

"Arriving in a police car! You really know how to annoy me! Have you no consideration for me? What will people think? I've only just moved here. We are different enough without this attention seeking. And you've come so late, dinner is stone cold. You can heat it yourself. I am done with you and your silly antics."

"I was running so late, I thought the police car and sirens would be the quickest to get me here. Azmi didn't mind giving me a lift in the patrol car. I had promised Ashu we would play his new Donkey Kong game before he went to bed. You are so strict about their bedtimes even on a Friday."

"Really, Tariq!" Hamida huffed.

"Calm down, Hamma!" said the good-looking man with a twinkle in his eye.

"DON'T call me Hamma!" said Hamida frostily but she knew each of his words was always calculated to irritate her; it had been the same for years.

Ashu and Munni looked at each other and giggled as their mother fumed. 'Hamma' was a childish word for a cow! They loved Tariq's weekly visits and were well-versed in this frequent diatribe. Their giggling irritated Hamida. "You two stop giggling or you are going to bed right now!" she glared at them. The children just laughed, knowing there was no substance in this threat, especially on a Friday night when Tariq was visiting. The children rescued Tariq from Hamida's wrath by gently pulling his arms and taking him through the foyer and upstairs into the living room, where the new game had already been set up. Hamida gave an affectionate, reproachful look at the retreating trio and followed them upstairs to reheat dinner.

After dinner was eaten, the game had been played, and the children had gone to bed, Tariq and Hamida finally had a chance to chat. "It has been a really good decision to move here. You know, I wasn't keen to leave our old neighbourhood, but we have settled in more easily than I expected, and the children have made new friends. And just going downstairs for work rather than driving through the city has made such a big difference. I dare say, all of you were right."

But Tariq's thoughts had drifted to a different topic. "Were you able to find out any more about that girl in the house next door? Preeti .... Rao? Although I have only seen her a few times, from a distance when I visit you in the evenings, I'm sure I have seen her somewhere. Just can't put my finger on it. I'm convinced *usko zaroor kahin dekha hai.*"

"Tariq! What do you mean '*usko zaroor kahin dekha hai?*' There is no way you would have seen or met her before this. Do you pay any attention to what I'm saying? I have told you before. Preeti Rao is from Calcutta and only arrived here a few days ago to begin work at Halo Advertising. She's staying in her brother's house while he and his family are in America. There is no way you have seen her anywhere in your wanderings in this city. You are such a flirt! First sign of a pretty girl and instantly you think *isko kahin dekha hai*. How can you have seen or known every pretty girl?"

Tariq, who was still thinking about Preeti Rao, refused to be drawn into this debate about flirting. "Well, if I could see her up close for a few minutes, maybe I would remember. She definitely looks familiar. I bet our paths have crossed before now. I never forget a face. Maybe you can invite her over when I visit next? Hmmm?" Tariq suggested mischievously. At first, Hamida looked shocked, then rolled her eyes, and it made him laugh.

In the neighbouring house, Preeti Rao was consolidating her notes and thinking the same thing. "If only I could get a closer look at the Impala man. Perhaps the police were on his trail tonight and turned away when they realised that the Impala was not parked in its usual Friday night spot? Did that mean he or Hamida were connected with the disappearance of the consignment? Maybe I should make up a reason to visit Hamida when he is there. Or at least go down and get a good look at the licence plate on the car, it's always parked at an odd angle and I cannot see it from my window."

Meanwhile, Mrs Barvay and Meena had hit upon the same plan. Mrs Barvay pondered, "Meenay, what if I send you over to Hamida's with a message next time he visits? Or maybe you can go to ask for your wages a week in advance or something like that. Then you can take a good look at the man and report back to me, of course. Then we can make a definite guess about their relationship."

Meena shrugged nonchalantly. She was not keen to highlight herself to this man with the posh car because she had a feeling, she had met him before and was unsure whether he had been a guest at one of her previous jobs or someone she had seen at the pawnshop. Rich people in fancy cars came to the pawnshop too, sometimes to pawn things and other times to get cheap bargains.

Oblivious to the stir he had caused with his Impala and the flashing police car and sirens, Tariq left the house much later that night. He drove away in Hamida's large new white sedan. By the time most residents awoke the next morning, Hamida's car was already back in her usual spot in her driveway. Only Preeti Rao had watched the car return. It was parked by a uniformed driver who handed the keys to Hamida at her front door and promptly walked out of the wrought iron gates and into the tree-lined lane.

✦ ✦ ✦

CHAPTER 8

Preeti Rao pondered, "Where was it? This missing consignment worth millions? Had it been passed on or made into smaller parcels for easy movement?" So far, her lack of progress about the consignment was frustrating. She had never made such poor advances on a task. Her boss had given her a file of information about the case that she had memorised by the time she got to Poona. Once she had noted her neighbours' routines, she had had them followed and their backgrounds checked. She had found out numerous things about them but nothing new or suspicious that was relevant to her task. However, some information was yet to come in from her boss and her own informants. She was still annoyed at the lost opportunity for exploring the Karamlegavraokars' house at their housewarming party.

"Had that strange watchful couple been private detectives? Plainclothes police? One of her rivals? Or had her boss put more people on the job, in addition to her, because the massive consignment was lost on his watch?" She shrugged.

Now she had no idea of how to poke about the Karamlegavraokar house without arousing suspicion. She had overwhelmed the Karamlegavraokar couple with compliments about the party until she got invited to see all the photos and videos of their housewarming party. The Karamlegavraokars were gracious and hospitable when she visited, but she sensed a strange animosity from Mrs Karamlegavraokar. Preeti had skilfully pocketed some photos of the watchful, strange couple and some large crowd shots. But when she showed them around in her work circles, no one knew anything about them. She continued jogging for hours along the stream and around the houses, staying home and observing the neighbours during different times of the day, but their routines showed no connections or patterns, and they had no new visitors. Hamida usually had a few new customers every day but Preeti's trained eye had immediately ruled them out.

She had investigated the Tulpules' outings in the flashy cars, including the car registrations and discovered that most of the flashy cars belonged to commercial companies and hire car fleets that took the Tulpules to corporate board meetings. The car that collected the shoeboxes every week was registered to Mrs Tulpule's mother. Access to the Tulpule shed and the contents of the boxes had remained elusive. The Tulpule's schedule was just too erratic for Preeti to find a 'safe window' to sneak in. It was hard to guess which of the Tulpules would show up or leave suddenly. Strengthening her resolve, Preeti made new plans to investigate the contents of the shoeboxes that Mrs Tulpule handed the car driver every week.

She had discovered nothing suspicious about the *Begum Boutique* tailor Darzi Master either. She had him followed home several times, had his house watched, and she had watched him every day at Tara Road Mansions. He simply cycled to work, then went home and stayed there with his elderly wife till the next morning. No one visited him. She carefully watched Darzi Master pedal up the driveway every morning with his steel tiffin and return every evening with two or three, small, flat parcels on the bicycle carrier and his tiffin on the handlebars. The parcels seemed too small to be tailoring work.

One evening, she timed her jog to coincide with the time Darzi Master left Hamida's house. She waited quietly in the shadows of her own house until Darzi Master started on his bicycle and then suddenly burst into his path, sending the old man flying off his bicycle; it clattered to the ground. The tiffin carrier bounced on the driveway and unhinged its tiered compartments, spewing food in every direction. The parcels from the carrier hit the ground at an odd angle. Their thin brown paper coverings tore, haphazardly revealing their contents as they landed on the rear wheel and its spokes. Darzi Master and the fallen items raised a small cloud of dust on the summer-scorched pathway.

Preeti Rao rushed up apologetically, pretending it was a complete accident. She helped the old man. He was shaken but mostly unhurt. She walked him to her house and sat him on the front steps. His grazed knee oozed a thin trickle of blood through his torn, once-white churidar. He looked much older and forlorn in the shrinking daylight; his crocheted skull cap was now askew, exposing his bald head. Preeti felt sorry for him as she picked up his strewn belongings. She felt guilty for considering that he could be in disguise and undercover like her. She straightened the bicycle first, as he seemed most concerned about it. The tiffin carrier, which she had assumed to be empty at the end of the day, had been full of soupy dal in one container and meat curry in the other. These contents lay splattered on the driveway, still smelling delicious. The brown paper parcels had torn, each revealing a stack of four or five rotis. The warm dusky air was filled with the smell of dust, curry, and dal. The entire meal was strewn and quickly soaking into the parched ground.

Preeti Rao felt ashamed for orchestrating this accident. Amidst profuse apologies, she asked in a kind tone, "Why is your tiffin full of food? Didn't you get time to eat lunch today?"

Darzi Master looked embarrassed as he said, "I eat my lunch every afternoon, and every evening, Hamida Bibi gives me dinner and something for the next day's breakfast to take home. My wife is not well, you see, and can barely cook my lunch every morning, and look after herself." Preeti Rao felt even worse. She told him to keep sitting on her doorstep while she ran to the main road to get a rickshaw to take the old man and his bicycle home. She gave him some money to buy food on the way home. She paid the rickshaw driver three times the fare to ensure he did not quibble about taking the bicycle as well as stopping on the way to buy food. As the rickshaw drove away with the bicycle wheels peeping out from either side, Preeti Rao sat down on her own doorstep with her head in her hands, dejected and desperate. The evening's plan had been a fiasco.

She heard faint, melancholy whistling and scuffling that seemed to be coming closer and closer. She looked up. It was Hamida's son, Ashu. He looked forlorn as he walked home with his head low and his hands in his pockets, his feet kicking pebbles in the dust. She frowned as she looked at him; he was usually quite cheerful and was coming from the wrong direction, from the Karamlegavraokar house rather than the rough cricket pitch by the stream. She beckoned him over before he reached his front door. She had made friends with these children, "Maybe a chat would cheer us both tonight," she thought glumly. They often told each other the silliest jokes.

"Hi Ashu, where's your sister?" she said kindly.

Ashu looked up. "Munni's at home; she's not well." He liked Preeti; she often gave them sweets.

"Ashu, no cricket today? Is that why you're looking so sad?"

"No. Maya Bai is out on an errand today, and Kartik and Kaveri are not allowed to play outside without her, so we played Lego and watched cartoon videos in their house."

"That's nice and cool. I know they have air-conditioning in all the rooms in their house. So, why are you looking so glum?"

"Because I have no 500-rupee notes. These are the new notes for the largest amount in our country! I only have 405 rupees and 25 paise."

"Wow! That's already a lot of money for someone your age. Why do you need a 500-rupee note? Maybe your mother could give you one when your savings total five hundred? You're not far off," she said, trying to cheer him up.

He shook his head sadly, "The Tulpule twins also came to play at Kartik's house and to show us their brand-new 500-rupee notes. Their grandfather gave them one each today because it is 100 years since the first Tulpule company was started. Then Kartik got annoyed because the twins were showing off so much and said he had lots and lots of them. We didn't believe him, so he and Kaveri took us to their parents' bedroom and showed us. There were stacks and stacks of 500-rupee notes. This much!" said Ashu, his eyes widening in disbelief as he remembered the stacks and indicated with one hand at his waist and the other level with his eyes. "Now I am the only one without a single 500-rupee note."

Preeti could hardly believe her ears! She patted the step next to her for him to sit down. She reached into her pocket, desperately feeling for a chocolate, a lollipop, something. She really needed it today for Ashu. Finally extricating a piece of bubble gum, she asked, "Are you allowed these?" He smiled wanly and nodded. She handed over the bubble gum as she expertly interrogated him.

"You saw these 500-rupee notes? Where?"

"They are in a safe behind the air conditioner. But don't tell anyone."

Preeti fought to keep the surprise from her face. "Are they really all 500-rupee notes?"

"Yes. We didn't believe it either. So, the twins and I flicked through the piles. I told you, there were stacks and stacks of them."

Preeti's eyes widened at this, and she had to remind herself to be calm and not show much reaction. Her mind was racing. Five-hundred-rupee notes had only come into circulation two months ago. As yet, she did not have complete information about Mr Karamlegavraokar. If this notes business was true, could it mean the consignment had already changed hands and payment was complete? Or could it mean the money was ready to be paid out soon? Surely this was black money. Otherwise, who keeps money hidden behind an air conditioner..." Her thoughts tumbled out but reminding herself that Ashu would not be available for questions later, she continued her chat with him, trying to find out as much as possible.

"Safe? Like a Godrej cupboard?"

"No. Like a safe from the movies. With a secret code and two little wheels on the door."

"Where is it?"

"It's behind the air conditioner in Uncle and Aunty's bedroom." Ashu was very happy to answer. It was rare that adults paid so much attention to anything that usually excited him.

"Was it locked? Is there a key?"

"There was no key, just numbers. The number is written in Uncle's bedside drawer. Kaveri read it out to Kartik because he had to stand on a chair and press the numbers and turn the little wheels on the safe. Then he took down some stacks and invited us to look at them. He said we could climb on the chair and look in the safe…"

"And did you?"

"Yes, we all took turns. All the stacks were really 500-rupee notes," said Ashu in a hushed whisper, awed by the memory once more. "Then Kartik put back the notes he had pulled out and locked the safe and clicked the air conditioner cover into place again. We asked him how he knew about the notes. He said he had seen his father put away some money from his briefcase one night when Kartik was ill and sleeping in his parents' room.

He had seen his father peeping into a bedside drawer before he opened the safe, so he looked in there a few days later and saw a number scrawled in pencil. One afternoon when Maya Bai was downstairs and Kartik and Kaveri were supposed to be doing homework upstairs, they had tried pressing the number on their new cordless phone upstairs, but nothing happened. Then they saw the safe had numbers too and thought the number might be for the safe. He and Kaveri stood on a chair and they tried the numbers on the safe, and the door swung open!"

"I am waiting for my Abbu to come home now. He has lots of money. Rupees AND dollars. He will give me a 500-rupee note. I am going to tell him to get a safe just like Kartik's father and keep his money in it," Ashu said determinedly, still smarting from his lack of 500-rupee notes. "And Abbu has promised to bring me a blue remote-control car this time and …"

Preeti sat with Ashu on her doorstep, pretending to be interested in the inane chatter about his father, how long he was away, his favourite chocolates, final exams, and comic books. She listened attentively; she did not want him to think the conversation about the notes had any special significance for her. She longed to ask him about the man in the Impala. but sensed this was not the appropriate time. They chatted until Hamida came to call Ashu home. As he ran to his mother, Preeti remained seated at her own front door, elbows on her knees and her face resting in cupped hands, wondering how fortuitous it was that she had met Ashu that evening.

✦ ✦ ✦

CHAPTER 9

That chat with Ashu had been a few days ago. Now dressed for her early morning jog, Preeti Rao sipped tea, thinking of that night when the police car had raced into the driveway, slowed down and driven off. She half listened to the local radio station as she remembered staring out from her bedroom window the next morning and seeing Hamida's white sedan arrive through the wrought iron gates of Tara Road Mansions in the flimsy morning light. As she had watched, the car turned into its usual spot, but instead of Hamida, a chauffeur had stepped out of the car and walked to Hamida's front door. Preeti had tried to make sense of the car arriving without Hamida or the children. She remembered seeing Hamida's car parked in the driveway as usual the night before, the police car slowing down near the roundabout, and then leaving. "Had something happened in the night to Hamida or the children? Who was this chauffeur? How did he get the keys to Hamida's car?" she had wondered and then chided herself for being too dramatic as Hamida opened the door and accepted the keys from the chauffeur before he walked away into the shaded lane.

Before she could dwell on this, she was distracted by local news on the radio in the background. There were reports of a spate of burglaries in a neighbouring suburb. She was suddenly alert and listened with interest. There had been several break-ins but nothing of any great value had been taken.

"Who were these burglars? It sounded like they were looking for something, just like her. Had her boss got it wrong all along? Had she been sent to the wrong place? Or was she merely an insurance policy, and he had known the correct area all along and put someone else there? Were these burglaries a 'flush out'? By whom?" she wondered.

She knew that criminals often used a spate of break-ins or burglaries so that people hiding stolen goods became insecure and tried to move the goods, and that is when they were 'flushed out.' She thought hard, rejigging all the facts she knew into another shape, but nothing was making sense. Then she had an excellent idea about using these burglaries to her advantage. She would pitch this new plan at the next Tara Road Mansions meeting. The meeting was imminent, as there was paperwork that needed to be signed, and someone would come around soon with a note about the date, time, and venue for the meeting. She decided not to wait. She would host the meeting herself; she began drafting a note about it.

✦✦✦

Mrs Barvay looked around her garden that morning with great satisfaction. She had forgotten about the police car that had driven up to Tara Road Mansions and was oblivious to Hamida's car leaving or returning to her driveway, and other happenings in the neighbouring suburbs. She gazed at the tulsi replanted from her old house. Its reddish-brown stems and deep green leaves were flourishing as the centrepiece of the traditional, *vrindavan-style* outdoor altar. The colourful herbaceous borders replanted from Barvay House to this garden were bright with gerbera and geranium blooms. "Well, those that had thus far not caught the attention of that wretched buffalo, at any rate!" she thought crossly. "I must write that down in the agenda for the next meeting of Tara Road residents, under 'any other business'—Sundari, the greedy buffalo" she thought unkindly.

She missed her old neighbourhood and friends, but they were only a short drive away in the next suburb. She had moved out of Barvay Mansion within a week of that nightmarish afternoon and said a quick goodbye to the street where she had spent most of her life. She had created a story that Avi had gone abroad for a few years to expand their business in America. The massive Barvay House with its art collections and antique furniture was just too big and unwieldy for her to manage alone (that bit was true), especially during the scheduled repairs and painting that were currently underway. This, although true, had been planned after that fateful afternoon and not before. She had told everyone that the paint fumes and dust played havoc with her asthma, so she had moved to Tara Road Mansions temporarily.

No one questioned these explanations, as it was not unusual for someone like Avi Barvay to go to America to expand a business that was the scale of Barvay Industries. Everyone also knew that the Barvays could easily buy a house at Tara Road Mansions several times over, and Mrs Barvay was a known asthmatic. Barvay House had been painted every decade as long as anyone could remember and she had never needed to supervise the workmen herself. She usually went away for a few months to Singapore to visit her brother or see other family members around the world, while Avi always stayed in the city to oversee the painting and renovations at Barvay House.

Mrs Barvay had bravely settled into this new house at Tara Road Mansions and set up familiar routines in her new home, pretending all the while that the awful afternoon had never occurred. She continued her life much as before, she went to the club every afternoon for cards, to the races at the weekends, and attended all the social events she was invited to. Every day, she smiled and laughed, and dressed exactly as she had for years. She had too much pride and discipline to let the world see her heartbreak, pain, and tears. For all appearances, nothing was different except for a temporary change in her residence. She was fine, on the outside. Inside, she was a broken woman. She often lay awake at night thinking of the events of that afternoon. "Was it her fault? Should she have anticipated it? Could it have been different? Were there signs she had missed?"

Her reverie was suddenly broken by the doorbell. She was not expecting anyone, but she hurried in from the garden to open the front door. Meena had gone out that morning to run some errands. At the front door was the Karamlegavraokars' ubiquitous Maya Bai in her standard, plain blue saree. She proffered a neatly written note on Mr Karamlegavraokar's ostentatious letterhead. Maya Bai waited patiently. She had been asked to ferry the note to all Tara Road residents and get their signatures on it. The note was about the next Tara Road Mansions meeting to be hosted by the Karamlegavraokars. Mrs Barvay read the note and signed it. She saw she was the first person to read and sign the note, so she scrawled, "I will telephone you." She did not want to write

'Sundari' on the 'any other business (AOB)' line and alert Mr Tulpule. "The buffalo problem needs to be addressed urgently; I cannot possibly be the only person whose garden is being chewed up," she thought.

Next door, Preeti Rao had just finished drafting her own note for the meeting and was getting ready to take it to all the residents when Maya Bai arrived with the note. As Preeti read the note, she was torn between going to the meeting and pretending to be ill on the day so she could sneak into the mysterious Tulpule shed while they were all at the meeting. But she needed to be at the meeting too, to try and launch her new plan. When she scribbled her suggestion in the AOB section, she saw Mrs Barvay's 'I will telephone you' scrawled there and wondered what that was all about. It sounded ominous.

"Was it some coded message? Was she missing a clue right under her nose or was she getting paranoid?" She shrugged. So far, she had only managed to check on some of the Tulpule family and a few of the Karmalegavraokar family members. Time was ticking, and any day now, her boss would ask for another update, and she had little new information to offer.

✦ ✦ ✦

The Karamlegavraokars had prepared extensively for the Tara Road Mansions meeting. They had read the note over and over to check for English grammar and spelling before handing it to Maya Bai. "Shivram, it must all be perfect! The first meeting at Mrs Barvay's house wasn't bad but we have to make our mark at least as equals," said Mrs Karamlegavraokar, always keen to disassociate from their extremely humble beginnings from anything they did, ate, bought or wore.

Deciding on the food to be served at the meeting posed a greater challenge. Mrs Barvay had put on a fantastic spread of traditional food, and most of it had been homemade. That left little for the Karamlegavraokars to outshine her menu. "Shivram, our food should seem effortless and exclusive, so it is clear that money was not an object. Maybe because Mrs Barvay did not know any of the neighbours, she played safe and had traditional food or maybe she is just old-fashioned…" Mrs Karamlegavraokar went on about asking close friends for recipes, caterers, and restaurants. "After all," she said to her husband conspiratorially, "Everyone knows that mostly only conventional, old-fashioned, and middle-class people actually like traditional home-cooked food. We will order from high-class places. Are you listening?"

Shivram Karamlegavraokar hauled himself back from his thoughts and nodded as if he had heard every word his wife had just said. He was thinking of the meeting agenda. Mrs Barvay's phone call about buffalo complaints, and Preeti's suggestion about a watchman; they were both valid points. Now that he knew the Tulpules were THE Tulpules and Mrs Barvay was Barvay Industries, he was trying to work out whether the buffalo problem should be aired at the meeting or resolved in private. He did not want to antagonise either of his very rich and influential neighbours.

The one-sided food discussion in the Karamlegavraokar household continued. "…have to make sure there is enough choice, that Preeti Rao and the Tulpules are vegetarian." He smiled encouragingly at his wife, knowing it was only approval she needed, not suggestions or critique. "Some coconut macaroons? What about those wine biscuits from the bakery in Camp? I can ask Maya Bai to make sandwiches, green chutney, cheese, and chicken. I am sure Mrs Barvay and that *Begum Boutique* lady are non-vegetarian and will appreciate the chicken..." Mrs Karamlegavraokar continued.

"Yes, that's good. Most things can be made before the meeting, so Maya Bai will be free to serve the tea, coffee, and juice to our guests. Then follow with the trays of finger food. Only seven of us, so it shouldn't be a problem." Shivram Karamlegavraokar contributed to maintain the illusion that he was still listening.

The near monologue from Mrs Karamlegavraokar went on, "I have told Maya Bai to make bite-sized vegetable cutlets and serve them with a dollop of tomato ketchup on top, just like we had at last night's cocktail party at Sulu's house but my recipe is better. Maya Bai makes them really well, more crisp and golden. And cheese and tinned pineapple with glace cherries on toothpicks. That will be very classy. Napkins. Posh paper serviettes or good linen? Paper, I think, will be more modern, expensive paper napkins. And people can use a new one with every food. It will feel almost like a sit-down cocktail party with tea and coffee," said Mrs Karamlegavraokar, very pleased with her own vision of the meeting.

"And Shivram, please stock the drinks cabinet, in case the meeting runs late, we can offer everyone a drink. Get some soda, Limca, and orange juice and some other soft drinks, in case the ladies opt for that. Cocktails might be a bit too much; it may look like we are showing off and that will never do…"

Mr Karamlegavraokar merely hmmed. Of late, he had been a little preoccupied with business. He seemed to be on the phone a lot more than usual. "Money begets money" thought his wife proudly, remembering the stack of notes he regularly added to the secret safes in their bedroom air conditioner and her wardrobe, in addition to their burgeoning bank accounts. "At this rate, maybe we can make a down payment on a holiday home in the hills, just like that showy Mrs Sathe at the club" she thought wistfully. She knew her husband was desperately trying to shepherd their finances towards this goal. They wanted to be part of the set that 'went down to the hill station' over long weekends and summer holidays, and invited people to stay at their 'cottage.' These 'cottages' were six- or eight-bedroom homes that nestled in the hills with stunning views of the valleys through the mist. They were comfortable homes with chic new furniture, a cook, some household help, and a gardener, all of it only a couple of hours away from the city. The Karamlegavraokars owned three large apartments and two shops in various parts of the city but those did not count. She knew that a holiday home at a hill station was the sign of a truly rich family.

✦ ✦ ✦

Emboldened by the welcome Hamida and her family had received at Tara Road Mansions, she dialled the Tulpule number and waited patiently as the phone rang in the eccentric household. Eventually, Mrs Tulpule answered in her laconic drawl, "Tulpule residence." Hamida began nervously, "Hello, this is Hamida. Meena is going to look after my children when I am at our residents' meeting at the Karamlegavraokars. I wanted to invite your children here so they can all eat dinner together and then play here or watch a movie on the video. Is that okay?" Finding no immediate resistance to her question, she hurried through the rest of her questions before she lost courage, "I am going to invite the Karamlegavraokar children too. I was going to make pav bhaji and fruit salad with ice cream because I know your family is vegetarian. Will your children like that for dinner?" She had let out her breath as quietly as she could, hoping she had not been too forward by inviting her neighbours' children.

Mrs Tulpule's reply was immediate, "Of course, they will love it. They will definitely come. And they won't have to be home alone. Thank you. What a good idea!" Hamida's shoulders relaxed; she was relieved that her invitation had been accepted so easily.

She began to dial the Karamlegavraokars' number with more confidence to invite their children too. She did not want them to feel left out just because the meeting was at their house and they would not need a babysitter. Hamida spoke with more confidence this time, inviting the Karamlegavraokar children. But Mrs Karamlegavraokar's response was calm, haughty, and firm. "Kartik and Kaveri have special dietary needs and eat an early dinner every evening, so they will eat at home. But I can let them join the others only for the movie. Maya Bai will drop them off after they have eaten."

Hamida's heart had dipped. "Had it been too forward of her to invite all the children? Was it because they were Muslim? Had she assumed too much from everyone being nice to her?" She had fidgeted nervously all the while Mrs Karamlegavraokar had spoken.

✦ ✦ ✦

Ashu and Munni were very excited about having their friends over for dinner and a movie, with just Meena supervising, especially while the adults were out. It made them feel very grown up, and they had hugged Hamida with joy and danced her around the room in little jumps before letting her go. They did all their homework and chores without complaint. Hamida had given in to Ashu and Munni's request to watch the latest Bollywood offering on video cassettes and had called the video library to book the movie video cassette for 24 hours. Ashu had already asked for 'lots and lots' of ice cream with fruit salad and strawberry syrup. "His sweet tooth seems insatiable these days" thought Hamida.

"If you keep eating so much sugar, then your taste buds will get so used to it that soon you won't be able to taste the sweetness at all after a few days. Then you will need more and more sugar every day, till one day, you won't be able to taste anything at all, Ashu" Hamida had lied, trying to convince him to eat less sugar. But she knew he just ignored her the minute she began that sentence.

✦ ✦ ✦

CHAPTER 10

The day of the meeting was stifling hot, making the outdoors feel like an open-air oven. Everyone complained of the heat as they laboured through their day. Only the Karamlegavraokar couple was ecstatic about this weather. It was perfect to show off the fabulous, new, expensive air-conditioning system in their living room. Mr Karamlegavraokar returned home from the office earlier than usual and switched it on; he wanted the room to be almost freezing when his neighbours arrived. Mrs Karamlegavraokar, who had taken the afternoon off, had already changed into a boldly patterned blue and white silk kaftan, of course, adding a sparkling diamond pendant and a huge pearl ring as accessories. Her tinted and highlighted hair was teased into curls and tendrils this week to match her new pearl drop earrings, and her makeup was perfect as usual. She looked like one of the 'smart but casual' models who lounged in advertisements for sofas or air conditioners in glossy women's magazines.

Her husband had changed into his new navy trousers and an imported blue and white designer t-shirt. They both looked cool and coordinated as they cooed at each other, rather like a preening pigeon pair. The children had been shooed upstairs almost as soon as they returned from school. Their living room had been rearranged by Maya Bai as instructed. Soft leather sofas and upholstered armchairs were pulled together in a circle around the Swedish, wooden coffee table to seat seven people in the centre of the large room. Bright, silk designer cushions strewn across the seats added a splash of colour to the scene. The coffee table had seven little notepads and pens, all boasting Mr Karamlegavraokar's company logo. The only bright lights in the room were those above the sofas and armchairs. The other lights in their huge living room were dimmed and cast a pale glow over the remaining furniture.

Mrs Barvay was the first to arrive, a little ahead of time. Resplendent in a maroon silk saree, she glided into the room like a ship in full sail with rubies twinkling at her ears and wrists. Mrs Karamlegavraokar seized this opportunity to rekindle their acquaintance before the others arrived. She fawned and fussed over Mrs Barvay and settled her into an armchair. She praised the older lady's punctuality, her jewellery, and her saree. Mrs Barvay had hoped to be the first arrival so she could have a quick discussion with Mr Karamlegavraokar about the buffalo before any of the others arrived. She was irritated with Mrs Karamlegavraokar buzzing around wasting time; the others were due any minute, and the opportunity to discuss the buffalo with Mr Karamlegavraokar would vanish.

Soon the Tulpules arrived, closely followed by Preeti Rao. As everyone hello-helloed their way around the room, Hamida arrived, and the meeting began in earnest. Mr Karamlegavraokar used his extensive corporate experience to begin the meeting.

The ubiquitous Maya Bai quietly moved around the room, offering everyone tea, coffee, juice, and soft drinks. Then, she hovered at one end of the room with trays of food till Mrs Karamlegavraokar gave her a nod, upon which she sallied forth, always approaching guests from the side so as not to interrupt the meeting.

Mr Karamlegavraokar passed around copies of the paperwork received from the developers declaring Tara Road Mansions as the property of the five new owners. A quick read of the paperwork revealed that the Tulpules were the original owners of Tara Road Mansion and still owned the neighbouring parcels of land, including the stream, paddock, and ruined pavilions up to the river. This information was a surprise only for Hamida, who looked at them in awe. The others simply sat smug in their knowledge.

Mrs Barvay's old-world money connections had ample knowledge of the vast wealth of the Tulpules, and for this reason, she had not directly tackled the buffalo issue with Mr Tulpule. She thought, "Just like I know about their money, do they know about my Avi? I most certainly do not want that thrown in my face at the meeting when I complain about the buffalo! I don't know the Tulpule family personally but gossip travels fast in business circles, although the Tulpules don't seem to know anything beyond their own businesses, children, and the wretched buffalo. The way Mr Tulpule carries on about Sundari, you'd think she was made of gold!" She seethed inwardly.

Seeing the Tulpules in a new light after the party, Mrs Karamlegavraokar had vowed to immediately pay more attention to the Tulpules. She constantly caught Maya Bai's eye and nodded that she should replenish the Tulpule couple's cups and offer them food again and again. She had decided that once she became close friends with the Tulpules, she could explain the Tulpules' oddities to her friends by saying that they had a different lifestyle. Immense wealth always made eccentricities and bad behaviour acceptable. "Goodness me!" she thought once more as she watched them. She had never expected these hippie-type people to be so loaded with money.

Mr Karamlegavraokar whizzed the residents through this meeting. He wanted more time for his neighbours to enjoy his hospitality and his air conditioner. He had prepared all the necessary paperwork, including membership and maintenance fees. Mr Karamlegavraokar and Mrs Tulpule offered to be the first chairman and first treasurer of the residents' committee. It was now time to discuss any other business. Expecting at least some disagreement, he had put Mrs Barvay's buffalo complaint as the last item on the agenda.

Preeti Rao's request was tabled first. She wanted to discuss employing a watchman. Most residential complexes had at least one for the day. But the minute a watchman was mentioned, Mr Tulpule leaned back into the soft cushions of his chair and began in his laconic tone, "Statistics show that burglaries…." He droned on about nights when the police sirens wailed across the stream and down the road that led to Tara Road Mansions. He talked of how this disturbed his sleeping children and his slumbering Sundari. He was just hitting his stride when he was cut short by Mrs Barvay. "Well, Tulpule, this was put up by Preeti, so let us hear what she wants to say."

Mr Tulpule looked disappointed, like an enthusiastic schoolboy who had been interrupted, so he continued speaking very fast now, afraid someone might cut him short again before he had said everything he wanted to. "Do we really need a round-the-clock watchman? Most of us are home at various times of the day, and so there is always someone alert and awake, and everyone knows that new houses have the latest locking systems and security grills. I don't think burglary is a real threat for us because ..."

As he stopped to take a breath, Preeti Rao recognised her chance and immediately began to speak. Her soft, calm, and rational voice almost cutting into the droning Tulpule sentence, and saying, "There has been a spate of burglaries in neighbouring suburbs. I feel it would be very easy for someone to break in here. The area from our backyards to the stream is wide open, and beyond the stream, there are bushes and tall grass; anyone could hide there. Three out of the five houses here have women who live alone, no men. It would make me feel safer ...." This was the idea that had come to her as she listened to the radio news about the burglaries in the surrounding suburbs. Her idea was to scare everyone into thinking they needed a 24-hour watchman, then recommend one of her men. This would provide an extra pair of eyes and hands to help with her own investigations at Tara Road Mansions, especially when she was 'at work.' Although maids, drivers, and watchmen were not usually given much attention by employers, they would definitely make friends with the watchman. Maybe they would make a chance remark to this watchman or he would see or hear something she never would. Maybe Meena would share some information with him or maybe he could better observe everyone from his post. She fervently hoped that her idea of getting a watchman would be approved at the meeting.

Initially, Mrs Barvay had questioned the need for a watchman. She did not want any extra people around. More eyes and mouths meant more gossip. "Most of us are home all day, and everyone is home at night. Is a watchman really needed?" But as everyone had agreed with Preeti about the large open unsecured area by the stream, eventually, Mrs Barvay began to nod her head, acquiescent to the idea of a watchman. She had been a brave, decisive, and stubborn woman until that fateful afternoon, when the world as she knew it had crashed. Now she felt vulnerable in ways she had never thought possible. Hamida adjusted her headscarf and gently said, "I don't mind, whatever gets decided, I am happy with that."

Mrs Karamlegavraokar had been keen to agree with the Tulpules, just to be on their side but she really wanted a watchman in a smart uniform in the same colour as her driver's uniform. She had very clear ideas about uniforms for domestic help.

Mr Karamlegavraokar, having anticipated that the residents would agree to a watchman, had made some calculations. He sat ramrod straight in his tall, wingtip armchair. The grey fabric of the upholstery was the perfect backdrop to show off his features. He cleared his throat as his wife politely gestured to everyone in the room to be quiet. Mr Karamlegavraokar made an unnatural yet practised turn of his head so that everyone could see the perfect cut of his close-shaven jawline in profile. "I think we should start with a watchman at night for a month. All the burglaries in the area and the police sirens going up and down our road, possibly to catch the burglars, have occurred under the cover of darkness. I feel there are enough of us at home in the day, and very much aware of any strangers in the vicinity of our homes. But night time is different. This way we can all sleep peacefully." Everyone murmured approval of this practical solution. Mrs Karamlegavraokar anxiously mouthed 'uniform' to her husband a couple of times but he had moved on to other things and she felt ignored.

"Also, as a newly formed society, we do not have sufficient funds to pay for a 24-hour watchman. We can decide in a couple of months whether we want a daytime watchman as well. At the moment, we should employ someone recommended by friends or family on a trial basis. The agencies charge quite a lot of money. Does anyone know a suitable person for a watchman? Maybe ask family or friends? Perhaps your Meena knows someone, Mrs Barvay? Please do ask around," he added expansively.

Preeti Rao could not believe her luck! A watchman was definitely on the cards; one recommended by family or friends, not from an agency. Perfect! She could definitely get in someone from her own contacts. The only downside was that she had been hoping for 24-hour surveillance by the watchman. She would ask her accomplice to ask for half the money, then maybe he would be offered daytime work too. Seizing the opportunity, she said, "I'll ask in the office. They often know trained people looking for these jobs."

Mrs Karamlegavraokar, keen to prove her identity as a career woman too, offered to ask in her clinic and some of her colleagues. She did not want her husband to admire that Preeti Rao again, this time for resourcefulness in finding a watchman. Hamida offered to ask her father and brother but her soft voice was drowned out between the Tulpules' fierce opposition to the watchman and the others trying to convince them otherwise. Preeti noted this strong anti-watchman stance and wondered about their reasons for it.

Mr Karamlegavraokar finally managed to quiet the residents and moved to the last item on the agenda, which was his least favourite — Sundari. Mr Karamlegavraokar was perched on the edge of his seat, ready to use all his diplomatic skills in the ensuing discussion. He was tense. He had already fielded another call from an irate Mrs Barvay about Sundari chomping on her flowers and making a mess in her courtyard again. His wife had also asked him to raise the matter of Sundari with the Tulpules but very, very gently. According to her, the young Karamlegavraokars' nutritious breakfast of organic, fresh fruit, and expensive bran muffins from the posh bakery were often pilfered by the leathery black beast as the children sat on the back porch every morning, soaking the morning sun for their vitamin D requirements.

"Our children, the poor dears, have not complained, but our ever-vigilant Maya Bai has reported that the buffalo visits the backyard most mornings and makes off with our children's food. Shivram, you have to do something about this! I don't like to complain about the Tulpules, especially since we now know who they are but our children's food… Or do you think I should order extra muffins for their buffalo?" For once, Mrs Karamlegavraokar had been unsure of what to do.

Mr Karamlegavraokar began the discussion, rather gingerly, "The next item on the agenda has been put forth by several residents. It is the matter of the much-beloved Sundari," he said, looking at Mr Tulpule, who sat up, his head cocked to one side. First, he was very pleased to hear that his beloved Sundari was an item on the agenda, but as he heard Mr Karamlegavraokar list the residents' grievances against Sundari, his face began to harden with anger. He glowered at his neighbours and said, "How dare you have the gall to suggest these things? How very dare you! All these accusations cannot possibly be true. Sundari is such a sweet and gentle soul. She would never steal food from children or eat your gardens! Especially not after the A-1 quality feed and straw I give her every morning and evening. She wouldn't even look at your things!" After this outburst, Mr Tulpule's homespun, pale, khadi kurta and bushy moustache trembled in agitation for several moments as if in a private earthquake.

Mrs Barvay forgot all her insecurities and was affronted by Mr Tulpule's suggestion that the complaints about Sundari were untrue. She leaned forward and glared back at Mr Tulpule as she began, "*Aaho* Tulpule! I mentioned this to you gently on the phone last week but you fobbed me off. Now I have made a formal complaint at this meeting. Your great leathery beast ambles into my courtyard and treats my garden like a buffet twice a day. I have no flowers for the altar and she even nibbles at the holy tulsi plant and other shrubs. Sacrilege!

As if that was not enough, she leaves little dung pats, actually, quite large pungent dung pats, all over my courtyard. And I think she eats some small clothes from other people's clotheslines too because last week's dung pats had bits of navy-blue socks in them! My Meena has to spend time cleaning off the dung and washing the courtyard every morning, and no sooner does she finish,

Sundari is back for the next performance. This has got to stop. I refuse to share my garden with your usurping beast." Mrs Barvay leaned back in her chair, spent by her outburst yet brimming with anger.

Preeti Rao, who had no idea that Sundari would be under discussion, gently added, "Yes, I often have to dodge Sundari's dung pats in my backyard and she does graze on my lawn too." Preeti did not care much for her garden; it was not hers, and she was not staying here for long. She had spoken in the hope that this conversation would show some cracks in her neighbours' appearances and alliances.

Mr Tulpule took further umbrage at Preeti's criticism of his beloved Sundari's behaviour. He stood up and loudly protested once again on behalf of his beloved beast.

Mrs Barvay's tone was now very chilly, "*Aggobai!* If you don't believe me, you can come and see the state of my borders and courtyard right now, Tulpule. There will be dung pats left from Sundari's afternoon and evening strolls" she said quietly, dropping the formality of saying Mr Tulpule.

"I don't need to see any borders or gardens and courtyards. I know that Sundari is too well-fed to go chomping at gardens and children's breakfasts. Maybe some other animals come across the stream to your backyard. Don't you know, there are goats and stray cows that currently have free run of the paddock across the stream, what about them? Has anyone actually seen my Sundari eating these plants that you are making accusations about? I can assure you ..."

Mrs Barvay was getting annoyed by Mr Tulpule's attitude and denial. Her powder-puff face was slowly beginning to lose its softer edges. Not to be outdone, she finally decided to repeat herself in a rather loud voice, "*Aaho* Tulpule, your darling pet buffalo walks past everyone's backyards in the morning, chomping away at flowers, leaves and anything else that can possibly be eaten, including some children's socks. In the afternoon, she ambles to my courtyard and proceeds to sit by my storeroom window in the cool shadows of the house. As she leaves for feeding time at dusk, she leaves behind her, a trail of dark, flat, thick, pungent manure pats or should I call them mats, that have some bits of other things she has chewed up in the day. As this defecation probably makes her hungrier, she eats more leaves and flowers from my garden borders on the way back to your house for her next feed. I have a witness; my Meena has seen her. Your buffalo will have to go if you cannot control her."

"Barvay Madam, my Sundari is but a mute beast. One of God's own creatures. How can you possibly accuse her of deliberately doing these things? And anyways, I own the land. Even the very land your house is built on is mine. Who are you to tell me what to do with my buffalo? Sundari will not go. She's a part of our family now." Mr Tulpule felt attacked and injured, as if one of his children was the accused.

"*Aho* Tool-le-pool-ey!" As Mrs Barvay's tone had risen, the niceties had dropped, and she elongated his name sarcastically. "I'm not accusing Sundari and I don't tell lies. I was merely stating facts and saying that you should control her wanderings and droppings better than this! After all, she is an animal, but aren't you, her owner, an intelligent human being? So, control your buffalo! As for the land my house stands on, you gave that land to us a few minutes ago when we signed those papers. Don't try and bully me!"

Mrs Barvay's fine complexion now matched the maroon of her saree. She was angry that a man half her age would doubt her honesty and argue with her. She was also angry with herself; she should not have lost her temper. Especially now, after Avi's behaviour, she could no longer be the righteous, outspoken person she had always been. It was paramount that she kept a low profile and not attract any unnecessary attention to herself or her family. The news about Avi needed to be hidden from everyone for as long and as far as possible. She abruptly stopped talking, composed herself and sat down.

Shocked at the outburst from the usually sweet-tempered Mrs Barvay, Mr Tulpule morosely looked around for support and finding none, drew his wife closer by putting an arm around her shoulders; at least it would look like they were in it together. But this unexpected public gesture of affection caught Mrs Tulpule unawares and her eyes widened momentarily. He knew that his wife shared none of his enthusiasm for the buffalo but he also knew that she would stand by him in public.

Mr Karamlegavraokar felt the control of the meeting slip through his fingers. The repetition of accusations and shouting by two of his richest neighbours made him extremely uncomfortable. Sensing his discomfort and regretting her complaint about Sundari, ever since her discovery that Mr Tulpule was a very rich man, Mrs. Karamlegavraokar generously said, "Well, Mr

Tulpule, maybe just take Sundari for a walk on a rope or leash and then take her back to the shelter, all problems solved! I can order extra bran muffins for Sundari too. She does seem to like them. Anyways, we are all new to each other's ways of living at the moment, so we will all take some time settling in." Mr Tulpule was grateful for some support from such unexpected quarters. Mrs Karamlegavraokar was simply pleased that fate had offered her a chance so quickly to try and smooth things out with the Tulpules.

Mr Karamlegavraokar tried to calm down Mrs Barvay, whose round face was red with anger and her mouth was set in a flat line. She was making her displeasure known by turning away in her chair so that she sat with her back to Mr Tulpule. Mr Karamlegavraokar waved Maya Bai over to offer some more snacks and tea to the elderly lady in the hope that maybe food would distract or placate her.

Mr Tulpule in turn, had dragged himself closer to his wife and was staring solidly at the group of people surrounding him. His wife was speaking to him in a low, soothing voice but he was irritated and kept flicking his wrist dismissively at her without looking at her.

The Karamlegavraokar couple looked at the group in despair. There was a very awkward vibe in the room; the meeting seemed to have reached an impasse. Hamida tried to soothe Mrs Barvay's agitation by placing a hand on her arm and saying, "Just let it go for now. As Mrs Karamlegavraokar said, we are all new to each other's ways. Maybe the watchman, when he starts, can keep an eye out for Sundari and stop her from entering your garden. Or maybe you can put in a fence and a gate at the back…."

While egos had been ruffled and were being cajoled and coaxed, Preeti Rao had quietly talked to Maya Bai and walked to the other end of the room, to make a call from the telephone in an alcove. She had no interest in the buffalo. She only wanted to see whether any fractions would develop between the neighbours. As the room quietened uneasily, they could hear Preeti speaking softly, "… Yes, yes, so we will need a watchman only for the nights to start with… when can he start? Can I have a contact phone number? I can organise an interview for him, the address is Tara Road Mansions. Yes, the new houses…"

Everyone looked at her in great awe. She was so prompt and efficient. No wonder she worked in such a big and famous advertising firm. Preeti Rao, on the other hand, was hoping to present someone as quickly as possible for the watchman's post so that her man got the job. Hopefully, her own contacts would send someone very soon; she had decided to keep her boss out of this. Her idea was that this man would only report to her (and not her boss) on all the happenings, especially at night. She could maybe solve the Impala man mystery too. Maybe she could break into the Tulpule shed at night with his help. Then, if she had any breakthroughs, she could take all the credit.

There was awkward silence in the room as Preeti finished her call. The last item on the agenda was finally laid to rest, albeit temporarily, as Preeti said to Mr Karamlegavraokar, "I just spoke to someone at work, they have given me the phone number for a suitable man, he may be able to come to see you tomorrow morning."

Sensing the mood in the room, Maya Bai scurried around the room offering fresh pots of tea and coffee. As instructed, she had now offered tea, coffee, and food to everyone. It seemed to have mollified some and pacified others. Mr Tulpule and Mrs Barvay still sat facing disparate corners of the room, refusing to move or make eye contact with each other, and they sulked.

Mr and Mrs Karamlegavraokar looked at each other uncomfortably across their living room. Both aggrieved parties were too rich and influential, so they did not want to be seen taking sides and wanted to remain friends with both of them. They made a great show of collecting the notepads and pens and then Mr Karamlegavraokar began to offer his neighbours alcoholic drinks, as his wife laid out a silver tray and an ornately carved, silver peg measure on the sideboard, and Maya Bai brought forth a silver ice bucket and tongs.

✦ ✦ ✦

CHAPTER 11

Preeti Rao hurried home after the meeting to call the number she had written down. She had already shortlisted a couple of men who would show up as soon as possible to be interviewed for the watchman post if tomorrow morning's man did not get the job. The phone was ringing as she unlocked the front door. It was her boss.

"Preeti, I have more information on the shoeboxes that Mrs Tulpule hands over every week to the driver of the battered car. She grows some rare plants and herbs used for Ayurvedic medicine. They are in great demand and expensive because they are seasonal, difficult to propagate, and only a specific part of the plant is used. But they are not illegal."

Preeti was glad he had been able to find out this information because she would have never known this without going to great lengths. With her training, she could only recognise whether the plants in the shed were illegal drugs.

Preeti's boss continued, "Mr Tulpule has been visiting a lot of livestock and agricultural fairs. He seems to be interested in several rare breeds of buffalo. They're worth a lot of money, you know."

Preeti groaned inwardly, "More Sundaris."

"And Preeti, be careful. The photos of the couple you sent from the Karamlegavraokar housewarming party, I circulated them, and no one here recognised the couple either. They were certainly not our people or our acquaintances, and that makes your work dangerous. Work harder and faster at this but make sure no one suspects a thing. I am just about holding off serious consequences for us because of this missing consignment. The new Assistant Commissioner is really burrowing through the unresolved cases, looking at all the details."

Preeti said, "I am working through this as fast as I can. I am being careful, and I carry my pistol on me all the time these days. Any more information about the Karamlegavraokars? The financial adviser and his orthodontist wife?" She inquired, trying to change the subject.

She was hoping to hear something that connected the Karamlegavraokar couple with the stacks of money that Ashu had told her about. She had not shared information about the hidden money with her boss. She wanted to see it for herself first and then take the credit for finding it. "It was definitely illegal money, ready to make a payment or received for illegal goods. When? And to whom? These were the real questions," she thought. But her boss had no new information about the Karamlegavraokars.

Hamida rang her father as soon as she got home from the meeting. When she told her father about the search for a watchman, he said he would check with their factory manager the next morning and suggested she should speak to her brother too. As she said goodbye to her father, she spotted Ashu's neat schoolboy handwriting on a note by the phone. She picked it up and had barely glanced at the note when the phone rang; it was Tariq.

"I've been trying to ring you all evening. I even told Ashu to leave a message by the phone, in case he forgot to tell you. Where have you been, Hamma? Ashu said you were out and he just had a gaggle of children in the house."

She winced at the nickname. She fervently hoped Ayaz would bring back an imported cordless telephone for her when he came back this time. It could show missed calls and record messages on the answering machine. Then there would be no need for handwritten notes and verbal messages.

"Tariq, Ashu has left a note by the phone and I'm just back from a Tara Road Mansions meeting. And I had invited the other neighbours' children here for dinner and a movie; Meena was here, babysitting them all. They weren't just a gaggle of children on their own. How would I leave them like that? Anyways, that's not important," she said in an irritated tone. "We have decided we need a watchman here for nights. Do you know someone suitable for..."

Tariq cut her sentence short and said "Hamida Begum, ..."

Hamida Begum! Her spine stiffened at her formal name; he always called her Hamma unless the matter was very serious. "The watchman is a very good idea. There have been several break-ins in your neighbouring suburbs. And I actually rang to tell you something more serious. Some nefarious characters have been seen near your road and the stream around Tara Road Mansions. Ayaz is away. Don't let the children walk alone to the bus stop, and make sure the children are always home before dark; I know they like to play cricket by the stream. Tell them not to talk to any strangers and to tell you immediately if they see any new faces around the place. You be careful too. Remember last year's incident? Make sure you lock up well every night, especially downstairs. I will keep a close eye on things; otherwise, maybe you and the children can stay with their grandparents for a few days? Don't say anything to Ayaz yet; he will only get worried..." As his voice trailed, Hamida shuddered at the memory of the incident he referred to.

Last year, at a family wedding, the children who were quickly bored with the wedding rituals were playing in the car park of the wedding hall when someone had tried to kidnap Munni. At first, they had all thought it was for the gold and diamond jewellery Munni was wearing, then they realised it was someone who wanted to get back at Tariq. Luckily, the scar-faced chauffeur who always accompanied her father had been minding the children like a hawk. He had whisked Munni out of harm's way and caused a commotion, attracting everyone's attention, so the kidnappers had fled. The perpetrators had never been caught.

"I am glad this watchman thing has been decided, Hamma. I do have someone in mind. He used to work with me but lost his job because he got an arm injury. He will make a great watchman. Very reliable man. I will feel better that he is there, watching your house. He can walk around the perimeter of Tara Road Mansions at night too. He worked with me on several jobs. I was sorry to see him go. He's found it hard to find work after he left here and definitely needs the money. Should he see you about the job?...

Okay, give me the Karmalegavraokar number.... Tomorrow morning?"

Hamida was unsettled by Tariq's call and the reminder about Munni's near abduction. She shuddered at the memory. "Should I have remembered that and insisted on having a watchman rather than being neutral about it?" she wondered before she fell asleep. She was glad Tariq had the situation in hand.

Preeti Rao, who had fallen asleep happily, secure in the knowledge that her plan for a watchman had worked and that her own man would be in that job tomorrow morning, would not have been impressed with the outcome of Hamida's phone call.

That night, the police sirens wailed once again across the river as the police chased yet another lawbreaker, but the residents of Tara Road Mansions slept soundly in the knowledge that very soon, they would have a watchman of their own.

✦ ✦ ✦

The next morning, shrill tones of the black telephone in the Karamlegavraokar living room pierced the peace of the household and its cordless telephone extension in the master bedroom played a soft, imported, melodious ring. The simultaneous reverberating was a nagging insistence to answer the phone. Downstairs, Maya Bai ran to the black telephone in the living room, hurriedly lifting the receiver with its curly wire and said "Haaluu." It was almost 8 o'clock in the morning, her employers were getting ready for work and would be annoyed with the noise and interruption. True to form, she heard Mrs Karamlegavraokar's muffled, insolent shout of "Maya Bai, PHONE!" from the upstairs bathroom at the same time as she heard Mr Karamlegavraokar on the bedroom extension answering with his usual crisp greeting, "Karamlegavraokar."

She hung up. "The Saheb could deal with the phone call" she decided. She had breakfasts to cook and school lunchboxes to pack, plus snacks for recess, and the breakfast table was yet to be laid. The children would come hurtling downstairs any minute, asking after mislaid hair clips, sports shoes, colour pencils, and other sundry items of a regular school day.

Minutes later, as Mrs Karamlegavraokar was putting the final touches to her make-up, she quizzed her husband about the phone call. She had caught the tail end of it as her husband said, "That's excellent, Mrs Sheikh, thank you. I can see him at 8.30 this morning." He paraphrased the conversation for his wife distractedly as he hurriedly put on his shoes, "Mrs Sheikh has recommended somebody for our watchman. He desperately needs the job. He might even be happy to work days and nights on a reduced wage. He's coming in the next half hour to see me. Lives close by, in that slum before we get to Gole Bridge, so no excuses for being late. Now, I need to eat breakfast before he arrives..."

Mr Karamlegavraokar was glad two candidates had been identified so rapidly for the position. This watchman business would be finalised very quickly and it would cement his importance with his new neighbours. Last night, once more, the police sirens had wailed several times, and the exposed scrub and bushes with plenty of hiding places that Preeti Rao had highlighted, now worried him.

Mrs Karamlegavraokar listened and waspishly said, “See? Hamida was better and quicker than Preeti Rao in finding a watchman, the man is even arriving earlier to see you.” She thought any remark that took the sheen off Preeti Rao from her husband’s esteem was worth making.

Mr Karamlegavraokar had noticed his wife’s jealousy whenever Preeti Rao was mentioned, so his tone was light and teasing when he said, “Last night, it had already been decided that Preeti Rao’s recruit was coming to see me this morning at 9.30, so she’s still impressive, my dear. I have asked Mrs Sheikh’s man to see me earlier because he lives nearby, and I can leave for the office by 10 o’clock as planned.”

Mrs Karamlegavraokar bristled and ignored her husband’s gentle teasing. She was annoyed that her husband seemed to be constantly in awe of Preeti Rao. “This has to stop!” she thought firmly. “Shivram, Preeti Rao is very young and from Calcutta. She’s still new in Poona. I don’t think you should trust her judgement about people for a watchman. After all, she is only suggesting what people at her office have said. What does she really know about anyone in this city? For all we know, the man could help the burglars!”

“Hmmmmmm” said Mr Karamlegavraokar, wondering where this conversation was headed.

“Hamida, on the other hand, well, she’s grown up in Poona, her family runs large businesses here for several generations, and therefore, they will know many people and have more trustworthy contacts. Her man would definitely be more suitable for the job.

Her family would vouch for their man or they wouldn't suggest him. I do wish you would see and understand this clearly, rather than constantly be besotted with everything that Preeti girl does." Mrs Karamlegavraokar drove her point home rather sharply. Then in a gentler tone she said, "And Shivram, don't forget to mention the watchman's uniform. It can be the same as our drivers. In fact, we may even have a spare set from one of our earlier drivers. Just let Maya Bai know."

Mr Karamlegavraokar was annoyed that his wife was so fixated on Preeti Rao. He shrugged, "Let's see how it goes, my dear. Let's find a man for the job first; the uniform will come much later. And even then, since it is only a night watchman, no one will ever see the watchman's uniform matching your driver's uniform," his voice was deadpan but his eyes twinkled and irritated Mrs Karamlegavraokar; he touched her shoulder affectionately as she gave her hair a final brush.

She pushed away his placating hand from her shoulder. "I have to leave for work now, Shivram. But don't let me come home to find out that you have employed Preeti Rao's man." Her fingers snapped back the perfume lid aggressively and she left the room in a cloud of his favourite French perfume. He groaned with pleasure and frustration.

✦ ✦ ✦

A couple of hours later, Mr Karamlegavraokar left for his office with a bounce in his step as Maya Bai ferried another note from her Saheb to the Tara Road Mansion residents. It read:

Dear Residents,

This morning, I interviewed two candidates for the post of watchman as suggested by Ms Rao and Mrs Sheikh. After careful deliberation of their experience and references, I have decided to employ Mrs Sheikh's candidate Tukaram Shinde, as he seemed suitable in every way. He lives ten minutes away near Gole Bridge and has agreed to work days and nights for the amount we agreed at the meeting for a night watchman, as he desperately needs a job and a place to sleep at night. His only conditions are that he gets an hour's break for lunch every day and another hour for dinner every night from 7 pm. He has agreed to patrol the area around Tara Road Mansions up to the stream, a couple of times in the day and three times at night.

He will begin work at about 8 o'clock tomorrow. In keeping with the class of Tara Road Mansions, I have given him a spare uniform belonging to one of our old drivers. Any further discussion about his uniform can be tabled at the next meeting.

Please note, Tukaram should not be given any jobs inside the houses or sent out of the Tara Road Mansion grounds on any resident's personal errands. He is a watchman and should fulfil that duty.

Yours sincerely,

Shivram Karamlegavraokar

Chairman, Tara Road Mansions

The Tara Road residents had mixed reactions to this note. Mrs Barvay felt a sense of relief; she would feel much safer about herself and her house with a watchman. The Tulpules had simply shrugged at the news; they were still not convinced a watchman was needed but had conceded to the wishes of the majority. Hamida was relieved that a watchman was in place after that unsettling call from Tariq about some sightings of nefarious characters in the area, and also glad she had been able to help Tukaram, who was in need of a job. Mrs Karamlegavraokar had been happy that the winning candidate was Hamida's recruit. However, she was more pleased that her vision of a watchman in the same uniform as her personal drivers was fulfilled. As the uniformed watchman would salute cars that drove in and out of the Tara Road Mansion gates, she hoped visitors would think it was their personal watchman or security guard.

Preeti Rao had been impatient that morning, waiting to hear from her recruit that he was the new watchman. She half-expected him at the front door to let her know he had got the job. Instead, she found Maya Bai on her doorstep once more with a note, "It's about the new watchman" Maya Bai said.

Excitedly, Preeti took the proffered note but her excitement turned to fury as she read it. Her idea had worked but her plan had failed. Barely twelve hours since she had pitched the idea of a new watchman at the meeting and a new man suggested by Hamida was already starting tomorrow. "Why did my candidate not get the job? I handpicked the man myself. Made sure he was suitable in every way for my plan and the residents' requirements. I had told him to agree to day and night work for a meagre sum and even sent him with impeccable references!"

She had not only lost an extra pair of eyes and hands but now had to contend with a new watchman added to the mix, so she would need to be extra careful. She was suspicious too. "Where had Hamida got hold of a watchman so quickly? Was he really a watchman? Why had he agreed to work so many hours for half the money? Who was paying the other half? How had they known her idea of the watchman working for half the wages so he would have the daytime watchman job too?" These doubts troubled her and always brought her back to an overarching question: "Were the residents together in this and protecting something or someone?" The urgency of finding the consignment gnawed at her. She needed to reinforce her efforts with more foolproof plans than the ones she had executed so far. She focused harder on the job at hand, clearly laying out each piece of information in her head and did not stop till she had a new plan to overcome her recent failures in strategy.

✦ ✦ ✦

That afternoon, Preeti Rao sprained her ankle at work. The sprain was so severe that she arrived home much earlier than usual in a taxi rather than the usual rickshaw. Meena was on her way to the Sheikh household to look after the children and Hamida was saying goodbye to a jittery bride at the front door, when they saw her. Preeti struggled to get out of the taxi, holding on to large ungainly crutches, trying not to put her crepe-bandaged foot to the ground, and clutching her handbag and some files. Meena and Hamida rushed to help Preeti out of the taxi. Grateful for their help, Preeti hobbled to her front door. Hamida unlocked Preeti's front door while Meena held the files and the handbag. The afternoons had become very hot and the three women hurried indoors into Preeti's cool house.

"Thanks, Hamidaji" said Preeti politely, hobbling behind them on her crutches and smiled gratefully at Meena as the young girl set down the files and handbag.

"I haven't even done anything to help you yet. Do you want me to call anyone for you? Relatives? Friends? Has your phone been connected now?" asked Hamida kindly because she remembered Preeti had gone to Mrs Barvay's house to make some calls after the housewarming party.

Preeti smiled sadly as she collapsed on a sofa, "Yes, the phone is connected now. Thank you. We have no family or friends here, just me. My brother's employers own this house; he signed a lease but the company transferred him to the US office for two years as soon as he started with them. Then I was offered a job at Halo and moved in, so I only know work colleagues here."

Hamida thought of Preeti's family far away in America and patted Preeti's hand, "Don't think for a minute that you're alone. I'm here, everyone at Tara Road Mansions is here, so of course, you are amongst friends. Just let me know what you need and I will get it."

Preeti shook her head and said, "I'm fine."

"Can I, at least, send you some dinner later on? Something vegetarian? Meena can bring it to you when she's going home after working at my house. She usually returns to Mrs Barvay's house by seven," said Hamida, ignoring Preeti's protests.

"No, no, it's okay. I have already eaten a big lunch this afternoon at a product launch party and I have a few leftovers from last night..." Preeti rambled on, trying to be polite but evading Hamida's questions and trying to avoid Hamida or Meena's repeated appearances at her house.

But Hamida had one more offer, she said, "Or even better, would you like to come and stay with us? Then you will have me and the children to help you. Honestly, you're very welcome, we don't mind at all. There is a spare bedroom ready and waiting. You can be our very first houseguest." Hamida went on to voice her concern about Preeti managing the stairs on her own with crutches.

Preeti shook her head determinedly. She had not expected such smothering from Hamida. "I will be fine; it's just this one flight of stairs. And those bannisters are strong if I need to lean on them. I will be able to make it upstairs easily. I will just sit on the lower steps and then lift myself up to the next step, and so on and do the whole thing in reverse to come downstairs. It'll be fine. I will take the crutches with me so I can use them upstairs. The sprain just looks worse than it actually is. I am planning to stay in bed and rest it, just as the doctor advised. And Meena will be here for cleaning every day, so I can always ask her for help."

Meena nodded vigorously, and Preeti reassured Hamida that she had already seen a doctor and finally convinced her to leave, promising to call if she needed anything at all. Preeti had purposely added the bit about staying in bed. It would deter well-meaning visitors because they knew she would have to come down the stairs to answer the door. She smiled slyly at the thought of the other things she had set in motion today before organising to arrive home in a taxi.

Preeti had planned to arrive exactly at a time when she knew the children arrived from school and Meena walked across to Hamida's house. Having Hamida at her door too, had been a bonus. She knew Hamida would help her but Meena would quickly spread the news of her sprained ankle, so no one would think it odd that she was no longer going for walks or to work. She needed to find out more about this new watchman before he saw her. Finally, after many instructions, Meena and Hamida saw themselves out, and as the door shut behind them, Preeti breathed a sigh of relief. At last, she could pull off the crepe bandage and stretch her ankle! It was beginning to feel quite itchy. The sprained ankle was only an excuse to stay home and keep an eye on her neighbours. Gleefully, she kicked at the crutches and skipped up the stairs. She still had a few more ideas to execute. She was determined to find the missing consignment. She was not going to be deterred by this new watchman.

✦✦✦

CHAPTER 12

Summer had set in, bringing long sweltering days. It was hot even at sunset when Sundari leisurely strolled past the cricket pitch on her way back from Mrs Barvay's garden to her shelter. She always walked with her huge hips swaying from side to side, as if in time to her own musical beat. The children often walked behind her in a line, hands on their hips, taking wide steps mirroring the buffalo and shaking their bottoms from side to side and giggling. They kept a safe distance from her, of course, to avoid her dung pats. Her tail swished and flicked over her bottom at irregular intervals, keeping her cool and punishing the impudence of erstwhile flies. The children had come to recognise Sundari walking home as a cue that it would soon be dark and time to go home. They usually hastened their pace of cricket when they saw her heading back to her enclosure and tried to squeeze out as much play as possible before they were all summoned home.

The afternoon Preeti Rao had returned with a sprained ankle, Kaveri had tipped her water bottle too far as she drank from it, and spilt water all over her dress. It was almost sunset, but not quite time to go home. It was too long to leave Kaveri in a wet dress, so an irate Maya Bai had marched her home to change, knowing she would have to hurriedly return to take Kartik home. He would not leave before it was dark. Ashu was batting, and Kartik wanted to get him out before they stopped play for the day;

otherwise, Ashu would get to bat tomorrow evening too. Kartik began bowling faster and harder than usual, knowing Maya Bai would be back any minute to break up their game and take him home. He hurled the ball rather haphazardly at Ashu who was making extravagant batting stances, just like the players he had seen on TV. Kartik's hurried ball was out of control, it completely missed Ashu's bat, whistled past Ashu's ears and spun away in a fluorescent yellow blur towards Mrs. Barvay's courtyard. The Tulpule twins immediately mimed and shouted 'Wide ball!' as their father was currently teaching them the signals for umpiring a cricket game. There was a muffled thump and a tinkling sound. Mystified, they turned towards the noise and looked in the direction of Mrs Barvay's courtyard. The fluorescent yellow tennis ball was nowhere to be seen. They walked in the general direction the ball had taken. They looked around the paved courtyard, in the low bushy borders of the courtyard and outside Mrs Barvay's garden by the overgrown grass near the edge of the stream. But the dusty, dry ground, and the drying grass did not have the fluorescent yellow tennis ball. They searched desperately in the fast-fading light, implicit in the knowledge that any minute they would all be summoned home but the ball was nowhere to be seen. As expected, Maya Bai came for Kartik, and the Tulpule twins left too, after promising to look for the ball the next day. Kartik, feeling guilty about the lost ball, offered to get a new ball for the next day's cricket. Ashu wanly smiled and waved goodbye to his friends, but he was worried.

Ammi was going to be furious! This was the third tennis ball he had lost this week. One had gone missing at school a couple of days ago. Yesterday, he had put a ball on the ground while he tied his shoelace, and Sundari had ambled past, slurped up the ball and chewed it, before unceremoniously spitting it out on the grass in a rubbery mess. "And now this one! Surely, this ball was here somewhere. At least Sundari was gone, so she couldn't eat it till tomorrow" he thought. He remembered the thump followed by the tinkling sound and looked worriedly at Mrs Barvay's house. As he had feared, a glass pane on one of the ground-floor windows had cracked and broken. There were several little shards on the paving where Sundari sat in the afternoons. He could not make out whether the ball had broken the glass and bounced back into the garden or broken the glass and fallen inside the room. He decided the lost ball must have gone through the window, as they had already searched the courtyard and the surrounding area of grass almost up to the stream. The thought of the broken window weighed heavily on his young shoulders as he gazed at the jagged glass that still clung to the window frame. Should he risk trying to go through the window? The jagged glass could cut his hand to ribbons as he tried to undo the window catch. He reminded himself again that this would be the third ball lost this week. His hesitation melted; today, he was not going home without his ball.

He knew Mrs Barvay was out every afternoon until late evening, and today Meena was babysitting his sister, Munni, who was not well. Ammi was very busy in the boutique these days. Summer was always wedding season, and *The Begum Boutique* had a lot of orders to complete. His mother was constantly downstairs in the boutique, finishing the embroidery, buttons, and alterations on the wedding dresses and sarees, long after

Darzi Master had left for the day. Ashu knew she had to finish a complicated order for a big wedding this week; she would not miss him for a while.

Ashu looked determinedly at the storeroom window. Through the jagged glass, he could see the little catch that loosely held the window closed. He wiggled his fingers in through the broken pane and tried to undo the catch several times, but could not reach it through the jagged edges of broken glass that still clung to the frame. He rattled the window in frustration and banged it shut; his action released a shower of tiny glass shards to the ground, and lo behold! The window swung open, startling Ashu. "Perhaps it had not been fastened at all" he thought. Furtively, he looked around, wondering if anyone had seen him shaking and banging the window. But no one was about, and all was still. He waited for a few minutes, then quickly climbed in. His shoes crunched the glass underfoot as they touched the floor.

He looked around. It seemed to be a storeroom like the one his grandparents had, except this room was smaller and newer, it had no peeling paint and did not seem as dusty. Oddments of furniture nestled amongst brass buckets. The beautiful bell of a gramophone looked like a dull metal flower in the dim light. There were battered suitcases, cardboard boxes, and a huge metal trunk with a padlock. Transparent new plastic boxes overflowed with papers, some printed, others handwritten, all old and yellowing. There were a few burlap grain sacks in various sizes, mostly full, and bursting at the seam where the pressure had just become too much for the hand-sewn edges to hold their contents. Each sack had some undecipherable green or pink stamp, just like the ones in his grandparents' house. The sacks looked exactly like the ones Ashu and his cousins sat on and giggled while they shared food they had purloined from the kitchen — handfuls of sweet, dark jaggery chunks, roasted peanuts, dried figs, raisins, even a fresh pakora or two, whatever the cousins had collectively plundered when the cook was not looking.

But being here in Mrs Barvay's room was different; it felt wrong. For one, it was not his grandparents' house, there were no cousins, he was alone, and twilight was quickly giving way to darkness. Ashu looked around desperately in the fading light, hoping the bright yellow tennis ball would somehow reveal itself quickly. He could grab it and go home. Never before had he broken someone's window and knew he should apologise immediately. He had never entered a room without knocking or permission. Ammi was very particular about these things. This was the house of a new neighbour, where he had broken a windowpane and brazenly entered the room. His heart was racing, he knew this was wrong, but losing three balls in a week was imprinted on his mind.

Suddenly, he spotted the errant ball, fuzzy and fluorescent yellow in the dusky twilight. It was lodged between two sacks. A large standard-sized burlap sack that stood almost as tall as his shoulders and about three times as wide with a couple of grains pushing out through the weave near the seam. The other sack was smaller, more the size of a large plump pillow. It looked exactly like the one containing walnuts in his grandparents' storeroom. As he lunged for the fluorescent yellow ball, his eye caught sight of the smaller sack's contents pushing through the seam. He was mesmerised. Like most sacks, one of the hand-sewn seams had come slightly undone and he recognised its contents in the fast-fading light. Sugar! Its tiny, pale, squarish translucent crystals beckoned him, glinting in the half-light. He could almost taste the sweetness even before he touched the sack. He craved it now, more than ever. Here was a whole sack full, albeit a small sack.

"Mrs. Barvay couldn't eat sugar because of the diabeety thing" he thought, remembering the large wedge of chocolate cake she had given away. "Surely she wouldn't miss a small amount, especially if he had a teeny tiny bit." He relished this thought. No one to say "Stop! Enough!" He had to have at least a taste. Before he changed his mind, his fingers had deftly pinched, pulled and poked the twine at the corner where the seam had split; he cupped his fingers underneath. "Thief!" his mind called loudly, but his traitorous body was not listening. A little trickle of sugar escaped the sack, reluctantly at first, then quickly sliding out in gathered momentum. His hand was sweaty, and the sugar crystals stuck to his fingers as they slid onto his palm. He wriggled his fingers and nudged the sack corner upwards to stop any more sugar spilling out, wondering what would happen if Mrs Barvay or his mother found out. "Could I be arrested for taking a bit of sugar?" His hands shook with fear at this thought, but unable to stop his hands, he flicked the sugar from his palm into his mouth, licking his fingers and palm with a slurp before he thought any more. He felt the grainy particles on his tongue as his heart pounded away and his ears strained for sounds of Meena or Mrs Barvay returning home. In his mind, he could hear himself reading what the Quran said about respecting other people's property. Yet, here he was. He had broken a window, climbed into someone's house and was now stealing sugar!

His mind was racing, and he waited for the rewarding sweetness of the sugar to hit his taste buds as he stood with one foot on the fluorescent yellow tennis ball. But he could taste nothing. "That can't be right" he thought as he wiggled another pinch of sugar from the sack onto his palm and into his mouth. Once again, he could taste nothing. No sweetness from the sugar and no saltiness from his sweaty palm. He was confused, but his brain was now fixated on getting a sugar hit. He could not believe it when his hands reached for the sugar sack a third time! "Maybe I am so scared of stealing that I cannot taste anything" he reasoned, "or maybe Ammi's warning has come true …that if I keep on eating so much sugar, one day I would not be able to taste any sweetness at all? Was Allah punishing him for all his sins of this evening? How horrible to never be able to taste sweetness again!"

His heart hammered harder with each thought, and he could feel a pulse in his temple now. He could not understand his own immoral actions. He was also scared someone would come in any minute, and yet he wanted to have another pinch to check whether he could taste sugar. His heart was now at full crescendo, just like the time he had put his ear to the large speaker at a wedding, in addition, he felt queasy as his stomach churned with guilt. He caught his breath again, "This was stealing! No two ways about it." His mind was truly terrified but his body was not listening. His hands reached for yet another pinch of sugar when he heard Meena singing as she walked to the front door. He panicked! He tried shaking the sugar off his hands by brushing his hands together to dust away the sugar but his sweaty palms stubbornly held on to the little particles. He looked at his fingers in dismay. Out of habit, he nearly wiped his hands on his t-shirt before realising Ammi would see the sugar and ask questions. Then he remembered these shorts had pockets. He carefully put his hands in his pockets and deftly wiped his sugary hands on the inside of his shorts' pockets, relief flooding him as he felt the particles detaching themselves from his fingers and falling into the cotton pockets. Once his fingers were sugar-free, he raised himself on tiptoe and lifted his bottom onto the window ledge. He used his hands to turn his body around on the windowsill and furtively clambered out of the open window and ran home in the deepening twilight without daring to look back. He had never been so terrified in his life! If he was caught stealing sugar from someone else's house after breaking their window, not even his grandfathers could save him from the wrath of Ammi.

Meena sang as she let herself in through Mrs Barvay's front door. She was disappointed with her evening. While she had been babysitting Munni, Meena had hoped the little girl would fall asleep while Hamida was downstairs, allowing her to steal at least a couple more of those Swari-something crystals that Hamida sewed on all the bridal outfits. They were always in Hamida's embroidery box upstairs in the living room. Meena was slowly building up a nice little collection. The crystals fetched a good price at the pawnshop near the railway station. But little Munni, now recovering from her illness, had been wide awake, asking for stories and lemonade, so Meena could not sneak around the rooms as much as usual. Not one to despair, Meena had managed to 'pick up' a small, gold-embroidered silk shawl from the top shelf of Hamida's wardrobe as she pretended to tidy up while Munni watched a cartoon. The soft silk shawl was delicately embroidered with 22-carat gold thread; Meena had recognised its value. It would bring in good money and definitely be a while before it was missed because it was still summer.

Once Meena was back in Mrs Barvay's house, she wanted to stow away the shawl before Mrs Barvay returned from the club. Still singing, she walked to the storeroom and stopped dead in her tracks. She gasped. The window was brazenly wide open! A part of the glass pane had shattered and bits of glass were scattered on the floor. Burglars? She hurriedly went to check the old pillowcase at the bottom of a bucket, where she had hidden the stolen jewellery and other goods, but the brass buckets around the pillowcase had not been moved at all. She lifted them and peered in; to her immense relief, all her loot was intact, exactly as she had left it. Her heart thumped wildly as she warily looked around the room, expecting an intruder, but there was no one. As her eyes trailed the windowsill, she caught sight of more shards of glass, and then she almost laughed in relief as she saw the incriminating bright yellow tennis ball innocently lying on the floor. Obviously, the children had broken the windowpane during their game of cricket. She remembered Ashu had not returned home by the time she left Hamida's house. She deposited the stolen shawl amongst the other loot and placed an empty box over the brass buckets next to the sacks. She swept up the glass shards inside and outside the window and covered the broken pane with a piece of cardboard and sticky tape. Then she went to the kitchen to start cooking dinner for Mrs. Barvay.

That night, when she told Mrs Barvay about the broken pane, initially, the elderly lady had turned ashen and looked worried. But when she heard about the ball, the colour had returned to her cheeks. She had chuckled and begun a cheerful tale of how her Avi, as a boy, had broken many windowpanes of Barvay Mansion when he played cricket with his friends. She told Meena to throw the ball into Hamida's garden later that evening, so the children were saved the humiliation of asking for it and apologising for the broken pane. Then she reminisced of a time when Barvay House had been alive with Avi's many friends constantly in and out of the house, eating the mountains of food that only teenage boys could consume. In her memories, those days were full of loud music, youthful laughter, bad haircuts, and silly fashions. Her eyes moistened as she thought of those days. She felt alone and sad and old as her mind brought her back to the present. "At least, I have Meena in this house. It's good to have a young person about" Mrs Barvay thought comfortingly. In a very short time, she had become very fond of the young girl.

Hearing Meena returning to the house, Ashu had raced out of the Barvay courtyard, through his own backyard and veranda and up the stairs to his room without interruption. That was when he realised that his stumps and bat were still on the cricket pitch, and worse, in his hurry to leave the storeroom, he had forgotten the incriminating ball in the storeroom. He kicked himself for the mistake. He ran down the stairs in a rush to retrieve the bat and stumps from the pitch but he bumped into his mother, who was walking up the stairs.

"Ashu! What is the hurry? How many times have you been told NOT to run on the stairs ....." After a mangled explanation about rushing home for the toilet and forgetting the bat and stumps, he walked slowly down the stairs as his mother watched and managed to return home quickly with the bat and stumps.

"Great!" he said to himself. Now he could also add lying to his mother to his list of sins. When he had gone to get the bat and stumps, he had glanced at Mrs Barvay's courtyard from the cricket pitch, hoping to retrieve the ball from the storeroom. But there had been a light in the storeroom and he could see Meena by the window. He kicked at the pebbles on his way home. "Why did I forget the ball in the storeroom? Because I had been too busy eating sugar!" His heart pounded hard in his chest as if it would burst out of its ribcage, his head hurt, and his stomach was churning again at the thought of stealing. How he wished they had wound up their game of cricket, instead of trying to eke out another over, when Sundari had walked past or when Maya Bai had taken Kaveri home to change her wet dress. If they had, then the disastrous events that had followed would have never taken place.

Ammi was so insistent that they always ask for permission even to enter each other's rooms at home and he had entered a near stranger's house without permission. In one go this evening, he had damaged property, lost a ball, entered Mrs Barvay's house like a thief, greedily eaten some sugar, wiped his sticky fingers inside the pockets of his new shorts so that Ammi would not know and then lied to her about needing the toilet. His stomach roiled again. If Ammi ever found out all these things, how was he ever going to justify any of his actions?

He lay awake for a long time that night, trying to think of ways to retrieve the ball and justify his immoral actions. He did not find any solutions to his problems as he lay in bed but the ceiling began to spin gently behind the blur of the fan, his heart kept hammering loudly in his chest, and he felt so ill that he decided to close his eyes and have a little rest. But he could not fall asleep and could not bear to keep his eyes open. He would definitely be found out, he decided. He could not have left behind more incriminating evidence, a bright yellow tennis ball with his initials 'AS' in his own handwriting to ensure no one could steal his ball at school.

Meena also lay awake that night, thinking uneasily about the broken windowpane. She tossed and turned restlessly, trying to figure out whether she should try and take all her loot to the pawnshop the next morning or change her hiding place. Finally, she decided to split her loot and stow it in two places in the storeroom, just until she got a chance to take it all to the pawnshop. Carefully finding her way around in the dark house, she took the flashlight from the kitchen drawer and made her way cautiously to the storeroom. She dared to switch on the flashlight only once she had firmly closed the storeroom door. She balanced the flashlight on a box so that it faced the ceiling. Swiftly, she moved the smaller, more valuable jewellery to one of the smaller sacks by carefully further unpicking a corner of one of the small sacks that already had a bit of the seam undone. Gently, she burrowed her closed fingers deep into the sack several times to deposit the jewellery and felt the reassuring granular sugary crystals around her fingers. Soon, she had buried some earrings, a couple of gold chains, a bangle, and silver coins from the Karamlegavraokar housewarming party into the sack of sugary crystals.

She had seen more valuable jewellery in Mrs Barvay's wardrobes. But she could not bring herself to steal anything from Mrs Barvay just yet. There was something about Mrs Barvay that reminded Meena of her mother. She saw the same energy, pride, discipline, and a constant underlying sadness and wondered about Mrs Barvay's sadness. Meena knew the reasons for her own mother's sadness were poverty and a drunken husband who had abandoned her. But Mrs Barvay seemed to have everything anyone could wish for, so maybe she was just sad about her dead husband or faraway son, Meena had concluded.

Upstairs in the same house, Mrs. Barvay was restless in her bedroom too. "What am I going to do about Avi?" she thought as she tossed and turned in bed that night. She had been much more unsettled by the broken window than she had let on. Broken windowpanes reminded her of Avi, and thinking of Avi nowadays made her heart ache. Her original plan for this year had been to find a suitable girl and get Avi married. Then the newly married couple could live in the huge ancestral Barvay House and she would move into the annexe. She would be independent and yet close to her son and his family. She had looked forward to relinquishing the responsibility of Barvay House to her daughter-in-law, just like she had handed the reins of Barvay Industries to Avi a few years ago.

Her husband had been a brilliant businessman and died when Avi was only ten years old. She had successfully run the huge family business and managed Barvay House singlehandedly until Avi was old enough to take over. She had brought up Avi to be a gentle, honourable man with plenty of friends, just like his father. She had trained Avi at the office, and ensured that she was involved behind the scenes in most of the business dealings he conducted. But with the happenings of just one afternoon, all her plans were now on hold, indefinitely.

Avinash Barvay, until that fateful afternoon, had been one of the most eligible bachelors in the state. Incredibly rich, unbelievably good-looking, and with an impeccable pedigree. He was well-educated, well-mannered, fashionable, respectful, honest, and had a superb sense of humour. He attended no wild parties and had no string of girlfriends. There were no unsavoury rumours about him and no one had a bad word to say about him, except that occasionally he was impulsive. But rich people like the Barvays could easily afford the vice of being impulsive – buying a racehorse on a whim, suddenly donating a valuable painting to a charity auction, booking out entire sections of the stadium for friends to see a one-day international cricket match, buying the latest car in a limited colour, surprising his mother and her friends with a month-long trip to Europe for her birthday, and inviting Bollywood's top stars to a dinner party at Barvay House. These actions by Avi were extravagant, harmless, and their expense barely registered a flicker in the vast Barvay fortune.

Avinash Barvay ticked every box ever created by any society matron who had attempted matchmaking. Mrs Barvay had been inundated by proposals from friends, family, and society's matchmaking matrons as soon as Avi had joined the family business. He had refused to talk about marriage. He wanted to settle into the family business before he considered marrying. She had agreed and waited until this year. Then, in just one afternoon, everything had changed. She was angry but did not know how it had happened and who was to blame. However rich you were, a stain like this on one's character could never be forgotten or overlooked by society. A good marriage would now be out of question. In that one afternoon, Avi had managed to lose almost a century of good reputation that generations of Barvays before him had always commanded in social and business circles for being conventional, honest, honourable partners and opponents with good traditional values, old money, education, and intelligence. She had no idea how she would shepherd Avi out of this mess and into his intended life. Could she help him at all now? A great surge of maternal love and the need to protect her only son engulfed her. It made her sad and furious. She wanted to fix this, make everything right for Avi, but she had no idea how she would go about it. She spun these facts round and round in her head and finally fell into an uneasy sleep just as the sun was rising.

✦✦✦

CHAPTER 13

Mrs Barvay woke with a start as the phone rang. She answered it, squinting at the bedside clock; it was already seven o'clock in the morning, but it felt like she had fallen asleep only a few minutes ago. She recognised Vijay Shahane's voice on the phone and was instantly wide awake. Vijay never rang before 9 am, although he was like family and called her *vahini* (sister-in-law). He had been her husband's best friend from their school days, and now was the general manager of Barvay Industries. He was also the only person who knew the truth about Avi's sudden trip to America.

"Hello, Vijay. All well?" she inquired warily, unable to hide the worry in her voice.

"Sorry vahini, I called so early, but something's happened that you must know. But don't worry, at least no one is hurt and nothing seems to be taken."

Mrs Barvay blanched as she suddenly sat up in bed. "Huh… Who..? Happened where? Where? Is it Avi? Hurt? What's happened? Something in one of the factories? What is it, Vijay? Tell me!" her voice urgent, alarmed and commanding.

"Avi is absolutely fine. Factories are all going well. It is Barvay Mansion that has the problem. Earlier this morning, one of the neighbours out for a walk saw the Barvay House watchman gagged and bound, lying on the driveway by the gate. They called the police, who found that Barvay House had been broken into; they are questioning the watchman at the police station.

Luckily, because the house painting is underway, all valuable art pieces have already been moved to the factory warehouses and no one was in the house. Some of the soft furnishings were slashed but those can easily be repaired or replaced. The burglars seem to have given the house a thorough going over. I am at Barvay House just now and nothing seems to be missing. But it would be good if you could come here later this morning to have a look before I complete the formal police report about missing and damaged items. The police said several similar burglaries have occurred in neighbouring suburbs. You must understand, this is not an isolated incident."

He continued, "I wanted to tell you this news myself, rather than the police who will visit you very soon this morning. I did try to dissuade them from disturbing you but the new Assistant Commissioner seems to have taken a keen interest in these burglaries and wants to do everything by the book. When can you come here to Barvay House this morning? I can organise a car accordingly…." Vijay Shahane let out a breath as he finished.

Mrs Barvay was now wide awake, and the news began to sink in. She felt like she was on a rollercoaster. First, she had been anxious about Avi being hurt, then of mishaps or a strike at one of the factories and then relief sluiced through her that it was none of these things. She hated the thought of an intruder or intruders in Barvay House and knew exactly what they had been looking for; although it seemed that nothing was taken, she felt violated and terrified. Her stomach lurched, and she retched as Meena walked into the room with the usual bed-tea tray.

Meena had heard the phone ring and Mrs Barvay speaking but had thought nothing of it. Mrs Barvay often had friends and relatives ring from overseas at odd hours. But now, as she observed the pallor on Mrs Barvay's face, the retching, and her shaking hands, Meena rushed to her side, settling her back in bed. She raced downstairs for an old enamel basin and brought a dampened towel to mop her employer's brow. Meena did not know what to do next. Once the colour had returned to Mrs Barvay's cheeks, Meena propped her up with pillows on the bed and handed her a cup of tea. While keeping a beady eye on her elderly employer, Meena rang Hamida, as she felt more familiar with her compared to the other ladies at Tara Road Mansions.

Hamida's house

Hamida called, "Ashu, wake up. Breakfast is almost ready." Ashu awoke tired and worried. His last thought as he had fallen asleep at night and his waking thought this morning had both been about retrieving the incriminating fluorescent yellow tennis ball from Mrs Barvay's storeroom. He had barely slept, waking many times, trying to think of ways to retrieve the ball, until he had fallen into an exhausted sleep.

Sitting up, he looked out through his window, focusing on Mrs Barvay's courtyard. He could see the broken windowpane taped with cardboard. As he looked away, his gaze caught an unnatural flash of fluorescent yellow in his own backyard. The tennis ball that had caused so much trouble was lying innocently in the muddy garden patch amidst the mud pies and battling plastic dinosaurs, its 'AS' faintly visible from Ashu's lofty perch. Relief flooded through him. Silently, he sent a prayer of thanks to Meena and Mrs Barvay for not complaining about the broken pane. He decided he liked Mrs Barvay for this kindness even more than he had liked her for the big wedge of chocolate cake sent after the first meeting. He relaxed as he realised that now, no one would ever find out about him entering the storeroom and eating a couple of pinches of sugar. He could simply pocket the ball from his own backyard when he left for school and forget all about yesterday's horrible events. He had definitely learnt his lesson. He never wanted to feel the terror, queasiness, spinning ceiling, and guilt of yesterday ever again.

Ashu went to the kitchen to have breakfast with a tired, pale-looking Munni. He was eyeing the sugar bowl while his mother's back was turned, when the phone rang. Hamida, who was cooking breakfast for the children, called for Ashu to answer the phone. Ashu was horrified when he heard Meena at the end of the line calmly asking for his mother.

"Was this nightmare ever going to end?" he wondered. He stammered as he asked Meena to 'please hold' while he got his mother. He briefly wondered if he should ask Meena the reason for her call but he already knew. Mrs Barvay must have asked Meena to ring his mother about the broken window pane. "Any minute now, all my sins will be listed and judged. Ammi will ...." he halted his thoughts. "What would Ammi do?" He had no idea. He tried to think of his worst escapades as he tried to gauge the scale of punishments for all his wrongdoings from yesterday.

Hamida wiped her hands on her apron and hurried to the phone. Ashu angled his chair so he could see his mother's expression and hear at least her side of the conversation. He watched intently as she spoke on the phone, bracing himself as he waited for the axe to fall. First, Hamida had looked a bit concerned, but she did not even glance in his direction when she said, "I'll be there in a minute" and hung up.

"Ammi was going over there, in the middle of cooking breakfast? This must be serious. I am in massive trouble," he thought, and his heart sank like a dead weight.

"Ashu, look after your sister, I'm going to see Mrs Barvay for a bit" Hamida had called over her shoulder as she left. Ashu was puzzled and simply nodded; his heart was beginning to pound again, and he pushed away the sugar bowl he had been eyeing on the breakfast table. "What about my breakfast? And school?" Two things Ammi never forgot. "Things are going to be very bad for me when Ammi returns."

Mrs Barvay's house

Meena was glad to see Hamida arrive so quickly. Mrs Barvay had insisted on getting dressed and coming downstairs to see Hamida. Meena watched Hamida as she sat on the couch next to Mrs Barvay in the living room, and managed to calm her after hearing about the burglary at Barvay Mansion. The older lady's distress and the mention of the police visit had unnerved Meena, but she managed to look very nonchalant as she openly eavesdropped on the conversation, pretending to hover nearby in case they needed her to fetch something. Meena had been relieved to know that the police would be here about the burglary at Mrs Barvay's old house, nothing to do with this house or its occupants. She had delivered another tray of tea, biscuits, and toast, this time to the living room and returned to the kitchen. Hamida was speaking in soothing tones to Mrs Barvay, encouraging her to eat and drink a little, when the doorbell rang, frightening Meena yet again.

Meena had no choice but to answer the doorbell. As expected, there were police on the doorstep. She stared at them. These were not the run-of-the-mill, bandy-legged, chubby constables in baggy shorts and white shirts, who usually directed traffic. Neither were they the young, newly minted smart aleck junior inspectors she had seen in the streets, handing out parking fines, managing crowds during religious processions, and trying to chat her up.

She stared at the tall man who stood in front of her. He seemed a bit older and more handsome than any inspectors she had ever seen. His khaki police uniform looked crisp and cared for; his cap and baton were under his arm. His beard was short, well-trimmed, his broad shoulders were decorated with many silver stars; there were colourful badges and a small rope was strung from his shoulders to the badges. His face seemed familiar, but she had never seen any policemen at such close quarters before this. She was startled to see two of the standard chubby constables standing right behind him. Now she stared in fear. She had never been confronted by three policemen in her life! "Have they come to arrest me? Have my thefts been discovered?" Her eyes widened in fright at the very thought.

But a calm, deep voice broke into her thoughts, "I am Assistant Commissioner Tariq Kareem. Is Mrs Barvay in?"

Still fearful and unable to speak, she merely nodded and extended her arm towards the living room. As she showed Tariq into the living room, Meena said to Mrs Barvay, "This is Tariq Saheb, the police inspector, comer, Kareem Saheb…". She could not say the big words he had said before his name, so she said 'saheb' twice, hoping that would make up for it.

Hamida, seated comfortably with Mrs Barvay, looked up when she heard the familiar name. She too, was surprised to see Tariq in the room, in full uniform. She had expected a junior inspector to arrive when Mrs Barvay said the police would arrive shortly, not the Assistant Commissioner himself. Hamida and Tariq stared at each other and then began to laugh. Mrs Barvay, taken aback by their behaviour and familiarity, had stared at him, her astute recollection taking in his tall frame, easy stride, and gleaming gelled hair.

"ACP Tariq Kareem" he said as he strode up and held out his hand to Mrs Barvay. She looked puzzled because she knew the Assistant Commissioner of Police. It was her cousin's podgy son whom she frequently met at family weddings, not this lean, good-looking man who stood before her. Forgetting her manners, she stared, confused. "Was this really the Assistant Commissioner of Police?" she pondered. Nothing had been the same since that fateful afternoon.

Smiling at the confusion on her face, Hamida turned to Mrs Barvay and introduced the tall, uniformed police officer.

"Mrs Barvay, meet Tariq Kareem, my brother and Poona's new Assistant Police Commissioner. He was appointed very recently."

Mrs Barvay gaped, then remembered Vijay Shahane had mentioned a new Assistant Commissioner. "But Hamida's brother? Now that was news." Momentarily forgetting her distress, she digested this information. In that moment, she had a flash of recognition, and she confirmed what she had suspected when he walked in. Tariq Kareem was the man in the red Impala. "And you have the beautiful Impala?' she asked boldly. Tariq nodded and smiled with pleasure at the mention of his car. Meena gasped, "That's why he had seemed familiar!"

Soon, Mrs Barvay left in the police jeep with ACP Tariq and his entourage, to inspect the damage at Barvay House while Hamida hastened back to her own home.

Preeti's house

That morning, Preeti Rao was intrigued as she watched all the arrivals and departures from her vantage point by the window. She had been standing next to the phone from the crack of dawn. The heat had been stifling even at that early hour. She had considered opening the window but decided against it, fearing her phone conversations could easily carry through in the quiet of the morning. She was waiting for a phone call about the Barvay Mansion break-in that she had staged in the hope of flushing out either the missing consignment or the people involved with it, including the Tara Road Mansions' residents. She could not afford to leave her post by the window today. She knew there would be a routine police visit to Mrs Barvay this morning about the break-in, and maybe people connected with the missing consignment would also visit other residents. She had expected someone would come to inform Mrs Barvay of the break-in but not the new Assistant Commissioner himself! The newly appointed watchman was also going to start this morning at eight o'clock, according to Mr Karamlegavraokar's note, and she wanted to observe him closely before they met.

Preeti was puzzled and impatient because her men had not yet called to report the Barvay Mansion break-in and the standard Tara Road Mansion morning routines had gone haywire. No Hamida walking the children to the school bus stop; instead, she had raced, shabbily dressed and without her hijab, to Mrs Barvay's house. Meena had opened the front door before Hamida rang the doorbell and let her in, quickly shutting the door behind her. It was too early for social calls. The children had not left for school nor the Karamlegavraokars for work. Preeti had watched with even greater unease when three police jeeps without blaring sirens had brought in the Assistant Commissioner. As she watched two constables hurry out of the jeep and stand at attention to their superior officer, she had a sudden flash of recognition. The Assistant Commissioner was the Impala man!

She stared in fascination; she had a glimpse of his badges as an ashen-faced Meena let him in and shut the door quickly. "The Impala man was Hamida's visitor and also the Assistant Commissioner? The Assistant Commissioner I know does not look like that." Then she remembered her boss mentioning a new Assistant Commissioner.

"Hamida was already at Mrs Barvay's house. Now the new Assistant Commissioner was here? What was going on?" she frowned with concentration. Soon, Mrs Barvay left with the Impala man in his police jeep, and the police entourage followed, once again without sirens. "Where were they taking her? Had she been arrested? Was this anything to do with the consignment? And here was Hamida hurrying back to her house again" Preeti observed.

A blur of blue in Preeti's peripheral vision distracted her. She watched as Maya Bai, in her blue sari, rushed out to whisper to one of the Karamlegavraokar drivers, then watched the police cars leave the gates and raced indoors. "What on earth is going on?" thought Preeti. She was riveted by the drama unfolding before her. There was too much unusual activity at Tara Road Mansions in one morning and Preeti's senses were on high alert. "Finally, things seem to be moving" she thought.

The new watchman walked through the gates almost immediately after Hamida had arrived at Mrs Barvay's house. He had arrived much earlier than expected and this seemed suspicious too. Preeti memorised every detail of the new watchman Tukaram Shinde. "Did he know anything about the consignment? Whose side was he on?" Preeti had wondered as she watched him walk up to the Karamlegavraokar house and ring the bell. He soon returned to the Tara Road Mansions gate with an old chair and settled himself in it. She was surprised when he did not go to Hamida's house at all, especially since her recommendation had got him the job. "Or did he already know she was not at home but at Mrs Barvay's?" He had smartly saluted the police jeeps as they drove in and out of the gates. Preeti was restless and her phone continued to remain silent.

Preeti was glad she had 'sprained' her ankle and could stay home to watch all these new developments at Tara Road Mansions. But she desperately wanted updates on her own investigations and the staged burglary too. That expected phone call about the staged break-in was well overdue now. She was agitated; the police had shown up right on Mrs Barvay's doorstep and taken her away, while she, Preeti, who had staged the break-in, was none the wiser about it.

Exasperated with waiting, she reached for the phone; she would demand some answers. But the phone rang as she touched it and she grabbed the receiver. Her shoulders sagged as she heard her boss's voice, calm, controlled but these days his tone always chilled her spine with its omnipresent hint of consequences, especially when she had nothing to report. She listened, glad her phone was next to the window and she did not have to give up her view while her boss droned on about a break-in at Barvay House, the police planning to visit Mrs Barvay etc. He had no idea that she had orchestrated the break-in. She let her mind drift; she already knew all this. Suddenly, she realised her boss's voice had become excitable to the point of being hysterical, and she focused on the call again. She listened intently, trying to make up for her earlier poor concentration. Preeti's jaw nearly clattered to the floor when she heard what her boss was saying. "What?" She almost shouted into the phone with shock, now glad she had not opened the window. "The new Assistant Commissioner of Police is Hamida's brother? Why didn't we know this earlier?" She trailed off her indignation as her boss continued speaking, "… a very new, very recent appointment, Tariq Kareem …".

She had told her boss about Impala man but now she did not tell him that the Assistant Commissioner was Impala man and that she had just watched him leave with Mrs Barvay in the police jeep. She did not tell him about her 'sprained ankle', her failed watchman plan, and the other things she had set in motion a few days ago, including the staged break-in at Barvay Mansion. Her failure to find the consignment despite all these efforts would only make her look inefficient and incapable.

The phone rang again almost as soon as she had replaced the receiver. Finally, it was the call about the break-in. She rebuked the caller for his tardiness and then listened intently, asked a few terse questions, and her shoulders slumped as she heard the answers. They had not found the consignment or any clues about it at Barvay Mansions, although they had ransacked the place thoroughly.

"Am I on the right track to find the consignment? Could it be at Mrs Barvay's house here? Hamida's brother being the new Assistant Commissioner of Police is a little too serendipitous, especially when he personally attended a trivial break-in at Mrs Barvay's old house and came here to pick her up. Or is that a clear sign that I am on the right track? Why had Hamida hurried over to Mrs Barvay even before the police arrived? Was she in cahoots with her brother? Whose side was ACP Tariq on? All my leads seem to take me to dead ends, but I will get to the bottom of this" she thought fiercely.

This was not the first time she had been given an important case. She had been naive earlier and had reported everything to her boss, which had resulted in someone else getting credit for her work. This time, she was doing things differently. She wanted a promotion over the young men who seemed to use her work to get ahead, although she knew she was much better at her job than any of them.

Determined to find out about the morning's events, Preeti rang Hamida. "Hello, Hamidaji, good morning…"

"Preeti? Are you okay? What's happening? Do you need help with something?" Hamida panicked at Preeti's voice on the phone early in the day and instantly thought of the young girl on crutches and her thoughts went into overdrive, picturing a hobbling Preeti needing help with something urgently. Then she realised Preeti had seen Hamida hurrying to Mrs Barvay, and the police cars, and simply called to ask if all was well with Mrs Barvay.

"I saw you rush and return from Mrs Barvay's house this morning and police cars driving off. What's happened? Is everything ok?" Preeti had managed to sound innocent, but she had strained her ears to detect any definite note of panic in Hamida's voice but there was none. Preeti was convinced this would have been another clue that she was on the right track if Hamida had something to hide.

Hamida told Preeti about the burglary at Barvay House and that Meena had panicked because Mrs Barvay was upset. "That's why I had gone over. Mrs Barvay has spoken to her doctor and just now she's gone with the police to Barvay House but she'll be home as soon as she has confirmed the damage, and missing items there and completed the police report. I think she's had a shock; it must be difficult with her son so far away. She shouldn't be alone, she's very shaken up. I wish I could spare the time to sit with her later today but it is the boutique's busiest season and Munni isn't well either. I have suggested Mrs Barvay call a relative or a friend. A bit of company will be good, I think" Hamida said kindly before hanging up. Preeti noted Hamida's omission that her Assistant Commissioner brother had arrived to escort Mrs Barvay.

✦ ✦ ✦

CHAPTER 14

An hour later, Preeti was still at the window, hawk-like, watching for Mrs Barvay's return. She was desperate to start searching Mrs Barvay's house, now that other possibilities were getting eliminated. Preeti's orderly mind ran the events related to the missing consignment in chronological order from the day it went missing to this morning's proceedings. The first part of the events was in the file her boss had thrust at her when she had been summoned to his office and told to go undercover in Poona as Preeti Rao.

The consignment worth millions was declared missing two days after it had actually disappeared from a truck en route to Poona. The drug cartel that lost the consignment was looking for it furtively and urgently. But after two days, when neither the police nor rival cartels had claimed possession of such a large consignment, panic had set in, and reluctantly, the drug cartel had declared it missing. Then the police and the two rival cartels separately began looking into the disappearance of the large consignment.

Three days after the consignment went missing, the body of a man was found in an expensive car; his body riddled with bullets. He had been identified as Tarun Tejani, the owner of the largest national trucking business Tejani Transport. He had recently made forays into property development as the builder of Tara Road Mansions. He had offered complimentary trucks from his transport company to all the new residents of Tara Road Mansions to move their things to the new houses.

The same two trucks that had carried the consignment until it went missing had also been the two trucks offered to the Tara Road Mansion residents around the same time. One truck driver had been arrested but he seemed to know nothing about the consignment. The other truck driver could not be found as he had left for his village for harvest season as soon as he had completed the deliveries, when the consignment was lost. He could not be contacted, and Preeti wondered whether he too, was dead. The trucking company only had his address in the city. Currently, another driver from the fleet was rostered on his truck.

After rigorous checks, Preeti's boss's men had found out that the drivers were unaware that some of their packages were drug cartel consignments disguised as ordinary packages. On tracking the movements of the two trucks that had carried the missing consignment and the residents' household effects to Tara Road Mansions for its residents, they had found that the trucks had never made any unscheduled stops or trips.

Tracing the movements of the car containing Tejani's body was tricky. But there were confirmed sightings of the car at the former residences of the Tulpules, Karamlegavraokars, and Avi Barvay's office before Tarun Tejani's body was found. However, several aspects of this part of the investigation were unclear. Had Tejani got hold of the consignment? Why? If yes, then had the consignment been disposed before Tejani was murdered or stolen after he was murdered? Why had Tejani visited some of the Tara

Road Mansion residents in their homes? Had the consignment exchanged hands or payments been made for it?

Connections between Tejani and the Tara Road Mansion residents were mostly to do with the sale of the houses and transport of household goods from their old residences to Tara Road Mansions. However, it had come to light that Tarun Tejani and Avinash Barvay were old school friends. Avi Barvay had bought the house at Tara Road Mansions at his friend's behest. That was the reason Preeti had staged the break-in at Barvay Mansion.

For years, Hamida's family had used Tejani Transport to move their merchandise all over the country, and the Tulpules owned a large number of shares in Tejani Transport. Therefore, other than the Karamlegavraokars, everyone had a longstanding relationship with Tejani, although only the Karamlegavraokars had cash stashed in their air conditioner. But the links between Tejani, the residents, and the consignment hit a dead end from there without any further connections with each other.

Careful searches of the former Tulpule and Karamlegavraokar residences and Avinash Barvay's office had not found the consignment or any clues about it. Then, in readiness for painting and renovations, all the artworks and other valuables from Barvay House were moved to the Barvay factory warehouses and a few vetted men known to Preeti's boss had gone undercover as movers for this job. They did not find the consignment or any clues about it either.

Mrs Barvay moved into her house at Tara Road Mansions around the same time. Her packing boxes were moved by the Tejani Transport trucks, as were those of all the other residents except the Tulpules. None of these families had ever had any connections with drug consignments until now. Hamida and Mrs Barvay were the only two people who had not moved all their belongings from their old homes into their brand-new Tara Road Mansion homes.

By conjecture, Preeti's boss had organised for all these families to be watched. Preeti's furtive hunt for Avinash Barvay had revealed that he had left for America a few days before Tejani was murdered and could not be reached despite all her boss's contacts in immigration and the police; the Barvay millions had ensured that. Preeti's thoughts whirled in her head. As soon as the consignment had gone missing, Preeti's boss had alerted their contact in the police department. Every bit of information and evidence was checked and rechecked. It had yielded nothing.

The Tara Road Mansions residents did not act suspiciously, and no people of interest had visited the Tara Road Mansion houses. The million-dollar consignment seemed to have literally vanished into thin air. The information in the file ended here, and Preeti had been asked to go undercover to Tara Road Mansions. Since Preeti Rao had moved into the Tara Road Mansions house, the Barvay factory warehouses with artworks and other valuables from Barvay Mansion had been secretly searched twice. Nothing had been found. Preeti's organised break-in at Barvay Mansion had found nothing either.

After the disastrous encounter with Darzi Master and nothing of interest about *The Begum Boutique* reported or observed, she had been ready to eliminate Hamida because Preeti had been unable to find anything suspicious except the Impala man. The information on Hamida's husband was still not verified, but now that she knew Hamida's brother was the Assistant Commissioner, it put everything in a different light. The whole family would either be squeaky clean or extremely involved in this whole illegal business.

The Karamlegavraokars were more implicated than ever after the discovery of the hidden cash. She was trying for an opportunity to snoop in the Karamlegavraokar household but with Maya Bai as an omnipresence, it was next to impossible. The hidden cash also meant that the missing consignment was not in the Karamlegavraokar household because the cash was either the payment to be made or received for the consignment. She needed to dig deeper.

Now that all the other possibilities were exhausted, the missing consignment had to be either in Mrs. Barvay's or Hamida's house at Tara Road Mansions or if the neighbours were all in it together then in one of the other houses in Tara Road Mansions, unless, of course, it had changed hands. By a systematic process of connections and reasoning, Preeti had eliminated the Tulpules. Preeti's mind brought her to the same tangled knot of information again, making her grimace.

She was going to begin again and start with Mrs. Barvay, especially after the staged burglary at Barvay House had been futile, yielding neither goods nor information. Preeti felt a rising sense of panic as all her orchestrated searches and even the staged collision with Darzi Master and the Barvay House break-in had hit dead ends. Things seemed to be moving but she was not in control and time seemed to be running out. Furiously, she stamped her bandaged foot loudly on the floor. When was Mrs Barvay going to return to Tara Road Mansions this morning?

Hamida's house

Hamida had left Mrs Barvay's house as the police vehicles drove off. Once home, she was pleasantly surprised to see Ashu ready for school. Munni was still not well enough to leave the house. But the ever-ravenous Ashu had only eaten a piece of toast this morning and she was astonished at the still-full sugar bowl and the unopened jam jar on the table. She had fully expected a near-empty jam jar or an empty sugar bowl at the very least, as there had been no one to censure Ashu. She could not puzzle over his behaviour for long just then, as Preeti had called to ask about Mrs Barvay and police cars driving away.

Meanwhile, Ashu had been in a private hell of his own ever since the phone call from Meena and all the while that Hamida had been at Mrs Barvay's house. He had remained seated at the dining table, rigid with fright. Every minute since his mother had left to see the elderly lady, his brain had conjured up conversations between his mother and Mrs Barvay. Every single one of these imagined conversations contained a list of his crimes – the broken window, climbing in, stealing sugar, and the evidence was the bright yellow tennis ball with AS written in his handwriting with a felt tipped pen. He imagined his mother and Mrs Barvay discussing severe punishments for him. He half-expected a phone call that summoned him to Mrs Barvay's house. He had tried to eat breakfast but everything turned to dust in his mouth. He had pushed away the sugar bowl and the jam jar that would have been so tempting on any other day. He had quickly eaten a piece of toast and dressed himself for school, hoping this good behaviour would placate his mother a little. He expected her to be livid when she returned.

So, he was amazed at his mother's calmness when she returned home. She acted as if he had done nothing wrong. She had simply said, "Ashu, I'm so glad you're ready for school. I am going to be very busy with boutique orders for the next few days, and I can't leave Munni alone at home when I walk you to the bus stop. So, I rang the Karamlegavraokars last night to ask if you could go to school with their children for the next few days. Let's make sure you are punctual and standing by their car. They are doing us a favour and should not have to call or wait for you." She said nothing else. Absolutely nothing else.

Ashu stared at his mother in amazement. "Is she so angry that she is not talking to me about anything else? Is she hoping I will confess to what Mrs Barvay has just told her? Is she so angry that she is going to stop walking me to the bus stop from now on? Is this going to be the punishment?" he wondered as he mutely nodded at the instructions for school. His heart sank even further in his stomach. "How on earth am I going to get into Ammi's good books ever again? What can I possibly do?" For the hundredth time, he cursed the ball that had hit the window, broken the glass, and gone into the storeroom.

Karamlegavraokar house

Maya Bai was irritated. "My mornings were busy enough until everyone left for work and school and nowadays, the phones seem to ring incessantly in the morning. My employers expect me to answer their phone calls, pass on their messages to each other, the children, the children's driver, the list is endless!" she shook her head in despair. "And despite these intrusive demands on my time, they all expect breakfast and all other morning routines to run smoothly on time. Plus, those two prospective watchmen arrived to see the Saheb that day and now, this new watchman arrived to see the Saheb. Then the Saheb told me to find the new watchman an old uniform, an old chair, and some cushions and give him some tea and something to eat before he starts work. I don't have time in the mornings to look up old chairs and make tea and breakfast for anyone the wind has blown in" she harrumphed loudly but did not dare say a word to her employers.

Grumpily, she had followed the latest missive from her employers and gone outside to remind the Karamlegavraokar driver once again that Ashu would go to school with the Karamlegavraokar children for the next few days. As she had opened the front door, several movements caught her eye. She saw a shabbily dressed, hijabless Hamida hurrying home on her driveway and the convoy without sirens driving out of the Tara Road Mansions gates, crisply saluted by the new watchman. Her grumpiness melted into wonder, "Had the police just left from Hamida's house? Is that why Ashu needed to go to school in their car for a few days?" She hurried inside. The children had finished breakfast and were chatting with their father; they would leave for school any minute and did not need her. She raced upstairs to tell Mrs Karamlegavraokar what she had just seen, then raced down to the kitchen again.

Mrs Karamlegavraokar shimmied downstairs in a tight green salwar kameez and high heels, just as the children said goodbye and left for school. “Shivram! Shivram! Don’t send the children to the car just yet…” she called impatiently. Her husband looked up distractedly from the newspaper as the front door slammed shut behind the children. She related Maya Bai’s observation breathlessly and looked at him expectantly. “Didn’t I tell you that very first day we met her, that Hamida’s husband was suspicious?” Mr Karamlegavraokar looked at her, trying to focus on the conversation; he could not remember her saying anything like that. His mind was still on the share market news he had just read. She always spoke too fast when she was excited or agitated. “I knew it! All this ‘away for long periods for work abroad’ is all smuggling. That’s why the police were here. Hamida’s husband is a smuggler! Maybe they have arrested him and she needs to visit the police, contact his gang, find a lawyer... that’s why she can’t take Ashu to the school bus for the next few days. I didn’t know about the police visit until a few minutes ago, so I said yes, of course, he could go with Kartik and Kaveri. She said she couldn’t take Ashu to the bus stop because Munni is ill and too young to be left alone. Now, how can we go back and say no? I don’t want our children to be associated with smugglers and criminals. I always thought it was a bit suspicious that they could afford to send their children to our children’s private school. And Kartik says they have the same video player and music system as us. Our things are all imported and so expensive. How can they afford them? Smuggling! That’s how. Otherwise, how can they possibly be our financial equals? Tara Road Mansions were top-tier prices, and that bridal boutique business, huh! It's just a front for black money from smuggling. I have always wondered about that Hamida and her suspicious smuggler husband and that money-laundering boutique of hers. I'm telling you, Shivram..."

Mr Karamlegavraokar shook his head dismissively and did not want to assume or discuss any illegal activities of his as-yet-unseen neighbour Ayaz Sheikh. Accusations of illegal activities were too close to home. He, Shivram Karamlegavraokar, more than anyone else, understood the lure of financial gain when it could be achieved so easily to support a lavish lifestyle. Peering at his wife and finding no hint of suspicion about himself on her face, he decided to take refuge on moral high ground, "Darling, calm down. We need to find out more before we say anything to Mrs Sheikh or anyone else. I don't like the police visiting Tara Road Mansions either, it makes me very uncomfortable. Why don't you give Mrs Sheikh a call? If she answers, just say you saw the police cars and ask if everything is okay. See what she says, then we can decide, hmmmm?" He knew his wife would not care to check any facts once her mind was made up. He returned his attention to the newspaper but the thought of the police arriving so close to his home had rattled him. He had been extremely meticulous and clever in his paperwork and all his business dealings; the police or income tax had almost no chance of tracing his money. But guilt was a demanding mistress, who frequently reigned supreme in his mind. As soon as his wife left for work, he hurried upstairs to check on the hidden safe behind the air conditioner.

✦ ✦ ✦

CHAPTER 15

Mrs Barvay was visibly very upset when she returned with Assistant Commissioner Tariq in the police jeep. She walked slowly to her front door. Her usual bravado was gone. Meena saw her stooped shoulders and sad face, so she did not ask any questions. She simply settled her in the living room and made her some tea. Mrs Barvay seemed to be in shock. She only gestured with her hands or nodded.

Just as Vijay Shahane had assured her, the burglars had taken nothing, just slashed cushions and mattresses all over the house, the dustsheets over the furniture had been flung aside with careless regard, and the contents of the cupboards had lain asunder on the floor. It had been very upsetting to see her beloved, well-cared-for home in that state. The police said the burglars were likely to be looking for something specific. The new Assistant Commissioner had watched her very closely as he said this. "Do you know what they could have been looking for?" he had asked, emphasising every word.

She had kept her head low and her face sad as she shook her head slowly, as if trying to think in a daze, making sure she never met his gaze. Because she knew exactly what he was asking about and where it was. Yes, she had moved it to keep Avi out of further trouble. It was the least any mother would do. Now, even Avi was unaware of its whereabouts. She was definitely not going to tell the police, especially a new Assistant Commissioner whom she did not know or trust as yet. Everything had happened so quickly that afternoon, she had reacted on instinct. She had done what she thought best in the situation. She had kept Vijay Shahane ignorant too, about this part of the story. She had no idea what her next move was or should be. There had been no opportunity to tell Avi about her actions or consult anyone about what to do next.

She sat in her armchair and closed her eyes. Her mind filled with the scenes of chaos from Barvay House earlier that morning. The viciousness of the slashes across couches, sofas, cushions, and curtains had shaken her to the very core.

Then her mind revisited the painful events of the rather ordinary afternoon that had turned her whole world upside down. That day had been completely unremarkable, forgettable even, until the events of that afternoon. Avi had come home from the office for lunch, as usual. He had laughed and chatted easily as usual, casually mentioning that his driver had delivered to the kitchen, some things a friend had sent down from his farm—fresh vegetables and a bag of stone-milled jowar flour. Avi had smiled as Mrs Barvay grimaced. Jowar flatbread or *bhakri* was Avi's absolute favourite, and she had always detested it!

Avi had numerous friends from all walks of life, not all of them were rich but Avi treated each friend with great love and camaraderie. They often sent him presents that they could afford, anything from a new horse to his favourite comic. "To Avi, the friendships had always mattered more than the gifts. Still matter" she checked herself. "But would these friendships be able to take the strain of the events from that afternoon?"

She and Avi had sat down to lunch as usual that afternoon and as dessert was being served, Avi had seemed a bit fidgety but that was not unusual. Like his father, Avi got restless when he wanted to get on with something at the office. "How precious these simple memories had become now!" She had smiled understandingly and said, "I can see you are in a hurry to get back to the office. Go!"

As Avi had pushed his chair away from the dining table, he said, "Can I have the farm vegetables for dinner tonight but don't open the bag of milled jowar yet."

"Of course, Avi" she had smiled indulgently, making a mental note of instructions to the cook.

As he stood up to leave, Lakshmi their old retainer had shown two visitors into the dining room, which was very unusual. "Saheb, they said they must see you immediately" she had said apologetically.

Visitors were usually asked to wait in the living room, especially if the family were at the dining table. Mrs Barvay remembered telling Lakshmi to bring tea for the visitors while Avi motioned for the visitors to sit down. The visitors were plainclothes police detectives and had not introduced themselves till Lakshmi had left the room. They had arrived quietly, no sirens flashing or blaring, no shouted orders or noisy footsteps like they showed in the movies. She and Avi had been completely unaware of their arrival until the officers had been shown into the dining room. Mrs Barvay's memories of the next few hours were dream-like, in slow motion, agonising her repeatedly and for much longer than the actual events.

Suddenly, the doorbell pierced Mrs Barvay's thoughts and she came back to the present with a jolt. Avi was gone. Barvay House had been burgled; she was living in Tara Road Mansions. Meena showed in Preeti Rao. Mrs Barvay shook thoughts of Avi out of her head and gazed at Preeti Rao in confusion. The girl stood before her, supported by crutches, and was asking something.

"Very sorry to hear that your old house was broken into. How are you, Mrs Barvay? Hamida told me about it, so I thought I would come and keep you company. I can't go to work for a few days anyway with these crutches."

Focusing on the present, Mrs Barvay realised it was kind of the young girl to visit, despite being on crutches herself. Preeti settled on a couch next to Mrs Barvay's armchair, refusing Meena's offer of tea. However, Preeti Rao happily accepted Mrs Barvay's lunch invitation on the condition that she stayed with her while Meena went to work at Hamida's that afternoon. She coaxed Mrs Barvay to eat some lunch and declared she was happy to stay with Mrs Barvay until the evening if Meena wanted to go to her other part-time jobs in Tara Road Mansions. Meena smiled gratefully at this kind thought. Mrs Barvay tried to tell them she would be fine on her own because she was going to take the mild sedative the doctor had suggested and a long nap in the afternoon. But Preeti won the argument, saying she would feel much better knowing someone was here with her, and it was decided that she would stay on.

The morning stretched slowly and tediously. Preeti chatted with Mrs Barvay, then they played cards for a while. Preeti pretended to read the book she had chosen from Mrs Barvay's vast bookshelves. She had hobbled slowly on her crutches, going through the bookshelves in the living room, pretending to look for a book for ages but secretly checking for concealed compartments, hidden catches, false fronts, and tampered books. She had also run a well-practised eye over the living room furniture while Mrs Barvay was on the phone several times that morning; and had scrutinised the floor and under the carpets as Meena had tirelessly swept and mopped the floors. Preeti had seen nothing suspicious. She had also inspected the living room under the guise of admiring the furniture and knick-knacks while Meena completed the polishing and dusting. Mrs Barvay had been only too pleased to recount the history of several pieces of furniture, while Preeti unabashedly peered and poked at all the items and fittings as she looked for clues.

It felt like ages before they had lunch; then Meena helped Mrs Barvay upstairs for a nap while Preeti sat demurely on the sofa, crutches by her side and a book on her lap. Preeti could not wait for Meena to leave and Mrs Barvay to fall asleep so she could go through the final remaining room downstairs, the storeroom.

Preeti bided her time while Meena got ready to leave, and as soon as the front door clicked shut behind Meena, Preeti raced to bolt it so Meena would not be able to let herself in with a key. Then she ran upstairs softly, carrying her crutches in one hand for appearances, in case Mrs Barvay was awake. Stealthily, she peeped into Mrs Barvay's room; she felt the chill of the air-conditioning as she saw Mrs Barvay's sleeping figure and heard gentle snores. Softly shutting the door, she raced downstairs and disdainfully pushed the crutches away with her foot until they rested on the arm of the sofa. Then she ran to the storeroom.

It looked exactly the same as before, small and filled with the usual paraphernalia of boxes, bags, grain sacks, and old photo albums. The beautiful bell of the brass gramophone caught her eye, and she told herself to focus. She began a systematic search of this room. She was convinced that this room would have the item she was looking for because all the other places had been thoroughly searched, including the freshly ransacked old Barvay residence.

She began with the stacks of large boxes, a quick rummage revealed that half of them were empty and the rest held frayed files and paperwork, old sarees, and some unopened bottles of beer. The room also had a couple of new mattresses still packed in plastic, and some old-fashioned pots and cooking vessels. Always known to do a thorough job, Preeti flipped through each file, checked the boxes for false bottoms and went through their contents. She prodded all the mattresses systematically and stood them up to shake them.

Suddenly, the window rattled. It startled her; she relaxed when she heard a lowing sound. Preeti realised Sundari had nudged the loosely fastened window as she lowered herself and sat down outside. She could hear the shuffle of hooves and the scrape of hide on bricks as Sundari settled herself in the shade. Then all was silent except for the loud *tchaah tchaah* sound as Sundari masticated the manicured plants she had eaten on the way here. Preeti blew out a long breath.

The room was hot and felt stale with stifled dusty air. Dust-mote-filled daylight filtered from the window pane. She longed to open the window but did not dare because she would be spotted snooping and without crutches. There was just enough light to look around. She made short work of the boxes of papers, old furniture, suitcases, and brass buckets. She found some silk shawls and sarees in the brass buckets and thoroughly patted them down before returning them to their spot. She turned her attention to the trunk with the padlock, deftly opening it with her penknife. Inside, there were photo albums of Mrs Barvay's wedding day and small silver idols of gods and goddesses, which were standard fare in most households but not much else. Disappointed, she shut the trunk softly. She rolled an unopened tin of oil from side to side to make sure it, indeed, had oil. The heavy tin had made a dull, slow thud of liquid hitting its insides, but no other noise. The heat was oppressive in the airless little room and beads of sweat joined to run as rivulets across her brow, neck, and down her back.

"Just the food sacks left to check, then I can leave this room" she thought. Wistfully, she thought of the fans in the living room. "It will be much cooler there, and light and airy too. Come on!" She encouraged herself. "Just the small pile of sacks left and then you're done." One part of her brain was crying out for a drink of water and a cooler room, and the other part was wondering, "If I don't find anything here, where can I look next?"

As she stepped up to the sacks, she stumbled over a suitcase. It was heavy. She undid the clasps and sighed; it was full of dusty video cassettes. She fingered them carefully, making sure nothing was hidden within them. She reached the sacks and prodded and squeezed the burlap bags as some of the grains squeaked in protest, but all she could feel was a uniform filling of grains, lentils etc., nothing else in them. She moved them aside to make sure there was nothing kept behind them. She stared at the jute and plastic sacks. Then she flicked at the jute seam of the large grain sack with her penknife, deftly unpicking half the stitches. The sack seemed to be full of wheat. She sat on her haunches and rolled up her sleeves, made a fist and slowly swivelled it downwards into the grains until her arm was in up to her armpit and her fist was in the grains, a few inches off the floor from inside the sack. There was nothing in the sack but wheat grains. She held the open edges of the sack together and firmly tied the jute string around it, closing the gaping mouth, so it did not attract attention.

Then she turned her attention to a little sack. The stitches Ashu had pulled instantly caught her trained eye. Some of the contents seemed to have spilt out but she could not make them out in the dim light. Once again, she used the penknife to undo a couple of stitches. Cupping her hand underneath the little opening, she nudged out some of its contents, just as Ashu had done, only a day earlier. She looked at the crystal grains in the palm of her hand and stared. She could not believe her eyes! She lifted her cupped palm to smell the sugar-like grains, then she picked a grain or two and lowered it on her tongue for a taste. She closed her eyes and pondered, then tasted another crystal again.

Once again, her brain confirmed what her mouth was telling her. She gasped and immediately stood up the tilted little sack so that the opening was right on top and not even the smallest amount of its precious contents could dribble out.

That was when she noticed some odd-shaped lumps in the little sack and wiggled a finger in the sack to reach the nearest lump. She pulled it out and stared at a large diamond-drop earring. It was not crystal or zirconia but a decent-quality diamond. She had definitely not expected this. She pushed it back into the sack again and knelt to check out the other lumpy shapes, careful not to pull out any more grains from the sack. She held up each item over the open sack so the grains fell back into the sack and she buried each piece of jewellery deep in the sack. There was a gold pendant, a thin gold watch, baby amulets, thin gold bangles, a sapphire ring, and a chunky wedding band. She was puzzled. No one had mentioned any jewellery alongside the consignment.

Staring at the little sack of woven hemp with its unpicked seam and strange lumps, she shook her head in total disbelief. "The consignment had been here, all along. In plain sight! Hell!" She was very sure the presence of the jewellery was strange and difficult to understand. But excitement about the crystalline grains in the sack eclipsed everything else. She took a slip of paper from her pocket and carefully folded some of the crystals into it. She laughed. She had never imagined ten kilos of high-quality cocaine worth millions would be lying here casually. No extra care, no protection, no fuss. For a few moments, she marvelled at the simplicity and audacity of it. "Did Mrs Barvay know the value of the contents of her storeroom?"

Preeti looked at her watch. "How can I move this 10-kilo bag out of this room and into my house without anyone noticing? Mrs Barvay could be up any minute and Meena would return soon. It was late afternoon, the children would return from school any minute, and then play cricket soon after. That damned new watchman was at the gate. He had a good view of the front and back of Mrs Barvay and Preeti's house, and the Karamlegavraokars would return home from work any time. Then, there were those Tulpules who had no fixed times for most things. I dare not ask anyone to come just now to help me move the sack."

Preeti's brain whirred in several directions like a massive piece of complicated machinery, trying to take in what she had learnt and fitting it with the other bits of information she already had. Her mind spun the possibilities. She had found the missing consignment! She knew exactly where the money for its payment was stashed and waiting, and if she could find out who had made these arrangements, she would find even the mediator of this deal, the very traitor who had led them all such a merry dance. This would surely impress her boss; she would get promoted and he would give her a bigger job next time. This staggering level of success was so overwhelming in her mind that she shuddered with pleasure.

Composing herself, she left the storeroom. She picked up her crutches, undid the bolt on the front door and sat in Mrs Barvay's living room once more, comfortably settled on the couch. She rested her 'sprained' bandaged ankle on a footstool for display, crutches by her side, and a book in her hands. This was going to be the hardest part; waiting patiently for Meena to return so she could leave. With the book still open and neglected on her lap, she took a deep breath and began to plan the covert relocation of the consignment and the cash.

Moving the consignment tonight would have been ideal. But as it was the watchman's first night on patrol, he would be awake and alert. She decided on a quieter time the next day.

She would need four trustworthy armed men. Two men would stay by the stream behind Tara Road Mansions to keep a lookout and the others would steal the sack from the storeroom tomorrow afternoon. They would pass it to the men by the stream who would take off with it. The two who were to steal the sack from Mrs Barvay would come to Preeti's house in the morning, disguised as carpenters. This would allow them to walk right past Tukaram with all the tools needed for the break-in and guns hidden under the tools. They would also bring a large box, pretending it contained a large mirror. All morning, they would hammer and bang things in Preeti's house so their presence would be noticed.

Late afternoon, when Tukaram went home for lunch, Mrs Barvay left for the club, Meena went to Hamida's house for the afternoon, and the children were still at school, 'the carpenters' would break into the storeroom, steal the sack, and pass it to the men by the stream. They would get a clear 30-minute window of opportunity to do this before the bustle of children returning from school. The theft would not be discovered until later that evening at the earliest. If Mrs Barvay knew of the sack's contents, she would definitely not involve the police. If she had no idea of the sack's contents, it would probably not even be missed for a few days at the very least.

The day after was Maya Bai's weekly day off. The 'carpenters' would return to Preeti's house and resume the hammering, sawing etc. In the evening, when the children went to play by the stream, the Karamlegavraokar house would be empty. If the adult Karamlegavraokars were not home, the 'carpenters' would break in from the back door, as it was out of Tukaram's view and take the money from the air conditioner, put it into a large work bag and bring it to Preeti's house.

The flat wads of notes would then be packed into the empty mirror box, and they would carry it out, walking straight past Tukaram once again. Preeti would escort them to the main road, under the pretext of going to exchange the faulty mirror. She would ask Tukaram to get her a rickshaw and ask him to help her load the mirror. Tukaram would not stop the carpenters and check their bags if Preeti was with them. They would be long gone by the time the thefts were discovered.

Even when the Karamlegavraokars discovered the money missing, such a large amount in 500-rupee notes would definitely have illegal connections, so they would hardly consider informing the police. Once it was discovered that the money had gone missing, the person who had masterminded the deal would be flushed out. She could tail the Karamlegavraokars and get to the mediator. Meanwhile, the sack and cash would be in a safe place. Her boss, had he known about it, would have been pleased with what he called a 'clean plan.'

The only uncertain part of this plan was whether the cash could be taken from the Karamlegavraokars on a chance that the couple would not be home while the children played by the stream. But it was too tempting, and Preeti decided that it had to be tried. If the cash could not be moved, then the carpenters could come another day for the cash in the air conditioner or she would have to think of another way to move the cash. Moving the small sack was the most important thing at the moment.

For now, as soon as Meena returned home and Preeti could leave Mrs Barvay's living room, she would tell Tukaram she was expecting some carpenters tomorrow and that he should let them through. Then she would take the grainy crystal sample from the small sack's contents that she had folded in paper, and have it tested to confirm it was cocaine. Maybe she would head home first to get her own snub-nosed pistol from its hiding place and tuck it into her little shoulder bag. She was taking no chances.

Soon Meena returned, Mrs Barvay came downstairs feeling well-rested and refreshed, and Preeti seemed to have almost finished reading her book. Saying goodbye to them, Preeti hurried out, her crutches clicking a steady staccato towards Tukaram's chair by the gate. She smiled sadly at him and said, "Please can you get a rickshaw from the main road?"

Tukaram had leapt up from his chair as soon as he had seen Preeti on crutches heading towards him. He shook out the cushions, then he smoothed them down and gestured for Preeti to sit on them. Then he ran down the lane to get a rickshaw for Preeti, who sat bemused, watching the man break into a lopsided run to the main road. She turned to the houses to double-check how much of each house and garden Tukaram could see from his post under the shady tree. This was important for tomorrow's plan to succeed.

Late that evening, when Preeti returned in the rickshaw, the summer heat was still relentless. Tukaram came running up to see if he could carry any bags to the door for Preeti. She told him she was expecting some carpenters tomorrow, and he should let them through. Then she handed him a packet of still-warm samosas and a cold drink before waving him away. She needed him to think kindly of her so that he would not be suspicious about anything she did. That would buy her some precious time to accomplish her tasks.

Time was of paramount importance now that she had found the much-sought consignment. But the heat and the charade with the crutches had exhausted her. Her 'injured' leg was tired from being kept off the ground, and her brain was tired from repeatedly reminding herself to hobble. Her 'good' leg was tired from constantly bearing her body weight and her ribs hurt where the unneeded crutches dug into them. She longed to be rid of them. "By this time tomorrow, I will have at least the consignment if not the cash from the Karamlegavraokars," confidently she consoled herself. Earlier that evening, she had made a telephone call to brief her men about tomorrow's plan. Two of them were to watch from across the stream after midnight tonight. Her laboratory contact had confirmed that the crystals from the sack were cocaine. She couldn't wait to be in possession of the consignment before she informed her boss.

She called her boss that evening to ask him to call off his men from the main road, the shaded lane, and the stream, before hers took up position. "I think we should call away our men immediately. There is a 24-hour watchman here now and we cannot risk any of our people looking suspicious and being recognised," she lied glibly. Her boss agreed.

Now she could put in her own trusted crew to watch the houses from beyond the stream. She wanted credit for finding the consignment, the money, and the traitor; that would complete her job. She was awake all night, alert for any sounds or movement. She ran through her plan several times in her head, looking for potential snags in it. It was simple and precise because of the countless hours she had spent observing the routines of the Mansions' residents.

✦✦✦

CHAPTER 16

Meena had viewed Tukaram the watchman with dread from the moment he began work at Tara Road Mansions. She had accumulated too many stolen items over a short period of time, and she was keen to get them to the pawnshop. Getting them past Tukaram was going to be a problem. He was a cheery fellow with a ready smile. He had set himself up with a rickety rattan chair from the Karamlegavraokars and an old, battered wooden bed from the Tulpules. His designated spot was under the shade of a huge tree by the wrought iron Tara Road Mansions gates. He smartly saluted all the cars as they drove in and out through the main gate, always ran up to help residents carry their shopping from their cars, and always checked the bags of drivers and maids as they left to go home.

How could she get all her stolen goods to the pawnshop quickly without attracting the attention of Tukaram or Mrs Barvay? Meena had turned this problem over and over in her mind urgently, like a restless Rubik's cube, after the appearance of the Assistant Commissioner in Mrs Barvay's house that morning. Watchmen were notorious for lording it over domestic help. Tukaram was spritely, cheerful, and never slept during the day. She had watched this morning as he had stopped Maya Bai at the gate. He had checked her bags as she walked past him with the weekly bundle of Karamlegavraokar clothes headed for the laundry on the main road.

Meena bit her lip, "What if Tukaram stops me as I try to walk past? If he searches my bag, he will find the stolen sarees, shawls, watches, and jewellery that obviously don't belong to me. Trying to leave the house via the courtyard and past the stream with a large shopping bag would look very suspicious since it was a long, overgrown and uneven path to the city streets through the scrub, no one ever went that way, and I will stick out like a sore thumb."

That evening, pondering her problem, Meena went to the storeroom to survey her stash. The seam on the little sack seemed a little more undone than she remembered. She thought she had left the bag lying on its side but it was upright now. "Maybe I propped it up this morning when I hurried in looking for lentils?" Her fingers wandered over the sack, feeling for the lumps. She counted them, they were all there. She exhaled in relief.

She decided to walk to the shops on the main road to return some empty soft drink bottles. This was not an urgent errand but she wanted to gauge Tukaram's reaction to her walking out with a full bag. He watched as she locked the front door, the bag of empty glass bottles by her feet. She smiled and said, "Namaste." Sure enough, he had stopped her and peered into the bag despite her comment that it contained empty bottles and tried to delay her making inane conversation. He unsettled her. It was very clear to her that it would be too risky to walk out with her loot of stolen items in a bag.

The solution to her problem came to Meena that evening as she folded numerous silk sarees that Mrs Barvay had worn to weddings and associated events she had attended in the past week. Summer was peak wedding season, and Mrs Barvay's many sarees were worn once, drycleaned, and only then returned to the wardrobe. Meena's agitation upon seeing the police on her doorstep ebbed away as she planned the details to get her loot to the pawnshop. She would take the stolen shawls, stoles, and sarees wrapped in the bundle of Mrs Barvay's sarees intended for the drycleaners. She would take the jewellery in her small purse she took with her to do errands. She usually bundled the sarees and went in the car with the driver and Mrs Barvay on their way to the club, and they dropped her at the drycleaner's shop. Tukaram would not dare to stop the car or check the bundle if Mrs Barvay was in the car. Meena could take the sarees to the drycleaners and then walk to the pawnshop. She smiled with relief at the solution.

Ashu

When Ashu had returned from school that afternoon, Hamida was busy with the final fitting of a bridal outfit, and Darzi Master gestured for him to quietly go upstairs for his snack. This was not unusual. But Ashu was now getting restless about his mother's lack of acknowledgement about Mrs Barvay's broken window and the scolding and punishment that should rightfully follow. He wanted that discomfort, like a tongue finding a painfully wobbly tooth. If she shouted, punished him, smacked him, shamed him, it would all be done and over. He hated this nothing-has-happened treatment. It was beginning to rattle him. He lingered in the boutique doorway. But his mother simply smiled gently and gestured for him to go upstairs. She, in turn, was puzzled by his behaviour. He was usually ravenous after school and bounded upstairs, always demanding his favourite snacks and ice cream, especially in this heat. He had made no demands for anything sweet in the past few days.

Ashu climbed the stairs slowly; maybe the punishment was upstairs. But upstairs, there was only a wan-faced Munni watching a video and sipping lemonade. "Ammi said that's yours, and your lemonade is in the fridge" she said, pointing to a covered plate on the dining table. He threw his school bag on the floor and uncovered the plate to find a big slice of cake and the tangy potato chips he loved. "Ammi said you can also have some ice cream if you eat an apple first. I have to make sure" she said, brightening at the thought of her important role.

He almost reached for the apple but admonished himself. He needed to be very good, so he picked his bag off the floor and put it in his room. He washed his hands and changed his clothes, then made a beeline for the food. Whatever strategy Ammi was following, he would be on his best behaviour, doing everything he was constantly reminded to do. "Everything!" he muttered under his breath.

"Ashu, for the next few days, don't play by the stream. Just invite your friends here or play in someone's house or garden but no playing by the stream" Hamida called from downstairs.

He frowned. "Was this the punishment? No playing by the stream? That was it?" But somewhere deep inside, he felt a bit better. "At least there had been some consequence, maybe there would be more. It was much better than trying to guess what was going to happen," he thought. Ashu sidled off to his friends' home after Munni had watched him eat the apple and the ice cream.

He came home when it was almost dark; he was hot, tired, and hungry. His mother was still busy downstairs. This was not unusual. In the old house, sometimes they did not see their mother for days when it was wedding season, their grandmother and aunt used to look after them. He had wondered how it would all work in this new house. Playing in the neighbours' gardens was not as much fun as their cricket game by the stream but at least he was still allowed to play with his friends.

Once again, Ammi had not spoken to him but left a message with Munni that Meena had cooked dinner; it was on the dining table, he should eat his dinner and then have a glass of cold milk with Rooh Afza. He loved the sweetened rose syrup with milk; it was a summer ritual. He peeped at the ice cream in the freezer but did not dare eat it. He showered, ate dinner, completed his homework and lay on his bed, waiting for Ammi to come and say goodnight. His sister had fallen asleep while he was doing homework.

Downstairs, he heard Darzi Master leave, and Ammi continued chatting with some women. Then nothing for a long time. He forced himself to be awake; he left his bedside light switched on to avoid falling asleep but did not read past his bedtime, in case it made his mother cross. He waited for Ammi to come upstairs, scold him, explain his mistakes, tell him his punishments, and kiss him goodnight. He waited and waited but she did not come. His eyes burned and his heart ached; he just wanted to feel his mother's arms around him. Tears welled in his eyes and ran down his cheeks in fat rivulets, making inroads under his chin and into his neck; his tears dried into stiff tracks on his face as they sped down to soak his pillow. It got darker and later, he felt very tired and fought to stay awake. Exhausted with guilt and heartbroken with waiting, he made a decision as he fell asleep – "Tomorrow morning, I am going to try to fix all this, in the only way I know I can. I will tell Uncle Tariq everything."

Oblivious to her son's distress and waiting, it was well after midnight when Hamida wearily climbed the stairs, the clothes orders were almost ready. She had been so busy, she felt she had not spent any time with the children. Munni had been ill, and Ashu, something was wrong with him. His exuberance had dimmed. First, she had put it down to the approaching exams and the heat but now she was beginning to worry. He had become too quiet. Maybe he had fallen out with his friends at Tara Road Mansions. The wedding season was almost done. She would finish these last few orders and then leave the boutique to Darzi Master for a few days to spend time with her children after their exams. She was grateful for Meena cleaning and cooking the meals, and the Karamlegavraokars taking Ashu to school and back in their car. Munni's health seemed to be improving slowly. Hamida was glad Ashu had some friends he could play with every evening. She peeped into the children's rooms before she sat down to eat dinner. Ashu, who had been acting strangely for the past few days, was fast asleep but his bedside lamp was still on. She switched it off and tiptoed out; she dared not kiss him, he had always been a very light sleeper. The click of the lamp had woken Ashu, who was only half-asleep. He saw Hamida's retreating figure leaving his room without giving him a kiss or a hug. He watched as she went into Munni's room across the landing. As Hamida adjusted Munni's covers, she marvelled once again at how different her two children were. Munni could sleep through anything. She kissed the top of Munni's head. Munni sat up, asking for water, and Hamida hurried back with it. Ashu saw this and the tears ran down his cheeks again, drying quickly in the hot night as he lay awake for a long time. "Ammi definitely did not love him anymore because of the horrible things he had done."

Mrs Barvay

Mrs Barvay lay awake too. Her mind kept going back to the afternoon when the plainclothes detectives had arrested Avi in her dining room but respected his wishes and not handcuffed him. He had willingly walked with them to the police car and left for the police station. The detectives said they were arresting Avi for embezzling money from Barvay Industries' public ventures.

Mrs Barvay had been aghast. "Why on earth would Avi embezzle from Barvay Industries? And when? I still shepherd most of the business deals he makes, albeit in a discreet behind-the-scenes manner." In that moment, Mrs Barvay was convinced this was either a huge mistake or Avi had been framed. A convenient scapegoat or a vindictive act by someone close. But she had had no time to ponder this.

As Avi left with the detectives, he had hugged his mother and whispered, "I guess, no *bhakri* for dinner." She had not understood what he meant then. She had been sure she had misheard him. *Bhakri* was the rustic unleavened bread made with jowar flour.

"Why would he talk about anything as mundane as flatbread for dinner when he had just been arrested? Especially the jowar *bhakri*, when he had definitely said earlier that only the farm vegetables were to be cooked for dinner that night. Did he mean this arrest was all a mistake and that he would be back in time for dinner?" she had pondered until evening. Their lawyers had assured her it must be a misunderstanding and they would have Avi out of police custody very soon.

Mrs Barvay had been most upset by the day's events but hid it well. She told all the house staff to go home for the day because Avi was not home for dinner. After the initial shock of the arrest, she started going through the whole day in great detail. She had a hunch that she needed to follow. She locked herself in the huge old house and then walked into the pantry. It was a cool, dark room with minimal natural light. She switched on the lights. Cupboards and shelves lined every wall in this room.

She looked around for the sack of milled jowar that had just arrived from Avi's friend's farm. She took a pair of sewing scissors and undid the stitches from the bag of jowar flour. Of course, as she expected, there was no jowar inside. Instead of the expected speckled brown and white flour, there were sugar-like, strange-looking, grainy, uneven crystals with a dirty translucence. She understood immediately what it was. Unopened, the sack could pass off as milled jowar. A quick look at the crystals in dim light could perhaps pass them off as sugar, and that had given her the idea. She had no idea how and why Avi came to have this sack. But she knew she had to act fast; once the police had taken Avi away, they could come back to go through Barvay House. She had no idea of whether there were any other illicit substances in her house but her maternal instinct was to save Avi first, then ask questions.

She dismissed Lakshmi, who had shown in the detectives and also worked for her since Avi was born. Lakshmi, now old and tired, had been asking for the past few years to return to her village. She wanted to spend time with her grandchildren and was very happy that afternoon when Mrs Barvay had finally given her a large cheque along with permission to leave for good. Then Mrs Barvay had rung Vijay Shahane, told him of Avi's arrest but not about the sack and its contents. She told him that she wanted to move to Tara Road Mansions as soon as possible. Together, they concocted the story about Avi's USA trip and renovations at Barvay House.

Avi had recently purchased the house in Tara Road Mansions because it was his old school friend Tarun Tejani's first foray into property development. The Tara Road Mansions house was to be used as a company guesthouse. Currently, it was empty, awaiting final interior design approval. Mrs Barvay put a hold on the company guesthouse plan and moved herself to Tara Road Mansions within a few days of that afternoon, taking with her some furniture, clothes, jewellery, and kitchen things; some dry goods, including the bag of 'jowar flour' and calling it a bag of sugar.

Her father had always said, "If you want to hide something, leave it in full view. No one will find it." So, she had not bothered with secrecy, special treatment or hiding; she had simply treated it like a bag of sugar. As she was diabetic, she knew it would almost never be opened. All she had to do was ensure that her weekly grocery order included more than sufficient sugar for her household.

Thinking about Avi made her furious and sad at the same time. "Did he know about the drugs? Why had he done this? Who were these people he was involved with? Or had he been framed? Avi and I will be ostracised by everyone. The newspapers would have had a field day with Avi's arrest and role in illegal activities. All the honour and respect given to the Barvays as one of the oldest business families in Poona gone because of one stupid thing!"

Then she had calmed herself. She still had some connections to the newspaper world, and she managed to call in all those favours. News of Avinash Barvay's arrest and charges did not make it to any of the large local or national newspapers. A few days later, only a couple of small regional newspapers ran a small article on Avinash Barvay's arrest. The news did not make it to the city or the national newspapers, and she thanked God for the money and goodwill of her ancestors that had made it possible.

She had visited Avi only once in prison, although she did write to him every week on an innocuous-looking inland letter. She made sure she wrote the address at the very last minute and posted the square blue inland letter herself. If someone saw her with it, they would assume it was to a distant relative. She had not mentioned the sack at all on her one visit to Avi but there had been a question in his eyes and she had simply said, "I will make your favourite jowar *bhakri* the day they send you home from this horrid place, Avi." He had smiled gratefully. He had understood that the sack was safe. She had no real plan. She had panicked and moved the little sack with her to this new house. But she had no idea how he had come by the sack or what she should do with it now.

The break-in at Barvay House had meant a hunt for the sack was on, and the police were literally on her doorstep once more. Since the sack was not in Barvay House, it would not be long now before this Tara Road Mansions house got burgled or ransacked. Should she tell the police? Or would that get Avi further into trouble? She could not decide. She felt trapped in her circumstances and her thoughts, which whirled around furiously yet offered no solution for disposing the sack or helping Avi out of his predicament. She tossed and turned as the hot night wore on despite the air-conditioning, once again falling asleep only at dawn.

✦✦✦

CHAPTER 17

The sweltering hot dawn was heralded by large swathes of orange across the sky. Yesterday's heat continued as though the night had been a mere change of light between day, night, and day. Even the birds sang quick, noisy songs this morning before fluttering off to find shady trees as the sun and the barometer climbed in competition with each other. The humidity had intensified and thick dark clouds had appeared in the distance. The relentlessly buffeting warm air and the slight creak of ceiling fans at maximum speed all night had fatigued the minds and bodies of everyone beginning the day. All over the city, first cups of tea were imbibed as fan blades whipped the air ineffectively and bare-chested men fanned themselves with the morning's newspapers instead of reading them. Despite the early hour, women alternately fanned themselves and wiped their brows with the waist-length pallus of their sarees as they made tea and breakfast for their families. Everyone peered hopefully and repeatedly at the sky in silence. It was too hot even to talk about rain; surely, it was imminent.

Ashu lay awake most of the night, alternately crying and fervently wishing for dawn. He crept into the kitchen and rang his Uncle Tariq as soon as he heard Hamida stir and then go into the bathroom that morning. Tariq could not keep the concern out of his voice when he heard his nephew's voice so early in the day. He heard the tremor and urgency in his nephew's voice. "You have to come here this morning Uncle Tariq, before school!" he whispered. "I have done very terrible things and now Ammi does not love me anymore."

Tariq smiled at the very absurd thought of Hamida ever not loving her children. Surely, Ashu had misunderstood things. "I'll come this morning, Ashu. With your favourite breakfast from the street stalls. How about that?" Tariq shook his head fondly as he heard the weak smile in Ashu's voice as he whispered a thank you and hung up.

Hamida was surprised to see Tariq at the door, bearing parcels of food just as she was about to make breakfast. "Hamma, I brought the children's favourite breakfast. I know it is wedding season and you must be very busy at the shop, plus Munni being ill and no one here to help you…" For once, Hamida did not admonish him for calling her Hamma. She felt tired and was grateful for his thoughtfulness and her brother never listened to her objections anyway. Graciously, she accepted the parcels of food and began laying them out on plates.

Ashu could not hide his relief at seeing his uncle within an hour of his phone call. "Uncle Tariq could and would fix everything." Ashu thought. Tariq saw the worry and sadness in his nephew's eyes and glanced at Hamida; there was no trace of anger or upset on her face. He wondered what was going on.

"Hamma, why don't you eat breakfast and go downstairs to work? Looks like Munni is still asleep. I will make sure Ashu gets to school on time; I will drop him. I don't have to be at headquarters till the afternoon. Night shifts again" he said as an explanation. Hamida smiled gratefully at her brother and served herself, "I will take this downstairs and eat while I do costings and bills. Just call out if Ashu can't find anything for school. Here's his snack for recess and he will be home for lunch, only half-day school now, it's almost exam time, so they get afternoons at home to revise."

Tariq asked, "Do your children actually revise? We never did, Hamma!"

She laughed and shook her head, "Some things never change."

Tariq waited while Ashu got dressed for school, and Hamida collected her things and went downstairs. Ashu had been acting quite out of character recently, and she wondered if she should have asked Tariq to find out what was bothering Ashu, she knew they were close confidantes.

As soon as Ashu reappeared at the dining table, Tariq pushed a plate of food at him and said, "Ok. Let's hear it."

In a low, hushed voice and with constant glances checking Munni's door was shut, Ashu recounted the whole sorry tale from his demand of a 500-rupee note to the broken window, lost ball, and the sugar sack. Tariq listened carefully, wincing, frowning and smiling at the narration. Then came the angst as Ashu told him how his mother had been ignoring him and withholding her affection. Ashu's eyes looked wide and worried. Tariq gave him a big hug and said things would be fine soon but Tariq was distracted.

Then he said in a serious tone, "How much of that sugar did you eat, Ashu?"

"Only two or three pinches, honest. I think I wiped more off my fingers than what I ate. My palms were so sweaty" Ashu replied in a sad, honest voice.

"Not owning up to the broken window was wrong. So was entering someone's house without their permission and helping yourself to their things. You know that. You should have just come home and told your mother since no one was at Mrs Barvay's house to offer an apology. Anyway, I will talk to Hamma, everything will be fine. But there will be consequences, young man."

Ashu's voice was low and serious, "I know, Uncle Tariq, but that's okay as long as Ammi starts talking to me and still loves me. I will never ever do any of these things again. And I will always come and tell Ammi everything after this, even before she finds out or someone tells her." The earnest note in Ashu's voice tugged at Tariq's heartstrings. Ashu leaned back in his chair and breathed a sigh of relief. Just talking to his uncle had made him feel much better.

"Take my advice, give your mother a big hug when you come back from school and see what happens" said Tariq and then asked "Ashu, what did you do with the shorts? The ones you wiped your hands in the pockets? Have they been washed?"

Ashu frowned. "How was that important?" But his uncle looked intent, so he answered. "Not washed. I hid them at the back of my wardrobe so Ammi would not find them for a long time."

"Bring me the shorts in a plastic bag and then eat up your breakfast. I will drop you to school." Ashu raced off to do as he was told. He loved a ride in his uncle's Impala.

While Ashu ate and packed his bag for school, Tariq made a few calls. The first of them was to the Deputy Income Tax Commissioner to tell him about the 500-rupee notes that Ashu claimed to have seen at the Karamlegavraokar house. "My nephew is only ten years old and could have easily mistaken what he saw but he would definitely not make up a story like this. He must have seen something. As a police officer, it is my duty to report this to you." He expected the Deputy Tax Commissioner to say a casual 'Thank you, we will check it out soon.' Instead, the sheer surprise in the Deputy Tax Commissioner's voice shocked Tariq.

He asked Tariq the exact address where his nephew had seen these notes and the first names of the Karamlegavraokar couple. Tariq rattled off the address but had no idea of the first names. "Thank you for the tipoff, Tariq. I think it is the same couple that we have been tracking for the last few years. The man seems to make several large deals in his financial consultancy business every year but his bank accounts and tax returns do not reflect this. His lifestyle and spending habits seem too opulent and out of reach for a man with his declared income and tax returns. We have followed the paper trail and interviewed him twice but to no avail. It's as if the money just disappears. Our informants say many of the deals are done in cash but we have never found any trace of it. We had even sent some undercover agents to his recent, lavish housewarming party. They had a good look around the house for hidden safes, vaults etc. but could find nothing."

Tariq was speechless. Hamida seemed to have moved into an enclave of rather risqué people.

"Obviously, our agents were disguised as guests at the housewarming party, so they could not start invasive searches but they had a very careful look at the other guests and around the house. A number of interesting guests were present that evening in the Karamlegavraokar house, including some faces from organised crime. Everything in the house is very opulent but nothing looked out of place or suspicious. They have two small safes, one in a wardrobe and another behind a painting in the study. Both had some jewellery and a reasonable amount of cash, but not the kind of cash or gold we were expecting. If your information about cash in the air conditioner helps us to get our man, I simply cannot thank you enough!"

By the time Tariq took Ashu to school and reached police headquarters that morning, a man from the police laboratory was waiting to collect the shorts for analysis. "Don't take one sample. Here, just take this entire bag with the shorts. The substance is in the pockets. I need the results of that extremely urgently! Get a few of your lab technicians on this job, test for everything. And the results given to me verbally straightaway on the phone first, then type them up for the files, these are direct orders," the man nodded, saluted and left.

"This new Assistant Commissioner certainly seemed to have his own way of doing things," he thought.

✦✦✦

CHAPTER 18

Preeti too, had welcomed the sweltering orange dawn with fierce determination. "Today is the day," she said to herself, hoping all went to plan. She had been disconcerted to see Assistant Commissioner Tariq roar up the driveway in his red Impala very early that morning and her heart had stilled in terror. When she realised he was not in uniform and carrying food parcels to Hamida's front door, she relaxed. Ever cautious, she had decided to watch from her window and heaved a great sigh of relief when Tariq drove away an hour later with Ashu sitting next to him. Minutes later, one of the Karamlegavraokar cars zoomed away too, with the children sticking their arms out of the window.

Tukaram had already saluted Tariq's car twice that morning as it drove in and out, so when he saw another silent police van approaching the gates, Tukaram eagerly saluted, his eyes scanning for Tariq once more. But the van had four police constables. Two Ambassador cars and a police jeep followed; they had an inspector and another man in civilian clothes. Tukaram noted that all vehicles had the Government of India flag on them and looked rather crowded with people. All the cars wound around the drive and parked outside the Karamlegavraokar house. Some policemen disembarked from the van and formed a cordon around the house and backyard before the man with the inspector rang the doorbell of the Karamlegavraokar house. Tukaram now began to watch with interest.

Mr and Mrs Karamlegavraokar were almost ready to leave for work when there was an insistent ringing of their imported doorbell. Mrs Karamlegavraokar was closest to the door and answered it, ready to admonish the visitor for leaning on their expensive bell. She was puzzled at the unexpected collection of strangers on her doorstep. There were some men and women in plain clothes and some uniformed police officers. Before she could get a word out, the man standing in front of her asked, "Karamlegavraokar residence?"

"Yes?" she said rather haughtily, as she shimmered in a purple silk saree while her large diamond jewellery caught the sun and glittered.

He proffered his hand, "I'm Vishwanath Tambe from the income tax department and this is my team ..."

She cut off his well-mannered introduction and leaned closer to him conspiratorially, "Income tax? I think you want the Sheikh family next door. They are a bit dodgy, all in all. We've never seen the husband. She says that he's in shipping. If you ask me, import-export is just another way of saying smuggling. And that *Begum Boutique* that she runs? It's probably a front for the smuggling. Otherwise, how can they afford so many things that we have? You know, imported expensive things?"

Mr Karamlegavraokar, who was walking down the stairs, glanced at the man in the grey safari suit, the standard unofficial uniform of the income tax department, and his heart sank. He silently prayed that his wife would stop talking and that the officers would conduct a quick, cursory search, a brief interview, and leave without finding anything, just as they had done last time when his wife and children were away. He had managed to keep that visit from his wife. Then he heard his wife's loud, confident voice going on about the imported, expensive things they owned. He nearly fell down the stairs in his hurry to get to the door. He cleared his throat very loudly as he approached and interrupted his wife's flow of accusations about the Sheikh family next door. He needed to take charge of this conversation immediately.

"My dear, I'm here now. I can deal with these people. You can leave for work. Don't be late, go. Go…" he said, smoothly entering the conversation before any more damage was done.

Mrs Karmalegavraokar smiled gratefully at her husband. "How gallant and good-looking he was, when he rescued her from dealing with the hoi polloi" she thought. "Thanks, darling" she said.

But before she reached for her car keys, Mr Tambe the income tax man stopped her and declared, "Sorry, madam, no one can leave this house or be admitted inside now. There will be no phone calls made or received from this house from now until my team has completed their job. I want all the members of the household who are indoors to come and sit here in the living room. Members who are outdoors should remain there. My officers will see to them. Mr Karamlegavraokar, you know the drill. Our records show that you have done all this once before."

Mr Karamlegavraokar blanched at the statement as his wife looked at the two men suspiciously. "What does he mean by 'once before'? Shivram? What's going on? Answer me!" Her voice rapidly leaving the posh dulcet tones that had dripped only moments earlier for a louder, harsher pitch. Mrs Karamlegavraokar looked from one man to another, but neither replied as she was shepherded to the sofa by a stern policewoman, and a dreadful feeling began in her stomach as she began to understand the scene before her. Her husband sat down next to her, and she snatched away her hand as he tried to hold it. Two policemen now stood guard over them while the rest of the visitors divided themselves into teams of four and went into various rooms. She could hear muffled sounds as they opened cupboards, yanked out their contents, unmade beds, and tapped walls. The carpets in the living room were rolled up and shoved out of the way as the income tax officers searched for God only knew what on the floors. Maya Bai tried to ask and help them, but they only glared at her and gestured for her to sit by her employers. They tapped the floors and walls listening for hollow sounds. They pulled off sofa cushions and sofa covers, patted, squeezed and even tore some of its padding.

They asked Maya Bai to clear the breakfast table, then escorted her to her employers as soon as she was done. People who had gone upstairs brought down jewellery boxes and began stacking them on the dining table. Maya Bai fidgeted with the pallu of her saree as she sat on the floor by her employers. She had no idea what was going on, and she watched in horror as the visitors opened her neatly arranged cupboards and shelves, rummaged through them and pulled out anything that seemed to take their fancy. They crammed the remaining contents back onto the shelves and slammed the cupboard doors shut. She winced. It was painful to watch her tidy, well-ordered things ransacked in this manner. The income tax officers shook off the stuffing from some cushions, and they even disturbed the neatly arranged books in the bookcases, flipping through the books, all the time looking for something.

Maya Bai's pain was punctuated by loud, indignant repetition by Mrs Karamlegavraokar. "Mr Tambe! You have the wrong house. This is No. 4. We are the Karamlegavraokars. Ka-ra-ma-ley-gaav-raao-kar," she emphasised for clarity, copying Mrs Barvay's style from the meeting. "You want the Sheikh house next door. They are the Muslim smugglers! We are honest Hindu people! Only one wife and an honest life. You have got the wrong family."

When this angle did not get a response from Mr Tambe, she tried a different one. "Mr Tambe, this is a private house and these are our belongings. Your people cannot throw things around. You have no right to do this. I will make a police complaint!"

"Shivram! Shivram, say something to make these men stop! Ring one of your friends in the income tax department or the police. This is an invasion of our privacy. They are plundering our well-ordered and well-appointed house. Don't they need a warrant for this kind of thing? And a reason! What have we done? ..."

"Shivram! That is my favourite jewellery! Mr Tambe, where are they taking all these things? They belong to me. My husband paid cash for all these things. They are mine!"

"No! NO! Those are the imported glasses and plates! Please be careful with them. And do you know, you are carting off modern art originals from America? Those are expensive pieces; please stop hauling them off like teenagers' posters. They are horrendously expensive paintings." Mrs Karamlegavraokar was almost in tears as she watched her precious items being carted off unceremoniously by the income tax officers. As there was no response from either of the men she kept addressing, her voice grew more shrill, louder, and angrier.

After a while, Mr Tambe from the income tax department grew weary of Mrs Karamlegavraokar's screeching protests. He had hoped her husband would calm her down or shut her up. He walked to the Karamlegavraokar couple and wearily shook out a sheet of paper from his pocket. "Madam, this is a warrant issued by the police for the income tax department to go through your house. This is an official income tax raid for unpaid and undeclared income and assets. Now, please just be quiet and let us get on with our job. Any more shouting from you and these policemen will escort you outside to your veranda, where you are welcome to sit in the heat."

✦ ✦ ✦

CHAPTER 19

By the time the Karamlegavraokar household had received unexpected income tax department visitors, Sundari had already ambled to Mrs Barvay's courtyard and settled into her shaded spot by the window. She had covered the distance between her shelter and Mrs Barvay's garden earlier and earlier as the hot summer days had advanced. The heat seemed to have made Sundari lethargic and slow. She did not eat as many plants on her way to Mrs Barvay's courtyard. Once she sat down in her favourite spot, she did not bother Meena or Mrs Barvay as they went about their morning routines and activities in the courtyard. In turn, Mrs Barvay and Meena had given up trying to get rid of the buffalo and allowed her to be ensconced in the shade by the storeroom window.

Meena was hanging out the washing, when she saw three workmen go into Preeti's house. They were carrying tools, cloth bags, and a large flat box; soon, there were sounds of hammering and sawing. Then she caught sight of several cars and some policemen standing in a circle around the Karamlegavraokar house. Scared for herself once more, she ducked behind the sarees she had just hung on the washing line and watched for a few minutes. Nothing seemed to be happening. But it was very odd that Mr and Mrs Karamlegavraokar sat in the rocking chairs on the back porch on such a hot day and Maya Bai stood next to them in the shade. Frequently, the trio mopped their brows, and their expressions looked angry, sad, and bewildered. Meena could see Mrs Karamlegavraokar gesticulating wildly in the air, saying something that Meena was too far away to hear. The policemen seemed to be watching them closely but ignored their discomfort in the heat. Meena was puzzled, "The Karamlegavraokars had so many air-conditioning units in their house, so why were they sitting on their porch in this heat? And what were the police doing inside their air-conditioned house for so long if the Karamlegavraokars were out on the veranda?"

The sun beat down on her mercilessly, although it was only ten o'clock, and she quickly retreated indoors to tell Mrs Barvay of the strange goings-on at the Karamlegavraokar house. Mrs Barvay had peered out of the front door just as several cardboard boxes and velvet jewellery boxes were carried out of the Karamlegavraokar house and into the boots of the waiting Ambassador cars. She took in the sombre mood of the box carriers and their attire, the Indian flags on the cars and the police presence, and wondered if it was an income tax raid or an arrest. She did not know whether to feel relieved that the police were not at her door once more or worry that the police were once again in such proximity to her own house, where she definitely had a sack of contraband.

✦ ✦ ✦

It was almost midday, Tariq paced his office like a caged animal as he waited for the phone to ring. He wanted to hear from the lab about results of the 'sugar' from Ashu's shorts. Impatiently, he barked orders for files from some older cases before his appointment as Assistant Commissioner to the city.

He had studied them intently before ringing the ex-Assistant Commissioner of Police. His mood seemed to worsen after that long phone call. His subordinates watched nervously. No one had seen him in such an impatient mood. He made another call, this time to Hamida. "I want you to stay indoors, keep Munni indoors, and have Ashu picked up from school and taken to our parents' house. Don't ask questions, just do!" Hamida tried to tell Tariq that Ashu's school was already finished for the day, and he was on his way home in the Karamlegavraokar car, but Tariq had already hung up. He was tackling the next task, ordering cars and armed officers ready to leave any minute for Tara Road Mansions. His subordinates scuttled about following his orders.

✦ ✦ ✦

It was almost lunchtime. Meena had cleaned all morning, dusted and polished Mrs Barvay's living room's innumerable knick-knacks. Beads of sweat formed on her forehead every time she moved out of the radius of the fan. She was not allowed to switch on the air conditioner unless Mrs Barvay or other guests were present. Today, Mrs Barvay had decided it was too hot to eat lunch or go to the club and had taken to her bed with the air-conditioning on full blast. This left Meena with no choice but to take the stolen things and the clothes for dry-cleaning tomorrow afternoon when Mrs Barvay headed to the club. "It's really hot today, nothing is going to happen in this heat, surely my loot is safe here for one more day," she thought, giving the windowsill a good wipe. She kept hoping to be called for errands in Mrs Barvay's cool air-conditioned bedroom.

✦ ✦ ✦

The dark bitumen in the driveway shimmered in the midday sun and tiny bits of it bubbled and oozed. The heat had defeated Tukaram too; he was slouched in his chair in a shady spot but was wide awake. He had already asked Meena twice for cold water from the fridge. Now she saw the object of her unease leap up from his chair and give a smart salute to another group of police jeeps quietly making their way through the gates of Tara Road Mansions. Meena stared, "What was this now? More police at the Karamlegavraokar house?" Meena watched the police cars wind around the drive and quickly turn in and park in Mrs Barvay's driveway. Meena's heart raced; she was frightened.

The windowsills Meena was wiping were out of the radius of the fan, and sweat ran into her eyes, making them sting. She wiped them with her sleeve and was about to report the police cars to Mrs Barvay when the doorbell rang. Meena nearly jumped out of her skin at the sound of the doorbell. She hurried to answer it, expecting Tukaram again asking for water.

She stared agape at the man standing there. It was the important inspector man- Hamida's brother again, asking to see Mrs Barvay. "Had he somehow found out about the things she had stolen at the last job or had someone at Tara Road Mansions reported missing the things she had stolen?" She stilled a shudder as she politely invited him in. He was puzzled at her discomfort and stared at her. She went upstairs to tell Mrs Barvay.

Meena hid behind the door, her heart thudded loudly as she listened while Tariq spoke to Mrs. Barvay about the break-in at

Barvay House and the possibility that the burglars were looking for something specific. She sighed with relief that it had nothing to do with her and nearly missed what he said next– something about his officers waiting outside, who would come in and search this house. He assured Mrs Barvay that he would stay with her throughout the search. "Searching this house!" Meena baulked at the very thought as she heard Mrs Barvay inviting him to search wherever he liked.

Mrs Barvay's practised pleasant expression had not wavered as she gave Tariq permission to search the house. But she sent up many fervent prayers that her father was right and that anything hidden in plain sight could not be found. Tariq looked at Mrs Barvay, puzzled. He could not make out whether she was simply bold or ignorant about the sack of cocaine. Tariq thanked Mrs Barvay for her cooperation. He spoke briefly to the policemen waiting outside, then sat down in his chair thoughtfully and continued talking with the older woman. He needed to ensure she did not make a quick getaway.

At the mention of several policemen searching the house, Meena had panicked. "Too many police were here these days!" she thought irritably. She had to get rid of the stolen items. Somehow. Now they were hidden all over, some were in the dry-cleaning bundle; the others were still in the sack of sugar or in the crate under the buckets in the storeroom. Her brain was processing all this information like lightning. Only Mrs Barvay would recognise the extra shawls in the dry-cleaning bundle, so they were safe. The stolen items in the small crate under the brass buckets were small enough to be ignored as items from the storeroom. But the stolen jewellery in the lumpy sack of sugar would look very suspicious. If that was discovered, it would raise many questions. She had listened in alarm as Tariq said officers would come in and search the whole house. That meant every room in the house but not the garden and courtyard. She raced to the storeroom and quickly reached for the small sack and hefted it onto the windowsill of the storeroom. She looked around cautiously before opening the loosely fastened window. She heard footsteps coming in from the living room to the kitchen and would be in the storeroom any minute. Deftly, she flipped the sack over the edge of the windowsill into the courtyard and firmly shut the window. Moments later, she heard footsteps approaching and the storeroom door flung open; she hastily knelt down pretending to fold yesterday's newspapers into a box full of old newspapers and magazines. Meena stammered out sentences about how she had come to put away newspapers, but no one was listening to her. Because as the two policemen walked into the storeroom, they all heard a bellow, scraping and shuffling outside. They ran to open the window and looked outside.

When Meena had flipped the sack over the windowsill, it had fallen unceremoniously onto Sundari's large, ridged back as she sat in the shade, napping and ruminating. She had not liked the sudden weight of the sack on her back while she had her siesta and had given an indignant bellow and flicked her tail. When the unwelcome weight did not move, she tossed her head, shook her neck, and flicked her tail repeatedly, but the discomfort would not go away. So, she stood up and stamped her feet to try to shake off the weight. But this movement only helped to settle the small sack firmly, moulding itself to the ridges and dips of her back and did not budge or fall. Sundari, feeling quite bewildered by the strange thing on her back, set off at an awkward pace with a loud bellow as she tried to throw off the weight. The policemen who had clearly been briefed about the sack were excited to finally see it and climbed out of the storeroom window, ineffectively shouting at the buffalo, "Stop! Stop!"

Seeing the policeman climbing out of the window, shouting and pointing to the strange sight of a buffalo with a small sack on its back, the awaiting policemen around Mrs Barvay's house chased Sundari too, waving their batons, although they had no idea why. The bellows of the buffalo had excited the cordon of constables around the Karamlegavraokar house too, and they watched wistfully. The chase looked far more interesting than watching the Karamlegavraokars, but they knew they could not leave their posts to chase a buffalo while a raid was on. They focused harder on the Karamlegavraokars as they sat under their sweltering hot porch.

Mrs Karamlegavraokar was glad of the momentary distraction by the buffalo. For the nth time she whispered to her husband, who sat with a pinched look on his face, "Shivram, it is so hot here. What's happening? Why are they raiding our house? It's going to be so embarrassing to explain this to our friends." But her husband had maintained his tight-lipped silence and his expression of mortified regret, so she continued angrily, "Shivram! We have six expensive air conditioners in our house, and yet we are sitting here, melting in this heat. Oh! I cannot bear to think that the odious Mr Tambe and his nosy team are comfortable and cool as they ransack our house. Our house, Shivram!" Then she worried again about how she would explain this raid to her friends. She wondered, "Could I pass off the embarrassment of the raid as a thing that routinely happened only to very rich people? And would that mean we have socially arrived?" But before she found an answer to that question, there were more shouts and bellows.

Tariq's officers gave good chase to Sundari, who had never encountered sudden weights on her back or people chasing her, so she was a little startled. She kept flicking her tail and tossing her head, trying to lose the strange feeling on her back as she ran from her pursuers. But the bag with its soft contents sat snug on her broad-ridged back. Sundari began an awkward scramble of running and shrugging to lose the heavy sensation on her back, but it did not budge. The sack had moulded itself to the central dip of her spine with almost equal parts of the sack hanging off either side. She bellowed again and peered around her broad haunches at the commotion behind her, and finding so many people yelling and chasing her with sticks, she tossed her head and ran as fast as her large, ungainly body and thin legs would allow. Hearing an animal bellow and constables yelling outside, Tariq abandoned his chivalrous yet detaining living room conversation with Mrs Barvay and ran out. Seeing the buffalo and sack, he understood the situation immediately and gave earnest chase too without stopping to consider why the buffalo had the sack on its back.

Preeti Rao waited anxiously by her window. She had been worried by the little cavalcade of police cars that had appeared throughout the morning and parked outside the Karamlegavraokar house. She had recognised it as an income tax raid when she saw people filling the Ambassadors with boxes containing numerous items from the Karamlegavraokar house. She had been able to recognise the strange couple from the housewarming party. "Income tax officers!" she had thought with relief, "That's who they were. Nothing to do with the drugs." She hoped fervently that they had not found the safe behind the air conditioner, as that would diminish her success in this job. Her chance to get hold of the cash was probably gone now, she thought dejectedly, but at least she would have the cocaine sack, she consoled herself.

She was waiting patiently for the afternoon when Mrs Barvay left for the club and Meena went to Hamida's house so the 'carpenters' could break into the storeroom. It was almost time. The 'carpenters' were sitting on the floor of her living room, taking a break from the fake hammering and sawing, engrossed in a lively game of cards as they waited for instructions from Preeti. But she watched in despair as another group of police cars arrived at Tara Road Mansions, and most of them stopped in front of Mrs Barvay's house. "Why today!" Preeti groaned. Oddly, one lot of police cars drove straight towards the stream. She quailed at the sight, because at that moment, in and around Tara Road Mansions were four of her armed men. They were now trapped amidst several jeeps full of policemen. She had barely digested this fact when she saw the tableau of Sundari with the sack on her back and chubby constables giving chase. She read the situation immediately and perfectly. She knew Sundari was going to run past Preeti's house on the way back to her shelter. She was glad she had briefed her men well yesterday. If she could steer Sundari towards her men waiting in the scrub and bushes, they could grab the sack and get away, even with the police hot on their heels. She opened the back door, dropped her crutches and began running after the buffalo, hoping she could steer the beast to her men before the constables caught up with Sundari.

✦ ✦ ✦

CHAPTER 20

Ashu and the Karamlegavraokar children, in their air-conditioned car, had seen all the police cars as soon as they drove through the Tara Road Mansion gates. Ashu had hopped out hurriedly as soon as the car stopped in his driveway; he was hoping to see his uncle again. He saw more policemen outside the Karamlegavraokar residence and wondered what was happening when he heard shouts and saw everyone running behind Sundari. He dropped his school bag at his front door and joined the chase. He had no idea who they were chasing and why, but the shouting and running looked like fun.

Finishing a fitting session with a bride behind closed curtains, Hamida pulled the window curtains aside, hoping to see dark grey clouds. Instead, a strange sight greeted her. Ungainly Sundari running with a small sack on her back, Preeti Rao chasing the buffalo effortlessly, running fast without crutches, but one foot still wrapped in a crepe bandage. Hamida stared. Preeti had been painfully limping on crutches only that morning when she picked up her newspaper from the driveway. Then she saw the chubby constables in hot pursuit. They were rapidly overtaken by her physically fit brother Tariq, who was also running in the direction of the buffalo. Hamida's mouth opened further in wonder as she saw Ashu running and gaining distance over Tariq and the constables. She felt a tap on her shoulder and realised the bride and her mother were trying to say goodbye. Apologetically, she closed the curtains again. It was bad enough that her clients had commented on the parked police cars at Tara Road Mansions. There was no need for them to witness buffalo chasing. Nodding hurriedly, she saw them to the front door and returned to her window to watch.

As Sundari heard excited shouts and the footsteps of more and more people running behind her, she suddenly changed direction in an attempt to shake off her pursuers. She was used to Mr Tulpule's soothing tones and Mrs Barvay's gentle shooing or spraying her with the garden hose. Never had she experienced the strange feeling on her back and a mad mob of ever-increasing angry voices and pounding footsteps right behind her. She was terrified and headed for the stream. Preeti Rao and Tariq, realising Sundari's destination, ran as hard as they could. Tariq shouted at Ashu to move out of the way of the huge lumbering beast.

Overhead, dark clouds had gathered quietly in the sky and draped the sun, shrouding daylight. There was a distinct rumble of thunder. It scared Sundari even more than the shouting and the people behind her. She increased her stride to a gallop as fat raindrops hit her and the chasers. Petrichor rose as the first drops of rain hit the parched earth, and without meaning to, the band of runners slowed a little to appreciate the rising fragrance of wet soil and the much-awaited coolness peppering their skin. But Sundari did not slow down; she continued her gallop, heading straight to the stream as the sky began its own rock concert with flashes of light and rolls of thunder. The rain raced down in thick, fast, slanting lines, making it hard to see or chase Sundari.

Within moments, Tariq, Preeti Rao, Ashu, and the chasing chubby constables were soaked to the skin as they got within touching distance of Sundari. Their wet clothes clung to their bodies making their movements difficult and before they could do anything to stop Sundari or change the direction of the big, bulky beast away from the stream, she tossed her head again, jagging her horns on the sack and tugging at it as she shook her horns free of the bag. She stepped into the stream and gently lowered herself into it, tossing her head back repeatedly, her horns catching the weave of the sack each time as she tried again and again to lose the uncomfortable burden on her back. Every time she tossed her head, her long, pointy horns caught in the weave of the sack, and poked another little hole. Every movement she made jostled the sack and a tiny bit of the sack's contents spilt out from the gouged holes.

Rain was soaking the sack and numerous tiny holes in the sack from Sundari's horns kept spilling out the contents. Sundari bellowed again as she tried to throw off the uncomfortable feeling from her back, as she sank blissfully in the stream and water began to claim the sack's contents. Sundari, having finally staved off the chasers, gently rolled on her side in the water with a long and content low, she was enjoying the cool stream and rain after running in the heat. Finally, she was happy; her back felt lighter as the sack with numerous holes fell into the stream.

Preeti and Tariq were frustrated by the restrictions of their wet clothing and aghast at the sack repeatedly spilling its contents. They tried to rescue the sack from the water as they navigated the rocks in the stream, avoiding Sundari's large body and spindly legs. Without meaning to, Tariq and Preeti helped each other in their efforts to reach and rescue the sack. They were breathless and floundered, hindered by the stream, the rain, and Sundari.

By the time they lifted the sack out of the water, it was a sorry sight, limp, torn, and half-empty. It had ripped from the constant digging of Sundari's horns and the jagged rocks in the stream. Most of the contents of the sack had flowed away, leaving behind a small, unrecognisable chunk of dirty, waterlogged crystals. Without speaking to each other, Preeti and Tariq stepped up on the bank, neither willing to let go of the sack. They peered into the sack and saw an assortment of jewellery amidst the remaining dirty, wet cocaine crystals. They stared at it, puzzled and dismayed, as the rain kept coming down in sheets, further soaking them, the crystals, and the assortment of jewellery.

Ashu reached Preeti and Tariq as they grappled for control of the sack. He was amused at the grown-ups engaging in such childish behaviour over a sack of sugar. Tariq looked at Preeti Rao soaked to the skin, hair plastered to her scalp. It was the first time he had seen her at such close quarters. "She really did seem familiar" he thought. A vague memory stirred, from days when he was a newly minted junior inspector. He remembered a younger version of Preeti's face, dirtier, shorter hair, a teenager's body in an oversized grubby shirt and rolled up men's trousers. He was running, chasing, grabbing handfuls of the shirt and the girl getting away. Girl? And later, a photo of the same girl, a little older and scruffier, had appeared on the police department's 'wanted' files."

Tariq stopped and stared at Preeti, and suddenly he knew who she was. "Rani Pattiwali!" he said triumphantly. The young girl who had sold *pattis* or strips of paper laced with cocaine on the streets of Bombay and then gone on to become a notorious criminal working with a well-known drug cartel. She was infamous as the only woman in these circles and had evaded the police on many occasions. Tariq dropped his hand from the sack and clamped it on Preeti's wrist while the other reached for handcuffs in his back pocket.

"You!" he said. Preeti's shoulders stiffened as she realised the game was up and held his gaze defiantly. She twisted her arm and her body, pushing Tariq with her free arm as she tried to loosen his grip and kick his shins. But Tariq held on to her wet slippery wrist. Their tussle was disturbed by the arrival of the tiny troop of puffing constables who had finally caught up with them. They stopped and came to attention, awaiting further orders, cautiously standing on the bank, reluctant to get into the water or close to the buffalo, who was now wallowing in the stream. "Shinde! Take this." Tariq handed the torn sack to one of the constables and handcuffed Preeti Rao.

The click of the handcuffs seemed to unleash something in Preeti. She tossed her head defiantly and let out a string of expletives and in rather crude language demanded they call her lawyers. *"Ey bhadvya, haat lavaicha nahi!"* She shouted at Shinde to keep his fucking hands off her. *"Maagey laag lass sangeen.* Rape *chi* case *karel."* She swore at Tariq and spat at him in fury. She threatened to report him, saying he chased and tried to rape her. She used the crudest words, insulting each inspector and constable individually, accusing them of taking blood money, extortion and other rackets. "*Harami, haftaa nahi mila kya? Har somvar ko Koliwada akey kya karta tu? Saangu ka saheybaalaa?*" She swore in Hindi, Marathi, and extremely crude Haryanvi, asking the men if they knew who they screwed at the *kothas*, did they even know whether the prostitutes were their daughters or their sisters? She tried to kick the shins of the constable trying to lead her away. "*Nustaa* yes sir, yes sir! *Boot chaatyaa behenchod*!" She shouted, hurled verbal abuse at everyone, called them fucking arse lickers who should fuck off! She looked at the last of the constables who had caught up and started afresh, "*Saalaa, ithey porey nangi bhukeli, bayko chaha saakhar udhari var ghete ani tu bhosadichya kar sutta, baatli, bai, aish!!*" She shouted that their children ran around naked and hungry, and their poor wives had to buy tea and sugar from the grocery on credit while they wasted their money on alcohol, tobacco, gambling, cigarettes, and prostitutes.

She inelegantly tied her waist-long straight hair into an ungainly bun and tore off the ankle bandage. She wiped the remnants of her makeup on her sleeve and sucked her teeth, as she looked at the police officers who had formed a circle around her. Gone were the polished manners, the demure body language and helpful, caring tone of the lovely young girl from the advertising agency. Now she looked like any crude, bedraggled criminal verbally abusing the police.

Ashu gaped at the arrest, the unexpected transformation of Preeti Rao and the crude words. He found it hard to believe that this was his friend, the well-dressed, well-spoken, smart girl who played cricket with the children, listened to his grievances, and handed out sweets and bubble gum.

For a moment, the uncle in Tariq shuddered as he thought about what Hamida would say to the language Ashu was being exposed to. But the Assistant Commissioner in Tariq was trying to work out where more drugs or Preeti Rao's accomplices could be hidden around Tara Road Mansions and whether through her shouting she was ensuring she gave them secret signals to escape to safety. He ordered some of the policemen to search Preeti's house and the bushes by the stream.

✦ ✦ ✦

CHAPTER 21

At the first hint of thunder and rain, Mr Tulpule had glanced at Sundari's shelter and finding it empty, he had run out to find her. "She will be terrified of the thunder and lightning! She should not be out in this rain; she will catch a chill," he had thought. He started looking for her, following the trail of the freshest dung pats as the rain came down in thick lines and the shouting voices came closer. That was when he saw the most bizarre scene unfolding. Sundari running to the stream with a small sack on her back. A group of policemen in khaki uniforms, shouting and waving batons, Ashu, and a suddenly fit Preeti Rao were all chasing Sundari. Angrily, he wondered what they were trying to do to Sundari.

"Had Mrs Barvay set the police on his Sundari after that heated argument about his beloved buffalo at the meeting? And what was that sack they had put on her back? Was it to slow her down?" He was speechless with fury and transfixed by the strange vista until he saw Sundari suddenly change direction, head for the stream, and immerse herself in it. Then she turned her head towards her pursuers and bared her beautiful white teeth that looked as if she was sneering at everyone. He laughed and watched with pride, like a parent watching their child suddenly take the lead in the race on school sports day. "It was okay," he thought, slowing down a little. Sundari had just shown him she could take care of herself. But he did not break his stride; he continued to walk towards Sundari just as an anxious parent would. All he wanted to do was make sure she was okay.

Sundari wallowed in the stream for a little while after the weight on her back had finally fallen off. She was quite content to lie in the water but there was more shouting from the bank of the stream and several people came quite close to her again. She had not enjoyed the proximity of the loudness and chasing any more than she had liked the feeling of the sack on her back. She rose from the stream with a sudden judder of her body, scattering the gathered people in all directions. Everyone tried to move out of her possible trajectory, not wanting to be showered with water, feel the thrust of her horns, a kick of her hooves or the bulk of her wet body against them. As the cluster of people parted, she saw Mr Tulpule running towards her, his arms outstretched; she could hear his gentle voice soothing her as he got closer. She hastened her stride towards him and soon they were both content as she stopped next to him and he bent awkwardly and put his arms around her neck and stroked it, while she gently nuzzled his shoulder. Mr Tulpule spoke to Sundari in soft soothing tones as if placating a child but he glared at everyone by the stream. He almost put his hands over Sundari's ears as he heard Preeti let forth more expletives.

The Karamlegavraokar children had wanted to chase the buffalo too with Ashu, but they had seen police cars in their driveway and worriedly hurried home. Maya Bai had shepherded them through the house very quickly from the front door to the porch. A shock awaited them. Their house was full of strangers and police officers. The tidy house they had left that morning was in complete and utter disarray. Couches and cushions lay helter-skelter and the contents of drawers and cupboards had been emptied on the carpets. Their parents were brought in by a policeman and sat at the dining table. They looked desolate as they were watched by a sombre man. Their mother sounded angry as she kept talking to their father and the strangers in their house but everyone ignored her. Maya Bai nudged the children and they ran towards their parents and hugged them. Their mother looked strange without her trademark large diamond jewellery and their usually cheerful father looked tired and sad.

The men were packing boxes of files from their father's study and many of their mother's jewellery boxes. They all gasped as they saw two men carrying down the whole safe from behind the air conditioner in the master bedroom. The sombre man spoke to their parents in a low voice, "You two need to come with us. The income tax office will be very interested in what you have to say. The children can stay here with the maid but they cannot leave the house." The bewildered children huddled around Maya Bai, who drew them closer protectively. She murmured something about getting them something to eat but the usually precocious Kaveri would not let go of her arms. Kartik clutched at Maya Bai's saree and Mrs Karamlegavraokar's eyes begged Maya Bai to look after the children.

"We will be back soon, kids" Mr Karamlegavraokar said reassuringly just as they were led out of the front door, but there had been no conviction in his voice. Maya Bai stared in disbelief at the change in her employers' attitude. She hoped for the children's sake that their parents would return home soon.

✦✦✦

CHAPTER 22

At the police station, Mrs Barvay and Preeti glared at each other mutinously while the duty sergeant wrote copious notes before the two women were led away to the holding cells. Mrs Barvay could not believe the language and mannerisms Preeti Rao now displayed. There was no hint of the soft-spoken, educated, caring girl she had seen in the past few weeks. Worse, was the easy familiarity between Preeti and the police. She had shouted upon arrival that she would be out very soon, within minutes, once they sent a message to Bhim Pawar. "*Arrey,* real security agency *hayey uski.*" The duty sergeant had laughed in her face and told her to shut up. She became acrimonious. She told the sergeant that Bhim would cut off his balls if she was not treated like a queen. "*Arrey, mera naam* Rani *hai*. Rani *minz* queen."

First, the sergeant ignored her but finally looked smug and said that they had caught her at last. Then he calmly continued to book Mrs Barvay into the arrest register. Preeti sat smugly, calmly braiding and unbraiding her damp hair, as if she was an errant schoolgirl simply waiting outside the principal's office for a minor misdemeanour. She felt safe and self-assured in the knowledge that she would very soon be saved by her boss Bhim Pawar or one of his men by making a mere phone call. The police would soon release her and probably apologise and organise a car to take her home.

She worked with powerful people who valued her. But she could not believe that her plan had gone so horribly wrong that she had been arrested! She had never been arrested. She prided herself on that. The boys at work were never going to let her forget this. Momentarily, she wallowed in some self-pity, "If only I had not become greedy about getting credit for the money and the drugs. It would have never come to this…".

Beside her, Mrs Barvay tried to ignore Preeti Rao as they sat next to each other on the floor with their backs to the wall and stared straight ahead; each of them pretending the other woman did not exist in that tiny cell. They looked like two schoolgirls who had got into a fight and been punished in class. Each one's face was a picture of superiority, sulkiness, and self-righteousness. Mrs Barvay had requested in her refined tones and already made her phone call to Vijay Shahane. He and her lawyers would soon get her out of this cell first and then out of this mess. She was sure this was also part of the same conspiracy that had seen Avi framed for embezzlement. She had decided to give the bare minimum information required by the police. The less they knew of anything, the better. She thought of her darling Avi in another prison cell, just like this one.

"What were these events of the last few months? They made no sense. One minute, they were going about their luxuriant lives in sprawling old Barvay Mansion and then a secret sack of jowar, police on the doorstep, Avi arrested, charged with embezzlement and not let out on bail. Now I am here, arrested too. And if I am here, who will try and salvage Avi's reputation and shepherd him back to his intended life? Will they really be able to pin anything on me? I can always pretend neither Avi nor I had any idea about the sack of contraband in my kitchen. I can say we have never seen the wretched sack before in our lives. Had someone done some black magic? Cast an evil eye upon Avi? What will happen to Barvay Industries in the meantime? Would Vijay Shahane be able to manage such a large undertaking singlehandedly?" The reply came to her instantly, "Of course, he could!"

And then an unbidden thought, like a hard cold hand, clamped around her heart and almost squeezed the life out of it. "Was Vijay Shahane behind all this? He had been her husband's friend for over 50 years. He could easily have orchestrated it. Avi's arrest for embezzlement? He certainly had been her confidante after she was widowed and knew the ins and outs of all their businesses from the very beginning of Barvay Industries. And she had foolishly confided in Vijay Shahane about Avi's arrest! Vijay said he had employed the best lawyers in the country to free Avi. Hah! Maybe I should have engaged the lawyers myself.

If Vijay was behind all this, then it was no wonder Avi wasn't even allowed bail. And, Vijay had power of attorney for Barvay Industries if the members of the Barvay family were incapacitated." Mrs Barvay shuddered as she remembered.

Her husband had trusted no one else outside the family and never anticipated that such a time would arise. "Just a failsafe, my dear" he had said to Mrs Barvay. "I trust Vijay with my life, my family and the family business." A new trail of terrible thoughts danced an evil procession in Mrs Barvay's head and she squeezed her eyes shut tight, trying to magic her way out of it all.

There was a commotion along the stone passage before they heard new voices. Mrs Barvay and Preeti had stared at each other in disbelief when the Karamlegavraokar couple were brought in by police officers. Mrs Karamlegavraokar kept asking, "Who is in charge here? I would like to speak to the police commissioner. Why are we here? We have done nothing wrong. It's that witch from *The Begum Boutique*; her husband is the smuggler. We are honest people. This is all a big mistake. Shivram! Shivram!"

Mr Karamlegavraokar tried to calm his wife from across the narrow passage, where he was in the men's holding cells. He was glad his wife could not see him because his hands were shaking and he could feel the threat of tears. He wondered how he was going to explain all this, first to the income tax department and then to his wife. He could not figure out which would be more harrowing.

Mrs Karamlegavraokar, in the meantime, had at first been taken aback to see old-money Mrs Barvay in the police station cell. Then she had taken comfort from the fact that if Mrs Barvay was here too, then it was perhaps a requirement of high society to be wrongfully arrested. This meant the situation could still be salvaged and explained away with aplomb. Sharing a cell, however briefly, with an old-money family member, who was a neighbour, was an accolade indeed. And surely two people arrested from one family were more credit than just one.

For the first time that day, she felt glad that she and her husband had both been meted the same treatment by the police. She moved a little closer to the older woman and pushed in between Preeti Rao and Mrs Barvay, settling herself on the floor, resting her back against the wall. Mrs Karamlegavraokar calmed herself down and thought, "This income tax raid must be a rite of passage, a sure sign that they, Shivram and Rajni Karamlegavraokar, had socially arrived and joined the league of other affluent, influential people. In fact, it was a bit like having that cottage in the hills that she so hankered for. She let her mind drift, planning a weekend with Mrs Barvay at the cottage that they would acquire soon. Should she have a dinner party to celebrate the release of Mrs Barvay? OR should they ask their friends to host a party in Mrs Barvay's honour?" She debated the options and logistics fervently in her head as she benevolently swatted a mosquito from Mrs Barvay's arm and smiled at her.

✦ ✦ ✦

Hamida had stared aghast at Sundari, Preeti, Tariq, and Ashu running to the stream when the rain came down in big slanting lines. By the time she found an umbrella, an excited, breathless Ashu came bursting through the front door and several police cars drove out of the Tara Road Mansion gates, their sirens blaring and blazing. Dripping with rainwater and excitement, he could not wait to tell her the events. He babbled about arrests, drugs, constables, and criminals, and Tariq and Preeti Rao and swear words.

Once Hamida had made sense of Ashu's excited chatter about the police, she sat down in shock. "Income tax raid! Drugs! Whatever next? And we all thought this was an excellent place for me to live with the children." Then she thought of the Karamlegavraokar children. "Poor mites!" She sent up a silent prayer for their parents' safe return. "And Mrs Barvay taken away? What a horrible thing to happen! Surely there was some mistake there and she would be home soon."

She tried to call Tariq to see if Mrs Barvay could be brought home but he was not answering the phone and the constable who eventually answered Tariq's phone after many many rings was curt, "ACP saheb busy. No personal calls" when Hamida explained she was his sister.

Then Hamida called Maya Bai, "Bring the children over to our house. They can watch a video with my children then eat dinner here. It will give you time to tidy up a little bit."

Maya Bai sounded relieved at the offer. She said "Can I bring them over now? They are upset. And cannot quite understand what is going on. They are scared that the police will put their parents in jail forever. They have never seen their house asunder like this." Hamida was glad to be able to help out. Her children could distract the young Karamlegavraokars until their parents returned or some relatives came for them.

Then she called Meena, who must be worried and alone too. "Meena, lock up the house and come over to my house. Bring your things to stay here until Mrs Barvay is back. Don't stay alone in the empty house. I have invited the Karamlegavraokar children over. I need your help with looking after them." Hamida thought keeping Meena busy and amongst people would be good for the young girl.

As Meena locked Mrs Barvay's house and headed to Hamida's house, she was still a bit shocked and thanked her lucky stars that her thefts remained undiscovered despite the dramas of that afternoon. She knew her stolen jewellery was lost and regretted not getting to the pawnshop a few days earlier.

The Tulpule household was awash with stories that night. Dinner lasted over an hour as Mr and Mrs Tulpule told and retold their tale. "It was only late afternoon and I was working in my study. Suddenly, I needed to switch on the desk lamp. I looked outside, and the dark clouds had gathered like an army. I heard distant thunder and just as I thought of Sundari, I heard her bellow. I raced out to find her. Her shelter was empty and she was not by her favourite spot by the stream. Then there was lightning. I heard her again. Sundari does not like thunder or lightning. Her bellow came from the other end of Tara Road Mansions. I turned in the direction of the sound and saw the strangest sight."

"Our Sundari had a small sack on her back and she was running to me. Behind her were a police officer, Preeti Rao without crutches, and your friend Ashu! After a gap, there were chubby constables waving batons! I realised that Mrs Barvay must have called the police to arrest our Sundari. But my beautiful girl was too fast for them, so they had thrown a sack on her back to slow her down. But she was just too fast for them and she went straight to the stream and lay down in it. You know, like she loves to. I stood on the bank and stopped the police. 'How dare you chase my buffalo?' I said. They were dumbfounded and looked scared. They never thought anyone would accost them. But Sundari is part of our household and of course, I will defend her!"

Mr Tulpule continued, "I turned away the police. They arrested Preeti Rao because I think they needed a scapegoat for the buffalo chase. Meanwhile, I coaxed Sundari out of the water and gave her a big hug before I brought her back to her shelter. People chasing her and the thunderstorm must have frightened her so much, but she was very brave about it all and settled quickly into her shelter and began on her evening feed. I tried to stay on and stroke her back for comfort but she kept flicking her tail at me, so I guess she did not need me there and was telling me, in her gentle manner, to leave. Once Sundari was back in her shelter, I made sure the police arrested Mrs Barvay for setting the police on my poor, harmless Sundari and making wild accusations about Sundari chomping garden borders and trailing dung pats. Hope they keep her in jail for that!" he said vociferously.

There, not wanting her husband to continue his rather imaginative tale, Mrs Tulpule picked up the story. "As soon as I saw your father running away from Sundari's empty shelter and towards the stream, I realised something was wrong. I stepped out of the front door to see if Sundari had wandered out on the other side. I saw some police cars and other official cars leaving from the Karamlegavraokars' next door. Then I saw many boxes being carried out of their house and suddenly realised it was an income tax raid. Then I saw Mrs Barvay being led away to a police car and then heard shouting from the stream. I recognised your father's voice and raced towards the stream. But by the time I got there, he was leading Sundari back to her shelter."

✦✦✦

EPILOGUE:

A few months before the consignment went missing

Avinash Barvay was frustrated. Today, another lucrative deal had been negotiated by Barvay Industries. He should have been proud and happy but he just felt frustrated. It was like being 12 years old instead of 28. His mother had been at the meeting, of course, as a Barvay Industries board member. Last week, she had promised him that she would take a back seat and let him run this meeting and complete negotiations, as he was now the head of Barvay Industries. But as usual, once the meeting was underway, instead of allowing him to navigate through it, she had subtly encroached on his role and played a major part in securing the deal. He understood it was her way of protecting him from making mistakes and sheltering him from critique. But he had studied at the top business schools in the world, been mentored by industry stalwarts, and she had taught and guided him well over the years. Now, he was confident and desperate to step out of her shadow and make his mark. However, his mother never let him complete any deal by himself.

For some time, he had been thinking about striking out on his own, doing some large business deals by himself, and only letting his mother know after he had been successful and posted a massive profit. Maybe then she would let him lead meetings and close the larger deals? He had worked out a way to extricate funds from Barvay Industries' finances without anyone's knowledge and this would serve as his capital. It had been hard to work this out, as his mother and Vijay Shahane kept a close eye on all the money in Barvay Industries.

Avi's friends, in India and abroad, frequently sounded out their investment ideas and ventures with him, always keen for his business acumen and often in the hope of investment from him. One such idea about buying a gold mine in South Africa had appealed to him. The location meant the venture could be kept easily from his mother and it would bring in profits large enough to suit his purpose. Thus, Avi became the owner of an existing gold mine in South Africa, which was for sale as part of a deceased estate. He visited the producing mine while he pretended to be on holiday in South Africa and saw for himself the rich, lucrative veins in the mountainside. The profits would be in his account in a financial quarter or two and he could easily 'put back' the 'borrowed' Barvay Industries' money before anyone realised it had been siphoned off.

Avi was excited as the first couple of months posted high profits but not to the degree he wanted to show off to his mother, so he decided to wait another few months. Then things began to go wrong at the mine. The miners went on strike due to working conditions, there was a regional change in the political situation, there were delays in the arrival of mining equipment; the list of problems began to grow steadily and rapidly. Avi tried to resolve the issues about miners' strikes, government permits, agents, managers, and union leaders but it was hard to do that from India without drawing attention or making repeated trips to South Africa. The days were whizzing by and the date when the auditors would go through the Barvay Industries' books drew closer and closer. Avi panicked and grew desperate to 'return' the 'borrowed' money.' Any day now, the chief financial officer would query the large chunk of money missing from the company accounts.

A few weeks before the consignment went missing

One evening, Avi walked into the Poona Golf Club's restaurant after playing a particularly bad round of golf. He had spent all day there. He was worried about his gold mine problems and avoiding his mother, so he headed to a quiet dinner by himself in his private club room. Because it was a weekend, the restaurant was full and noisy. Several people waved and nodded at him to join them as he walked through the restaurant; he declined all invitations. He was startled by an ebullient shout and a sudden, heavy, python-like arm weighed down his shoulder. Avi relaxed as he recognised the voice of his school friend Tarun Tejani, who seemed louder and happier than usual that evening.

Tejani addressed the room at large again as he waved a half-empty bottle of Scotch whisky, "I have it in my blood. Success! Bijness! Trucksss and bussses, bijness and the most expensive real estate development scheme bijness, and this golf hole-in-one. Everything! I've done it! I can do it. I can do it all. I can do it alone. My parents left me aaallll their money. And my girlfriend left me aaallll alone. Ditch. Bitch. I can do it alone, I don't need a girlfriend … I'm the best, I'm the best, I'm the best, …. yes I am the best! …" sang Tejani, whose singing was as terrible as his golf handicap.

Tejani always had a string of girlfriends and he changed them as regularly as society women discarded handbags. Tonight, he was celebrating his rare hole-in-one from the golf course. Tejani's exaggerated drawl and slurred words told Avi that Tejani was newly single yet again, and the celebrations had been underway for a while at the bar. Avi smiled indulgently as he cajoled his school friend to his private room to make sure he ate some food before he drank any more and made a further spectacle of himself. Tarun Tejani always created a scene after one of his breakups with the latest girlfriend.

Once inside the private dining room, Tejani continued his off-key singing and slurring. Avi rattled off a food order to the attending waiter without consulting his friend. He knew it was important that Tarun ate straight away. Once the waiter had left and shut the door behind him, Avi tried to calm down his friend. "Tarun, everyone knows you have been very successful. Did you break up with Dolly?" He got a loud protesting yell in response. Realising his mistake, Avi tried again' "Did you break up with Asha? Just speak softly now and no! No." Avi coaxed gently as he wrestled the bottle of whisky from Tarun's hands and put it out of his reach.

"Not Asha. It was Suparna, the transport minister's niece. She dumped me! Who dumps Tarun Tejani, *yaar*? I do the dumping… I have never been dumped in all these years." Tarun trailed off his sentence and slouched in his chair after making another lunge at the whisky bottle. "She said it had been fun but she had found someone else … beer company owner! Huh! I'm never drinking beer again from now on. Just whisky" he said, lunging for the bottle once again.

"No. No more drinks now till you and I have eaten dinner. The food will be here very soon. I've ordered all your favourites…." Avi Barvay patiently explained to his friend, knowing his own chance for a quiet dinner by himself was gone.

Tarun began singing again, "I'm the best! I'm the best! Suparna can go to hell! I can send her in one of my trucks. A very old rickety truck. With punctured tyres. I'm the best! I'm the best" and leaned back in his chair. Avi willed the food to arrive quickly. He decided he would keep talking to Tarun to stop him from singing.

"Tarun, the Tara Road Mansions project is almost complete, I hear. Good profits made on your first real estate deal? Tarun? Talk to me." Avi knew Tarun always loved to talk about the business.

Tarun chuckled. "Yes. Yes. Tara Road Mansions done. Profits. Good profits … Profits?" he slurred. "You want profits?" Tarun sat up in his chair, suddenly alert and leaned forward to speak in a stage whisper. "I will tell you about proffitsshh. And I am not telling this to anyone. Especially not Dolly or Asha or Suparna. It's a secret. A very big secret."

Tarun stopped speaking to look around and make sure they were alone. Then he looked around for the whisky and continued speaking when he could not find it. "Am telling you, Avi, only because you're my bessshhht friend. You're my bessshhht friend because you didn't tell Miss Baxter when we were eight that I threw the paper ball at her and shouted 'Boring'! Her English lesson was so boring, *yaar.* So boring. And you helped me hide my cigarettes from Mummy and Daddy when we were on holiday with my family when we were twelve. Avi, best friend. My best friend. I will tell you about profitsss..." Tarun slurred and his head lolled. His eyes were closed and he had finally gone quiet.

Avi relaxed and settled in his armchair. "At least the shouting and singing had stopped. Maybe he's fallen asleep. If only the food would get here quickly now" he thought.

But then Tarun suddenly woke himself and went on "The secret for profitsssss.... Avi, are you listening? The seeeecret to profitssss is trucks. Not any old trucks. My truckssh. Only a few special trucks. No, no. No! Sorry, sorry. Only a few special packages on selected special trucks. They are worth millions! The rest of the packages are useless! Worthless! Normal packages that people want to send here and there. They become the decoys. And the best part? No one knows anything about the special parcels. None of the staff in the warehouses, none of the truck drivers, almost nobody. No one needs to know anyway. The most special package, the motherlode! It's arriving very soon. This one package alone is worth at least two million dollars! Not rupees, dollars."

Avi suddenly sat upright and began to pay attention to his friend's drunken ramblings.

"It arrives on my favourite truck, the green one with my birth year. It's coming on Wednesday from my delivery depot in Bombay to the warehouse in Poona. The truck will have lots of packages. Lots of packages, but this important one will have the registration of my car as its billing code and package number. Mother lode! Two million it's worth. And profits. You know my cut? Twenty percent! Of the two million dollars. Just for getting the parcel to them. They just let me know the parcel number when it is sent on the truck. I have many such parcels delivered every week so I can tell you all about profits. But thisssh one is big. Biiiig. When the special package is delivered to a different address each time, I just send a telegram to the name and address on the shipper's code saying 'Arrived safely.' Then I give them a different address each time to send my cut. And BOOM! I get my cut the next day. Delivered as twenty-four carat gold coins. You know, the ones embossed with various religious shim shymbols. The type everyone gives as wedding presents or housewarming gifts. There is noooo money trail. So no one susshh sushpects a thing."

Tejani's slurred words gave Avi Barvay's desperation a shining beacon of hope like nothing else had in the past few weeks. He savoured this knowledge, treating it with the utmost care. This was his golden egg. He needed a plan to hatch it. Tarun's ramblings had given Avi Barvay's brain real possibilities. "Two million dollars will more than tide me over nicely. I know Tarun's date of birth and his first car's registration. But how can I extricate the package from the truck without anyone noticing?" The next morning, Avi mulled over his idea of stealing the consignment. As he sat in his luxuriant office, he ironed out the kinks carefully and soon Avi finalised a definite plan.

In the following days, he discreetly acquired a dilapidated Tempo van and some old clothes like those worn by truck drivers.

He would pretend to be a Tempo driver who was given the wrong package at the Bombay warehouse. He would follow the truck with the motherlode package away from the warehouse and exchange a useless package with the unsuspecting truck driver, away from anyone watching the depot. Avi gift-wrapped an old printer from his office and asked his secretary to get the shipping number from the courier company but not send it. He wanted it back in the office; he explained it was a prank on a school friend. Avi's office, of course, routinely used Tarun Tejani's company. Avi addressed the useless printer package to a friend in South India. Currently, this friend was away in Australia. This would be the useless package, complete with a shipping number, that Avi would exchange with the truck driver. It would look as authentic and ordinary as any other package from the warehouse, as it would be duly processed and stamped.

He checked his plan against the dates for the Barvay Industries company audit. Once Avi stole the parcel from the truck stop, he planned to 'cool' it for a few days at home. Then he planned to sell it to a dealer that several of his drug-partaking friends had mentioned. A man called Bhim Pawar, who ran a large state-wide security agency as a front for his drug trafficking business.

Avi thought, the consignment money when added to the profit he had already acquired from the mines, would be more than enough to cover the Barvay Industries shortfall and give him the impressive profit he had in mind to show off to his mother.

Avi thought Tarun Tejani does not need the money from this consignment as much as I do. He will grumble a bit when I tell him I took it, but I can return the money to him soon enough. He's such a good sport! He will love the cloak-and-dagger drama and the idea of surprising my mother with the goldmine profits. Avi just hoped that no auditors at Barvay Industries would discover the amount he had embezzled until his plan was complete.

The first part of Avi's plan of stealing the consignment had worked out almost too easily. So, he had not accounted for the next part of the plan to fall apart as it did. No sooner had he got the consignment home, disguised as the sack of milled jowar, he had been arrested for embezzlement of company funds. It meant he never got a chance to sell the consignment.

Instead, Tarun paid heavily for Avi's mistake. Tarun was killed brutally, shot several times mercilessly and his bullet-riddled body left in the car. When Avi heard of Tarun Tejani's death, he wept with remorse and regret about his own actions and for the untimely, violent death of his loud, funny, flirtatious, endearingly mad, rich, childhood friend. Avi's loud keening sobs burgeoned and crescendoed in his jail cell.